I0698826

THE DRAGON'S LANCE
THE SAINT GEORGE CHRONICLES
VOLUME TWO

M.L. EADEN

Copyright © 2023 by M.L. Eaden

All rights reserved.

No part of this publication may be reproduced, distributed, or transmitted in any form or by any means, including photocopying, recording, or other electronic or mechanical methods, without the prior written permission of the publisher, except as permitted by U.S. copyright law. For permission requests, contact author@mlea den.com The use of this book, the contents, and art in LLM and/or AI training is also prohibited.

The story, all names, characters, and incidents portrayed in this production are fictitious. No identification with actual persons (living or deceased), places, buildings, and products is intended or should be inferred.

Print ISBN: 978-1-962655-04-0 — Douglas Illusions

eBook ISBN: 978-1-962655-03-3 — Douglas Illusions

Edited By Victoria Rose: flickeringwords.com

Cover Concept by M.L. Eaden: mleaden.com

Dragon and Iconography designs by Martin Whitmore: martinwhitmore.com

2st edition 2024

Content Warnings: *This story contains explicit sex (including teratophilia and dragon sex), violence, secondary character death, drug use, confinement/incarceration, withdrawal symptoms. For more details, visit mleaden.com*

QUEER STORIES BASED IN MYTH, LEGEND, AND SCIENCE FICTION.

Reader's Note

The Universe you are entering is a contemporary one with magic, myths, and legends living and working alongside each other. There are many sentient and varied species. Some of them are out in the open while others are not. However, everyone knows they existed, knows there's magic in the world, and knows that whether something walks in the light or goes bump in the night, it's as real as the sunrise and sunset.

It's a world where science and magic work hand-in-hand, creating advanced technology and building a day-to-day life where you could easily meet a dragon astronaut, an orc mage specializing in medicine, or a fae working as a tailor. Moonbases exist, sustainable living is a reality, and promises which seem to be mere figments of imagination are woven into the fabric.

Enjoy!

TO DISCOVER MORE:

MLEADEN.COM/BOOKS

CONTENTS

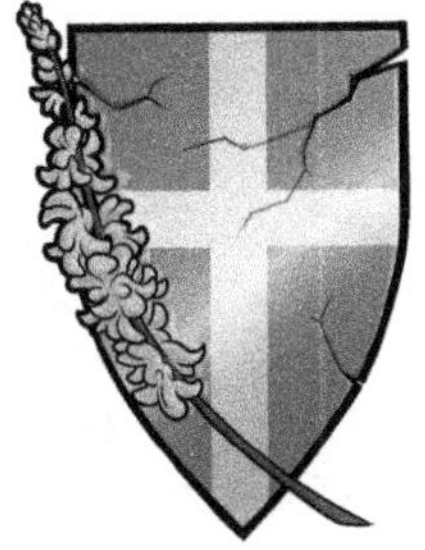

PAID LEAVE

GREGOR

I grumbled as I carefully closed the door on Xavior's very expensive vintage luxury vehicle. He was trying to be romantic, but I couldn't help but feel like I had been hijacked on a road trip to the middle of the desert. He had driven about three hours until we ended up at some massive, exclusive resort so hidden by wards and camouflage magic that Xavior needed directions via a magical wayfinder plugged into the vehicle GPS.

It took forty-eight hours after what the press and everyone else was referring to as "the phoenix incident" for decisions to be made and Xavior to make arrangements. I was still unsure about leaving the city. It felt like we were running away, even though we did nothing wrong.

"Welcome to Firebaugh Resort," Xavior said as he pulled into the circle drive that led to the resort entrance.

"Couldn't we have stayed at home or at your estate?" I complained, not for the first time. This place looked like it would cost me an entire year's salary for a single night's stay.

"We could have. Then we would have been dodging journalists, Captain Lang's efforts to coordinate what happened with the city, and anyone else that might take an interest," Xavior said as he exited his side of the vehicle. "We agreed to let the administrative folks figure things out. Between the local vampire coven trying to take us out, my phoenix event, and us explaining to Captain Lang that we're dating, two weeks off with pay seems like a blessing right now."

"Yes," I agreed, as I had every other time the topic came up, "but we could have spent it with my parents or at your estate." The amount of magic the resort gave off made my skin itch.

"Greg. We both agreed. Philip and Jennifer don't need the attention. My estate and the people I employ don't need it either. They didn't sign up for harassment."

"But this is too much, Xav." I looked at the entrance and watched as well-dressed individuals drifted in and out of the doorway. Many of them were obviously not human. I was wondered if I was really welcome here when Xavior blocked my view.

He reached up and placed his hands on my face, and my focus narrowed to only him. "Greg. Listen. I'm a member here. This is the least I can do for us right now." My nerves settled slightly as he kissed me softly. "I don't want you to worry about doing anything but relaxing. That's all I ask. If you don't like it after a day or so, we can leave, and I'll find another place for us to stay."

I took a deep breath as Xavior wrapped his arms around me. "Alright. You're right. But places like this remind me of where my mother would take us for vacations." Resorts that were clearly meant for one species, very exclusive, and designed around the training I endured until I was nineteen. The Saint George Knights weren't the only hunters in the world. The Van Helsings. The Winchesters. The Harkers. The Colts. The Remingtons. Plus other smaller groups which made a living by hunting magical humans and non-humans alike.

"Oh." Xavior held me tighter. "This won't be like that. I promise."

I embraced him and gave him a kiss. "I trust you." He rubbed my back, which helped my anxiety.

He smiled as I relaxed in his arms. "I don't want to rush you, but the attendants are waiting to valet my vehicle and take our bags. Are you ready to go in?"

"Yeah, okay." After that acknowledgment, everything was done with a level of precision I'd only ever seen around military operations. Someone took Xavior's key fob, and another individual ushered us inside, where someone instantly handed us drinks, an iced tea for me and some kind of bubbling beverage for Xavior which I'd never seen him drink before. Xavior held my hand as we followed yet another attendant down a long hall to an elevator, then up a couple of floors to a suite. The attendant instructed both of us to thumb the bioscanner at the entryway, then opened the door. We followed them into the most opulent suite I had ever seen.

The attendant waved their hands, and windows opened while a holo turned on and displayed a 3-D map of the resort. They inclined their head toward Xavior. He handed them something small, and the attendant gave a small bow and left.

"What did you give them?" I was looking around the room. The view looked spectacular from the balcony which was large enough for a dragon to fly from it. The suite had a massive kitchen area, a living area, and a bedroom hidden by sliding doors. There was one bathroom for guests near the entrance and another, much larger one off the bedroom.

"A fragment of silver," Xavior said. "From here on out, everything is included, so you shouldn't have to worry about having money or tipping anyone unless you buy something from an independent dealer."

"Like what?"

"Drugs. Rare magic. Artifacts."

I spun to look at him. "You can't be serious." He gave me a small smile. "You are serious."

"Why are you so surprised? The resort has a supply of just about everything on the market at the moment. Some people deal in uncommon things. It's unregulated, a little shady, and the resort doesn't necessarily step in to stop it, though they don't tolerate their guests being bothered, either."

"What if people find out we're public safety officers?" Xavior walked toward me, took the tea from my hand, set down our drinks, and put his hands on my hips.

"For the next two weeks, we aren't. Besides, if you don't want to leave this room, that would be fine with me." His hands slipped lower, and I laughed.

"Oh, so this is an expensive ploy to get me naked?"

"Well, I wouldn't call it a ploy exactly. More like setting a mood. It's our first vacation together." Xavior smiled as his hands continued to wander. "First and foremost, I want you to relax. Which is exactly what I'm going to do. Second, you can have anything you want."

"Anything?" My insides heated with the idea of taking the next step. My body literally ached for him. We'd been relatively careful with each other. But the whole almost-dying-and-coming-back because he was lucky enough to be a phoenix dragon crystallized how much I already loved him, and I was ready to make a more serious commitment.

My libido warred with my guilt. It was too dangerous for us to be together. And too cruel to both of us to be apart. If I was smart, I would have told him to save himself. Instead, I stood in a very expensive suite, being held by one of only a handful of individuals in the world that cared about me enough to risk his own life to do so. And when I thought about it that way, too many emotions caught in my throat.

For the last couple of months, we had put off the inevitable for the sake of making sure we both understood the consequences. Not only with his pheromones, but also our jobs, families, and everything that implied.

If he felt a fraction of what I felt when I looked at him, when I kissed him, when I shared a bed with him, then his willpower was nothing short of colossal. Mine crumbled a little more every time I was near him.

I could imagine the scent I gave off as I leaned toward Xavior and pressed my lips to his. He sighed into my mouth as hands reached for clothes and undid buttons. Xavior pulled back.

"Wait, wait."

"What? Really?" I asked, confused.

"I don't want some quick fuck. That's not what I want for us."

"Was that all bravado a second ago?"

He pushed his hands through his reddish-brown hair. "No, no. I meant it. But I also know I want this to be . . ." He took a breath. "Perfect."

I stifled my amusement. "Well, this is a switch." I dropped to the couch and watched as he paced the room. "Xavior, come sit with me." He stopped walking and flopped down next to me, without a question, argument, or joke. I blinked. Seeing him so subdued and nervous gave me pause.

I cupped the back of his neck and gently pulled him closer. "Listen to me. It will be perfect because it was meant to be. If you're not ready, then we wait. I'll wait, just like you've waited for me. It's only fair."

He nodded. "Fair, but ironic." A slightly sarcastic smile curved his lips.

I couldn't help but smile too. "Maybe." I let go of him. "It means you're taking this seriously. I appreciate that. It reassures me."

"Right now, we're attracted to each other. But because I've marked you with my scent, going any further initiates biological changes. Some of them are fairly quick; others take time."

"We've talked about the other stuff." Like biological addiction and increased libido. "Do you mean the possibility of you becoming pregnant?" If Xavior had doubts, now was the time to talk about them before we did anything else.

He blinked at me. "What? Wait. How do you know that?"

"You think I spent the whole time with my mother's family in combat training? They taught us about dragon aging cycles, anatomy, and physiology. I know dragons are sequential hermaphrodites. You are your most vulnerable in an aging cycle when you are unmated. You're the most dangerous when in your dens, and even more so if pregnant. And by law, you're not allowed to hunt a pregnant dragon, so you have to recognize the signs of one when given a proclamation of execution."

Xavior sat back. His body language told me he was in fight-or-flight mode. It was the most I'd spoken about my training. In many ways, I've always known how much I could hurt him, and how much we could hurt each other if we mated. He could be dead right now because of me. Xavior's phoenix half saved him from a vampire's blade I couldn't properly control. Would it save him the next time I made a mistake, or someone put us in harm's way?

I watched as he came to the same conclusion I had months ago. Working together was a risk. Being mated could get us killed.

PREGNANT PAUSE

XAVIOR

I could only stare as I processed Greg's words. In my head, the Knights were nearly a myth themselves. I'd never met one until Greg. My parents talked about how deadly they were. I don't know if they, or anyone, ever suspected how much knowledge they had about dragons.

He sat patiently and waited for me to say something. I swallowed my fear. No one had ever scared me before, and now I was terrified of the one person I wanted more than anything. I stood. "Why are you saying this?"

Greg laced his fingers together and rested his arms on his knees. He looked at the ground. "This is the first time you've had doubts." From his smell, he had no doubts. As a matter of fact, he smelled relieved.

"What about you? Did you do this on purpose? Did you want me to doubt myself?" I fidgeted, torn between moving farther away from him and the need to be near him. He didn't tell me anything I didn't already know, and it was information I wanted him to have. So why did it make me feel so vulnerable and angry?

"No. I want us to be together. Moving forward and starting a biochemical connection we can't undo? We have to be sure we understand the consequences." He sighed. "We know a lot about our families, and about each other, but we didn't talk about this. Not really." He ran his hand through his hair. "Attraction isn't going to carry us through those changes, and I'll be more dangerous to you if we're connected."

"How so?" I spread my arms. "We've worked together for over a year. You didn't hurt me on purpose, Greg." The wild thought in the back of my head was that if he did, at least I would come back. Or at least I thought I would. I didn't know if my phoenix ability worked like my mother's or not, and I wasn't too keen to test it.

He shook head and turned away from me slightly. "Maybe not this time, but what about the next time, or if my family finds out?"

The smell of worry shot through his desire. I wrinkled my nose. He didn't mean Philip and Jennifer. He meant his mother, Narissa, the woman Philip warned me about. "We deal with it when and if that happens."

I sat down and reached for his hand. He gave it to me willingly. "Remember when you asked me in your parent's kitchen why I didn't tell you my suspicions about you being a trap?"

"Yes." He turned slightly to look at me.

I wanted to kick myself for my moment of odd panic. All this back and forth didn't matter. There was only one thing that did, and I had to tell him.

"It didn't matter because I'm in love with you. I've been in love with you almost the whole time we've known each other. So no, it didn't matter. If it had been a trap, I would have figured it out and still hoped we would be at this point where I could tell you, and you'd believe me."

Greg stared at me for a long time. I swallowed and waited. His hand squeezed mine, then eventually, he nodded.

"I knew." He smiled with that confidence that I loved so much. "When we were under the ward, all you could do was stare at me. I knew if I'd asked, you would have told me."

"And now?" I asked, almost afraid, but I had to know.

"I fell for you in the first month I knew you. The dinner with Keith and Vanessa was the first hint of my mistake. The more I pushed the idea away, the worse things were between Keith and me." He shook his head. "I think Keith was waiting for me to admit it. But at the time, I could barely admit he and I were over, let alone that I was in love with you."

I chuckled and shook my head as I moved closer and touched my forehead to his. "You wanna say that again without mentioning your ex?"

He nodded slightly. "Yeah, if you repeat it without talking about traps."

We kissed, and then Greg was under me, and the memory of what we did at my house flashed through my mind. I kissed him again. "Gregor, I love you."

His hands came up to cradle my face. "I love you, Xavior." We continued kissing, wrapped in each other's arms. I wasn't sure when we fell asleep, but the sun was completely gone when I woke, still on top of Greg.

I sat up as something pulled at my senses registering the intrusion. Someone was in my den.

"You're tense. What is it?" Greg was staring at me in the dim light.

"I need to check something. Will you come with me?" I stood, went to my bags, and pulled out a rock about the size of my hand.

"Okay. Where are we going?" he asked as he stood and came to my side.

"Someplace you probably know about but haven't seen before." I walked over to the sliding door that went to the balcony and traced the frame, spelling the door with an old chant my family used for such things. Once I was done, I stepped back.

Greg gave me an odd look, noticing the rock in my hand as I played with the weight of it, tossing it into the air a couple of times. "Xav, what are you doing?" His curiosity wafted through his scent.

"You'll see," I said after I finished the chant, then threw the rock at the glass door.

"Shit!" Greg yelled and flinched, covering his head with his arms as the sound of breaking glass echoed around the room. "Wait, it's still there." His eyes went wide when he looked at me.

"Well, kind of. The glass broke, but it reformed to hide a portal." I offered my hand. "Wanna see my den?"

He relaxed and smiled as he took my hand. "I would be honored."

"Hold my hand and keep walking. Okay?" He nodded. I held onto him as I walked steadily toward the glass door.

"Xavior!" My name on his lips turned into a gasp as he crossed the threshold of my den.

I turned toward him and smiled. "Gregor Lyndon, welcome to my home away from home."

He looked around. "It's a library."

"Well, yes, and no. These are my journals. Everything I've ever learned. All the mysteries I've solved. Maps of places I've been to and how they've changed over the years. Objects I've found that I wanted to keep safe."

I led Greg past my small reading room that contained a comfortable reading chair, a side table, and a little magic-powered lamp. The shelves around it were packed with books and things, though not really organized by any method a librarian would recognize.

We continued down a foyer area lined with shelves until we reached the back. The floor was piled with furs and pillows in roughly the circumference of—well, me, but in my dragon form.

"Holy shit. This is your nest."

"Yes, Greg." I grinned at him.

"It's more fluffy than I'd imagined."

"Fluffy? The floor is stone. It's cold to sleep on. The rugs, furs, and pillows keep me from losing body heat."

"Um, hmm." Greg chuckled.

I let go of his hand. "What were you expecting, a pile of objects?"

He shrugged.

"Holy elements, sometimes I loathe how people have twisted the myths all up. How uncomfortable would it be to sleep on gold, let alone artifacts or whatever else in a dragon's hoard?

I mean, pillows and shelves are way more practical, and I can move them however I want."

"You mean none of this is real?"

"No, it's real, but it's also magic. Watch." I took a deep breath and turned my pile of rugs and furs into a couch.

"Whoa." Greg went and sat down. "I have to admit, that's impressive."

I waved a hand and watched as everything returned to its previous state, dropping Greg about a quarter of a meter onto a large pillow. "HEY!"

I laughed as he flopped around in the mess of nesting. When he finally stood, he came over to me and drew me into a hug. "Thank you for trusting me with this. It's amazing, Xavior."

"It felt right. Besides, when and if we decide to . . ."

Greg looked over my shoulder and went still. "What happened over there?" I knew what he saw as I turned to look. The conjoined space. While Denis and I weren't conjoined twins, somehow, as we came into our ability to create our own pocket dimensions, a connection had appeared between our dens.

We hadn't told anyone about it. When my sister had twins, I wanted to ask them if they had a similar thing, but dens were very personal. Even other dragons were wary when they entered each other's dens unless they were mates. Denis, however, was different. He always had been.

There was a pile of wood planks on the floor, which looked as if they had exploded from the wall. "Denis and I have a connection point between our dens. I woke earlier because I sensed a change."

"Did he tear part of your den down?"

"Yes. The blocking ward was supposed to make it harder, but he's pretty talented in his own space. It doesn't surprise me he broke through it. I wonder what was so urgent that he ignored my ward for the first time in nearly a hundred years." I waved my hand to put the wall back to rights. The wall melted back together, the planks reforming and settling to place. I hadn't noticed Greg take a few steps away from me until the conjoined space was sealed again. He picked up what looked like a package.

"I think he left you something." The package he handed over had my name scrawled across it in neat cursive. Inside was a note and a box. I pulled the note out first. Denis's distinct writing stood out.

Brother,

I am currently occupied with packing for an urgent trip, so I used the most expedient method to reach you. I assume you can fix whatever I destroyed to place the package in your den.

Inside, you'll find the culmination of my work with your partner's blood. The Knight's blood has some surprising properties. We can discuss those further in person. However, I have found a solution to your high risk association. The Knight's ability is dual-sided. They can kill as well as heal. It makes me wonder if their original ability had something to do with healing, and somehow it was altered. Alas, that is research for another time.

For the moment, I have devised a way for your Knight to use his abilities to heal instead of harm. The box contains a ring that should allow him to channel his internal magic at will.

You might have to properly motivate him if he's not a natural magic-user. He has enough inherent latent magic ability to be exceptionally talented if he'd ever had the chance to be trained in that direction.

In service,

D

"Is that Spanish?" Greg asked.

"Yeah. It's from Denis." I pulled out the small ring box.

"Your brother sent you a ring?" He sounded surprised, which, given what I had told him, made sense.

I turned toward him and held the box out. "Actually, it's something I asked him to do for you."

He shook his head, confused. "Why?"

"Well, when we first started working together, you were tense about us being in dangerous situations. I wanted to find a way for you to control your ability around me. Denis is one of the best scientists on the planet. If anyone could figure it out, it would be him. Looks like he did."

Greg took the box out of my hand and opened it. "Is this a joke?"

"What do you mean?"

He turned the box toward me. "It has my family crest on it, Xavior."

"What's wrong with that?"

"Oh, nothing except it stands for everything that is a danger to you and shunned me most of my life." He shoved the box back at me so fast I barely caught it. "I don't know what your brother's playing at, but it's gross."

"The note says the ring would let you focus your ability. Your gift is dual-sided. You can kill or heal with it. This ring would act as a focus and let you heal." How had this gone so wrong? If Denis had only figured out Greg's abilities sooner, maybe I wouldn't be so desperate for him to have the ring.

"I don't give a fuck what it would let me do. I'm not wearing the damn thing." His voice was strained as he took a step back and crossed his arms over his chest. The smell of his anger was akin to a physical blow.

"Okay. We'll shelve that idea for now. I didn't mean to upset you, Greg." I closed the box and pushed it in my pocket. Leave it to Denis to make a dig at someone when you least expected it. He didn't know about our relationship, though he had suspected. I wondered if he added the symbol on purpose to remind both of us exactly what we were dealing with. Given what we'd discussed a few hours ago, I was going with Greg on this one. I marshaled my calm and reached for Greg, but he stood stock-still. "What's wrong?"

"How did he discover information about my magical ability? The Order doesn't even know that information, Xavior, or if they do, they've kept it to only the highest ranks. How did Denis find out?"

Crap. I dropped my hands and realized how much I had fucked up. I should have told him, or at least asked. I hadn't been sure of anything then. Now, I knew better. I glanced away and took a breath. Greg deserved the truth. We couldn't move forward without it. "Remember the blood drive at work right before your birthday? I might have pilfered some of your blood for Denis to study."

Greg's voice sounded perfectly calm, which underlined his disbelief. "You did what?"

"I know it wasn't the brightest idea, but I was worried about you, about us. I did it for a good reason."

"You never thought to run this scheme past me? You thought you'd show up one day with information or a magical whatever, and suddenly my ability wouldn't be a problem?" His steady voice was starkly different from the anger and betrayal I smelled. It frustrated and confused me.

"Yes, actually, that's exactly what I thought." I raised my voice. "Do you blame me?"

He shook his head. "You're scared of me. You have every right to be, Xavior. I did gut you, after all." He walked away from me, and oddly enough, in the correct direction toward the den's exit. I followed.

Guilt crawled up my throat as I grabbed his arm to stop him. "Greg, please."

He yanked out of my grasp. "Don't." Anger and tension filled the space between us until Greg turned away.

I stood in my reading room, with its cozy lighting and soft chair, and watched Greg leave my den with no help whatsoever. The fact that my den recognized him as my mate gave me a tiny pang of joy, which soured from the regret I felt for betraying his trust.

CONJURED THOUGHTS

GREGOR

"Fuck!" I let all my anger pour into that one word as I stood on the balcony, staring at the gorgeous view of the whole resort lit for the night. I wanted to scream, throw up, or both. I couldn't breathe.

Xavior lied to me. The truth of it weighed on me like gravity had shifted. Given everything I'd been through with Keith, how could he have done that? Even if he'd done it to protect us, he should have told me.

A rational part of me knew Xavior thought I would be elated that he had solved our dilemma, and recognized it for the gesture of care he wanted it to be. Regardless of whatever the ring might have represented before, it certainly symbolized our trust issues now.

When I was young, I saw my mother and father argue too often. When Philip and Jennifer dated, they made a point of not fighting in front of me. If an argument was on the verge of developing, they'd take a break, talk it out, and then talk with me. I knew I needed to figure myself out before I talked with Xavior again. Yelling wouldn't help.

When I saw Xavior out of the corner of my eye, I wanted to tell him I wasn't ready to talk. Instead, he moved past me at a slow jog that changed to a run as he went for the end of the balcony. He easily scaled the railing, naked, then dove off. I yelled his name as I reached the railing. A dark dragon shape I recognized all too well flew over the resort toward the desert.

My dazed mind refused to believe I'd just watched Xavior literally jump off a building and fly away.

I had no idea how soon he'd return, if at all. The shiver that rolled up my spine from the cool breeze reminded me I couldn't stand out on the balcony all night. A very petty part of me wanted to do something drastic.

When I grabbed the handle to open the balcony door, the magic from the den's portal pulsed. I stuck my hand through and pulled it back out. An even worse idea presented itself and I shook it off. Destroying a small part of anything in his den was reprehensible, and I felt ashamed for even thinking about it.

I went inside the suite instead, closed the balcony door, and locked it. We both trusted each other enough to cause irreparable harm. He left his den here. For a dragon, that was unheard of unless he thought it was safe. I was in unfamiliar territory. This was more than "I love you" or sex. For the first time, I'd trusted someone with all of me and Xavior had done the same.

Keith never knew about The Order. I was careful with him. Let him have what he needed and didn't press for more, because I knew I could physically hurt him. Maybe I thought it was some kind of penance, letting myself play a role. Maybe that's why we never worked. I wasn't there, and neither was he.

This relationship was different. Even how we approached it was different. Xavior let me set boundaries and dictate how fast or slow we took things. He knew the biggest parts of my history I'd told no one about. He trusted me in a space probably few had ever been in, and still did, based on the fact the portal was open to me. Each realization hit me like a brick, one after another. For each thought that roosted in my head, I ordered a menu item.

As much as I ordered, once it arrived there was little I wanted to eat. I ate from a couple of the plates but didn't feel hungry. I drank a beer, watched some holo, then tried to nap. When I woke later that night, still tired, I opened the massive sliding doors hiding the rest of the suite. They revealed a room with an ocean-sized bed, a mountain of pillows artfully splayed across the surface. The idea of sleeping in such a gigantic bed alone turned my stomach. Instead, I retrieved an extra blanket and went back to the couch.

It had only been a few days since Xavior's phoenix event. The whole altercation played out every time I closed my eyes, but instead of him resurrecting, he turned to ash in my hands as I slid the knife into his guts. I jolted awake, screaming, checking my hands. Unlike that night, they were still clean. Without Xavior the suite seemed like a cavern with no comfort. I stood with no idea where I was going, only that I needed to move, stumbling and trying my best to avoid the furniture.

All I could think about was how irrational my reaction had been. He had lied, yes, but he tried to explain. He hadn't hidden the truth once it was in the palm of his hand. He knew I'd be angry. On some level I knew he was upset with himself or he wouldn't have taken a flying leap.

"Shit," I yelled as I tripped over something on the floor and nearly face-planted. I was on the verge of exhaustion, a breakdown, or both.

A dim light slowly filtered into the room. It might have been voice-activated, or sensed my presence. I'm not sure which, but I was grateful not to be in the dark any longer. That's when I realized I was in Xavior's den.

Standing next to his nest, I looked around. Xavior's clothes were in a pile on the floor nearby. He had decided, right here, that he'd take off for a while. Before I realized it, I had his clothes in my hands and pressed my face into them. His earthy, smokey smell was there, along with something else I couldn't identify. When I folded his pants, the ring box fell out. I picked it up. I took a deep breath and opened the box.

The symbol stared at me. It was an icon that represented everything I hated about myself, how dangerous I was to Xavior, and knowledge I had which I could use against him. The training which had been too rusty to turn the knife quick enough to stop the vampire that used my momentum to follow through. The loud snap of the box echoed as I closed it.

I sank into the soft pillows and blankets. The stress of the last few days came out in tears, sobs, and snot and I wiped my face like I was five. I hadn't cried this hard when Keith broke up with me. I had been depressed, but not devastated, not like this.

If I'd lost Xavior that night, I wouldn't have come back from that. The realization alone should have me out the door and as far away as possible. Instead, I tipped over into his pillow pile and grabbed a fur to pull around myself. It turned into a blanket in my hands. The gesture from his den gave me some measure of comfort as I fell asleep.

INESCAPABLE TRUTH

XAVIOR

Dragon dens were magical pockets of space and time. When I first discovered mine, I was twenty-two. It was no bigger than a closet, and the connection to Denis's den was the size of a knothole. I never saw anything through it and assumed he blocked the tiny connection, which grew to the size of a medieval tapestry as we both aged and grew into our magic. Whatever had him in such a hurry, I hope it was important enough for him to violate my space like that. The last time he ignored my wards, he dropped some kind of coded message he wanted me to keep until he asked for it. He never did, so I kept it with the many other things I'd collected over the years.

After I calmed down, which flying always did for me, I came back to our balcony. I didn't bother to shift as I walked into the glass. The portal shifted and the surrounding space expanded to keep my bulk from destroying anything as I moved through. It rippled back into place once I entered my den.

While I was flying, I felt another pull from my den. I thought maybe Denis might have sent something else through, even though I sealed the wards again. What I didn't expect to find was Greg crying in the middle of my nest. He hadn't realized I was there. I watched as he clutched at my clothes and then pulled a fur around himself. The need to take care of him overwhelmed me as I turned the fur into a blanket and lengthened it so it would cover him completely.

How he'd found his way back into this space was a mystery. Maybe that was part of my attraction to him besides the pheromones. He was an endless mystery that kept me wanting more.

When I knew Greg was asleep, I moved toward him and conjured more pillows and rugs to make the nest larger and quietly curled myself around him. I must have dozed off because I woke up with Greg's hand on my snout. He was stretched out next to me as his hand gently passed along my scales. His face loomed in my field of vision.

"You scared me."

I hadn't meant to scare him. I made a sad tone and pulled away from him slightly as he sat up.

"I'm sorry I yelled at you." He sighed. "Even though you lied, it wasn't with the intent to hurt me." I made a slight affirmative noise. "The past few days have been a lot for both of us."

Greg looked around. "Your den has several human lifetime's worth of knowledge here. I can't help but think about what happens if we follow through with this. We'd have fifty years together, maybe less. On top of the risk to you because of the pheromones. Plus, if we had children, they'd barely be adults when something happened to me or both of us."

He looked at his hands instead of me. His scent was muddled because of his emotions. It frustrated me, but I understood. He was right, and I knew there was only so much I could do for us. The concept of the ring had been part of that.

"The idea of us makes no sense. Yet, I can't let you go. I know I should, but I can't."

In the space it took him to bury his face in his hands, I shifted. I pulled him into a hug, and he wrapped his arms around me and continued to cry.

"We're not dead yet." I caressed his face and kissed his cheek. "We could have died a couple of days ago, or elements willing, we could die peacefully together in our bed. None of us knows how long we have. But what I have, I want to spend with you." I took a breath and continued. "The doubts and the problems we'll figure out. We're good at that. As long as we know we want to be together, we'll figure it out."

He gave me a slight nod and held me tighter. I continued, determined to apologize as best I could. "I won't promise to not do something foolish when it comes to protecting you or being concerned about your welfare. I can promise that I'll do my best to at least try to let you know I'm planning a bonehead thing before I do it."

That got a small chuckle.

"I love you, Gregor. More than anyone I've ever known. As long as we're together, as long as we love each other, we'll figure the rest out." He looked up at me, finally, and I put my hands on his cheeks, using my thumbs to smooth the tears and worry away. I gave him a gentle kiss and met his gaze. "I'm sorry I hurt you." In his eyes, I saw forgiveness. It was worth more to me than anything. "I can only promise to try not to do it again."

He nodded. "I love you, Xavior." He kissed me with heated tenderness as his hands moved along my shoulders, pressing his body into mine. I let his weight carry us back onto the pillows.

I don't know what I expected. When Greg lifted himself a little to take off his shirt, he returned for another kiss as his warm flesh pressed to mine. This wasn't new. We'd shared a bed before. My breath caught as he moved slightly and slipped his jeans and boxers off. I grabbed the blanket and pulled it over both of us to keep him warm.

"Thank you," he said softly as his fingers drifted through my hair.

"You're welcome." I kissed him again. We were naked, together, in my den. There was no way I was awake, and this was reality. Or that's what I thought until his hand ventured below my waist and wrapped around my cock. My throat went dry. I croaked, "Am I dreaming?"

"Xavior." Greg kissed me and teased my mouth open with his tongue. He took my hand and placed it on his chest. I was too astonished to do anything else. He stopped kissing me long enough to let my brain catch up.

"Do you want to stop?" His hand stilled, and I was keenly aware of how hard I'd become.

I shook my head, unable to trust my voice. I'd had sex before. Why was this so different?

"Xavior, open your eyes." I did, and Greg's dark brown ones brought me back to the moment. His hand had picked up where it had left off. I groaned and moved my hips. "That's it. That's the face I remember. Seeing it in person is even better."

"Has anyone, oh fuck, Greg . . . has anyone ever told you . . ." I bit my lip as I tried to hold back, to make myself last. Elements have mercy on me, I couldn't speak. The way he took control was intoxicating.

"What are you trying to tell me, Xav?" Inexplicably, he squeezed me a little more, then slowed down, and all I could do was groan into his mouth. "Come for me," Greg whispered. His fucking voice wrapped around my brain as sure as his hand was wrapped around my dick.

Over the last couple of months, it's always been his voice that brought me, my imagination filling in the blanks. He kissed me, and I came hard, as I made noises I'd never heard before. Desperate, relieved noises to finally be in this moment with him and still want more.

He moved on top of me before my orgasm faded. I felt him slide along my oversensitive dick as my cum painted us both. "Fuck, Greg." I groaned.

"Too much?" He slowed. I shook my head and urged him to continue.

I reached between us and wrapped my hand around him. Greg's hand snaked into my hair as he thrust his hips. I couldn't help but moan. I was desperate for him to add to the mess we'd already made.

My free hand wrapped around his neck as he looked at me with a desire and need so deep, I was fairly sure it could drown us both. I knew he was close when his body tensed and his grip on my hair tightened. I distracted him with kisses instead of words. When I nipped at his neck, his orgasm took him in a full-body shudder. We held onto each other until our breathing returned to normal.

It was perfect.

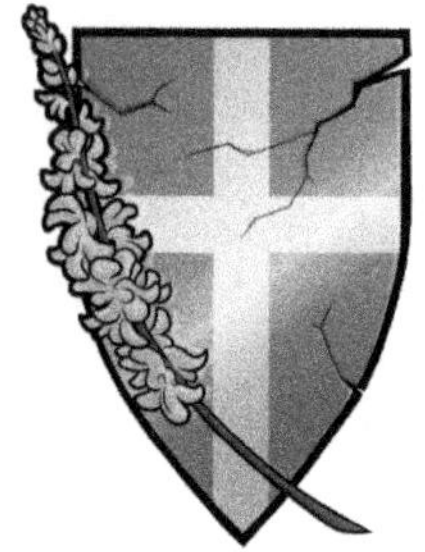

NEXT STEPS

GREGOR

We kissed, and held each other quietly for a long time. I finally whispered into the silence because I was afraid I'd die of curiosity. "Is that it?"

"Is what it?" Xavior responded as his fingers traced my face.

"Are we connected now?"

"Oh." He chuckled. "Yes, but only in the most tenuous sense."

"What do you mean?"

"It's not instantaneous. We've spent a lot of time together, so it won't take long, at least for me, but we'll have to see what happens where you're concerned."

"Oh." Was that disappointment in my voice? What had I expected? I knew it wouldn't be instantaneous. Like any drug, it took time to manifest changes.

"Look at it this way; the more sex we have, the more the connection takes hold." He moved, pressing himself closer, semi-hard already. Oh God, would I be able to keep up with him? The thought of trying excited me.

"So you're saying we're going to turn into sex addicts for the next two weeks?"

"We do have to stop for food and water, maybe a shower, but sex for two weeks doesn't sound like too much of a burden considering how long we've both been without, wouldn't you agree?"

"Fuck yes," I blurted. We laughed and kissed more. "Why did you get an expensive resort suite if we could have stayed in your den?"

"A few reasons." He rolled me onto my back and laid on top of me. "One, my den doesn't have facilities. Showers and bathroom breaks are necessary. Two, I can't conjure food. I don't want to survive on protein bars alone. And three, there are some really fabulous amenities here like hiking trails, a salt lake, several swimming pools, dance floors, bars, nightclubs, restaurants…shopping." His emerald-green eyes danced as he smiled. He was excited. I was excited about one of those things he mentioned.

"Dance floors?"

He nodded. "Plus, by the way you're shivering, sleeping on a stone floor, even with this many rugs, blankets, and pillows would be short-lived."

"I admit, you were right. It's cold." I chuckled. "Also, I'd like a shower, and I'm hungry."

"Mmm hmm." Xavior moved off me and sat up. "How about I start the shower, you order us whatever you want from the menu, then come join me?"

"Okay." He stood and offered me a hand. I let him help me off the floor. When we headed for the den's exit, I stopped him. "What about the mess we made?"

He gave me some shifty eyes and a sly smile as he put his hand on my back and continued to walk us out of his den. It dawned on me that he wanted our smell in a confined place, at least for a while. It had to be a dragon mating thing.

As I ordered lunch, I heard the shower start. I set the delivery time giving us an hour before our food showed up. The mess on the dining table from the previous night made me feel a little guilty, but I'd read somewhere that the resort composted everything, so hopefully it wouldn't be completely wasted. After finishing up with the holo menu, I followed the sound of water to the entrance of the bathroom.

While the bedroom was huge, the bathroom was unlike anything I'd ever seen. The sheer size of it was not unlike something you'd find at a gym, but instead of several toilets and shower stalls, there was a massive rain shower system that could accommodate at least fifteen people or several large individuals. Which made sense since I'd seen some half-giants and larger trolls in the lobby earlier.

The tub looked more like a small swimming pool with a water circulation system. There was a toilet and bidet in another space with a door. And a large vanity with two sinks and a giant mirror. The vanity was marble and contained an enormous basket of complimentary hygiene products, towels, and other implements.

Xavior was already in the shower. The steam fogged the glass doors. I opened it and stepped inside. Some of the fog dissipated, and I saw him under a larger spray of water.

His brownish-red hair was slicked back as the water cascaded down his solid muscular structure. When the water hit his skin, scales flashed and moved underneath as they responded to the heat. It was like watching a living work of art. Xavior turned around. He had tone and muscles in the way some species had without a lot of effort.

His eyes were still closed, but Xavior had to know I was watching him. I bit my lip as another ripple of iridescent scales danced across his skin as his hands slid over his face and down his body. He opened his eyes and looked at me as I walked over to join him.

"Has your boyfriend told you lately that you're sexy as fuck?" I said. I meant to tease, but it came out lower and needier than I intended.

"Not recently, but he gave me an excellent handjob not ten minutes ago." The grin on Xavior's face softened to a sweet smile as we kissed.

An array of bottles sat on a shelf nearby. "Give me a sec," I said. Xavior raised an eyebrow and stuck out his lip as I moved to select one. I opened a couple and found a shampoo I liked. I poured some in my hand and brought it back to Xavior.

"Close your eyes." He did, and I proceeded to wash his hair. He turned around and leaned against me as I continued to slide my soapy hands over his scalp. I continued down his neck, along his shoulders, and across his chest as his small, comforting moans encouraged me.

When I slid my hands across his stomach, his scales surfaced for a moment, then faded again. Fascinated, I let my hands drift along Xavior's body, amused not only with his scales but how erect he was from my touch.

"You're being playful." Xavior said softly, as he smiled.

"It's your scales. They seem to be chasing my fingers." He opened his eyes, and I demonstrated for him.

"That's unusual."

"Why? Isn't that your dragon side responding?"

"Yeah, I guess, but I've never responded to someone's touch like that before. It feels . . . it feels like you're caressing me and my dragon form at the same time."

"Do you want me to stop?" I was concerned that I had inadvertently caused something to happen he didn't like.

"No, I like it." He relaxed a little, but not enough.

I gently turned him around so I could look him in the face. "It's alright to be scared. We're both in pretty unfamiliar territory at the moment."

Xavior's face changed. Something I said alarmed him. His eyes widened as his mouth opened slightly before he spoke. "How did you know I was scared?"

I closed my eyes and focused. "You're a little scared, but concerned, aroused, and the slightest bit hungry, but I can't tell if that's because you're aroused or actually hungry." I opened my eyes to look at him.

"Both." He reached up and touched my face. "Adoration, concern, a tiny bit of fear, and an ocean of lust." Xavior's eyes widened. "That happened much faster than I expected it to."

"What happened?" I pressed his hand to my face.

"It seems we can sense each other. At least to some extent. It's part of what the connection provides. I expected it to take days, maybe even weeks." He shook his head slightly.

"Are you sure that's what it is?" I asked.

He nodded. "Unless you had some kind of empathic abilities before now, yeah, I don't know what else it could be."

I chuckled. "No backing out. You're mine, asshole."

Xavior dropped his hands and wrapped his arms around my waist. "The same goes for you too, asshole. No turning back."

I kissed him again as steam and water cascaded around us and our senses intertwined, opening us to a deeper understanding and empathy than we'd ever experienced before.

ELEMENTS OF SURPRISE

XAVIOR

I was still in a daze after the shower. I hadn't expected visible evidence of our connection, let alone sensory proof. It was too soon. Rather, it was too soon for me. Greg seemed pleased with it. The conflict I felt kept me quiet through our meal, then more so as we got into bed and laid next to each other.

"Hey, talk with me," Greg said as he kissed my shoulder. "It's not like you to be so tense."

I rubbed a hand over my face and turned to look at him. "It feels too fast."

"What does?" His even-toned voice was a warning. If I wasn't careful, I'd hurt him. I could feel him brace for rejection as his hand settled on my arm.

I took my time to think of the right words. They had to be the right ones. The last thing I wanted was for Greg to regret what we did. I didn't regret it, but it scared me all the same. He'd wanted to talk about procreation earlier, and I changed the subject. Now, with the possibility right in front of me, I had to tell him and explain what might happen.

"I expected more of an adjustment period. I thought the changes would be more gradual. That we'd be able to ease into our connection."

"Are the changes overwhelming for you?" He held onto his even tone. I'd heard him use the same voice to talk with people that were panicked or not in a good place mentally. The kind of tone that encourages you, and at the same time, lets you know you're safe. From Greg, I mostly sensed and smelled curiosity and a tiny bit of fear.

"A bit, yes. The biochemical changes should have taken longer." I paused for a moment and bit my lip. "We should take precautions."

"By precautions, do you mean protection? Because I'm not sure I could handle abstinence again. That sucked."

I chuckled. "Yeah, it did." I kissed him, trying to reassure him in some small way. "Protection would be a good idea for now. If the biochemical changes were this fast, I'm worried the physiological ones will be too."

"Oh," Greg said as I watched understanding dawn on his face. "What do the changes look like? How careful do we need to be?"

"Um." Fuck, I never thought I would be too embarrassed to talk about this. "Condoms should be enough. As for the other, dragons are born with egg pouches and penises. Normally, it would be a matter of sensing who's in heat first. We don't develop eggs as often as sperm."

"Let me guess, dragons develop eggs every twenty-five years?"

"The aging cycle tends to be part of it, though off-cycle re-production is possible."

"But, since I'm human and we haven't entertained the idea of sex with you as a dragon," Greg shook his head, "which I'm not even sure how that would work, are we fairly safe with you in your bipedal form?"

"It's harder, but not impossible," I admitted, then rushed to explain. "In our dragon form, we have penises and seminal canals. It's why any dragon can mate with another dragon regardless of their bipedal form. Dragons choose their bipedal genital presentation, or lack thereof, after their initial shift into their bipedal form. It allows us to mate with other species. When in our bipedal form, if we present female genitalia, the vagina acts as a conduit, though female-presenting dragons still produce semen. If we present with male genitalia, a meatus develops between the testicles and the anus."

Greg's eyes went wide, though he had a slightly amused look on his face. "Wow. I knew about the genital duality of dragons, but I didn't know it was so complex. So, if you suddenly present with an extra hole, we'll have a decision to make."

I nodded. "Basically." I wondered if he picked up on my embarrassment. I rarely had to explain dragon reproductive systems to my partners. Jordan might be the only exception to that since he was rather pointed about avoiding me during an aging cycle, this year notwithstanding since it was early, but I hadn't entered a heat yet, from what I could tell.

"Can you change your bipedal form?"

"Maybe, but I've never felt the need to. I've heard others have over time. Our bipedal form is primarily magic, with some genetic pointers. There's lore that thousands of years ago, we weren't shifters. No one knows for sure what happened, but shifting lets us interact with more species and protect ourselves better. It gave our bipedal form things like hair, belly buttons, and nipples that are completely useless to us otherwise." A soft laughter echoed between us.

"That makes sense." He touched my hair, and I could almost see the wonder in his eyes as he took in this new information. It amused me.

"Do you want children?" he asked.

While the question wasn't a surprise, I wasn't sure how to answer. With everything that went on in the last few months, we hadn't discussed children until yesterday. I knew Greg wanted to have children. My family heritage was secure because of my sister Faith and Trevor, her mate, and their brood. "I hadn't really thought about it. I've never been with anyone consistently enough to worry about it beyond preventing it." My heart beat faster as I stared at the ceiling. Greg's hand touched my cheek and gently brought my gaze back to his.

"It's okay if you don't know right now. We'll use protection and decide what's best when we actually need to decide."

"You sure?" Greg liked plans. The whole time we worked together, he preferred things planned rather than pushed off until later. This wait-and-see approach was new.

He nodded. "I know I pushed yesterday, but considering everything we've been through, and now that I know more about how things work, we can make that decision later." He paused and took a breath. "When we were taught dragon anatomy, it's not like they told us how to have sex with one." Greg grinned, and I chuckled. "It was mostly so we wouldn't assume, based on a dragon's bipedal appearance, what was and wasn't possible."

"Considering everything else, that's surprisingly enlightened for The Order."

"Maybe," Greg said. "I'm sure there's a fucked-up reason somewhere in there." He wrapped his arms around me, then pulled me close and kissed my forehead. "How about we take a nap? Whoever wakes up first can give the other a blowjob." I chuckled and settled next to him. Things were going a bit fast, yes, but Greg was right here with me, and that's all that mattered.

HIDDEN MEANINGS

GREGOR

Something teased at my senses before I was completely awake. A light touch, a smell, and soft breathing all drew me from my cloud of sleep to what the dragon next to me was doing to get my attention.

"Hello, sleepyhead," Xavior whispered as his tongue teased my right nipple. To say my body responded would be an understatement. "Oh, this is going to be fun."

"Whadya mean?" While I wanted an explanation, I was pretty sure nothing sensible actually came out of my mouth.

Xavior chuckled into my chest. "Our vid chats were a good primer." He licked, teasing a sensitive spot he found. "However, it seems you were holding back. Your nipples are way more sensitive than you let on. I'm wondering what other spots I could find."

"Find where?" *What a dumb question, Greg.* Between Xavior's tongue and the sleep fog, if I made any sense at all, it would surprise me. My hands hovered in front of me, intending to reach for Xavior, but I hesitated to see what he did next.

His soft brownish-red hair was a mess from sleep. I could see the finger furrows he'd likely made when he woke. The small detail delighted me. Did he do something similar when he woke as a dragon? I cataloged each gesture, recognizing his body language. It was a comfort that in the short time we'd been together, I had come to know him on such an intimate level.

Now that I was more awake, I folded my arms under my head so I could take in the very excellent view I had of my partner working his way down my torso.

"That's better," Xavior said as he kissed my abdomen. "You're always so tense, even when you sleep. Did you know that?"

"I . . ." He kissed and slowly licked lower. "I know. I'm working on it." Therapy had helped some, but between how I grew up and my previous relationship, my trust issues wouldn't fix themselves overnight.

"Well, hopefully, I can help." The offer threatened to derail what we were doing as a snarky comment sat on my tongue. I bit it off rather than ruin the moment. Xavior caught it all too quickly. "Nope, don't do that. Something I said annoyed you. What was it?"

"Xav." I pulled at my hair, frustrated with myself.

"Greg. Talk. We need to talk, or all the things we pick up about each other through our senses will turn into much larger things for us to be angry about later. Talk with me. What did I say?"

I sighed. "You were trying to be helpful. It annoyed me because you're too helpful sometimes, like with the ring business. Then, I was annoyed with myself because I should ask for help. It should be alright to do that, and I shouldn't be upset with you or annoyed because of it."

"Ah." He gave me a soft smile. "It's not just the ring, though. It's more. I've created a power imbalance. I do too much sometimes." He folded his arms across my abdomen and rested his chin on them as he looked up at me. The rest of him was stretched out across the bed, gloriously naked.

"Sometimes," I admitted. "But sometimes you get it right. You stayed out of the house business with my ex and haven't pushed me to move in with you. And we've maintained a mostly normal working relationship."

"Those are large boundaries. It's easy to see that crossing a line there wouldn't help either of us. The ring was probably another, but that, I admit, was for selfish reasons." He sighed. "If I'm honest, I asked Denis to make something because I wanted you, though I tried really hard to ignore it. Also, you represented something I hadn't faced before."

"Oh?" I reached to smooth his hair. I sensed a mild satisfaction from Xavior as I touched him, but it shifted to what I might describe as introspection as he spoke.

"My mortality. I didn't know what would happen or how much time we would spend together. If fate put you in my path, then I refused to be idle and let it control everything."

I took a deep breath and let it out. "The ring wasn't a bad idea. If you'd asked me, I probably would have agreed to it. What Denis discovered is remarkable. If they ever tested me for magical aptitude, I don't remember. Magical items always give me headaches, but I thought it was because I didn't have any magic."

"You had headaches because the items weren't attuned to you."

"What? It can't be that simple, can it?" I don't know what face I made, but Xavior chuckled in response.

"The items and things you've used were made for non-magical beings. Different magics have a signature, right? So if two signatures, like wavelengths, are trying to sync and can't, they cause a resonance. When you use something for a while that wasn't made for you or attuned to you, that resonance can have an effect, like headaches. Spelled items can shift signatures, but it takes time and practice." Xavior continued his lesson while he drew a circle on my chest. "Take your shield spell. You've used that for a while now. Do you still have headaches when you use it?"

I thought about it. "No, I haven't for a few years." When did I realize I didn't have a headache using my shield? I practiced with it enough.

"It's probably because it's attuned. It definitely made a difference in the vampire altercation. Your shield held a lot longer than it should have. You were likely reinforcing it with your own magic without even realizing it."

"Huh." It made sense. Those spells weren't meant for long-term use, especially if you're being hit by someone or something more powerful than you. They deflected and reduced the impact of the blows.

"Brains, talent, and sexy as fuck," Xavior said. I smiled at his comment and ran my fingers through his hair again.

The shield spell was supposed to let you maneuver out of a fight, not stay in one. It was a subversive decision to stay in the fight instead of leave, drilled into me by my unconventional upbringing, and Xavior's next question told me he had noticed. "How often are you still training?"

He didn't mean the gym, workouts, or even our training sessions at headquarters. "Once a week. I have a course set up in the woods near my parent's place. At least, I did before I invited you to weekend dinners." I shrugged the answers off with a smile as if I hadn't said something concerning.

Xavior nodded with a gentle smile. My senses picked up a tiny bit of something I'd call trepidation. "We're taught to disarm in public safety training, but you did something different. You handled the vampire as if that wasn't an option."

"It's not. Anything with teeth or claws has weapons you can't get rid of. The vamp was intent on the knife, so I kept his focus there instead of letting him get the idea he could bite me. It was a mistake on his part. Though if the vampire tried to use his fangs, there's another maneuver I could have used. It would have likely cost me my job and I'd face charges for excessive force."

Xavior held my gaze. "Why are you still training if you loathe it so much?"

He was right. I did. Every time I trained, I hated myself for it. "It's all I had from my mother. I thought that if I kept up with what I learned, someday my training might make a difference. To preserve a life instead of taking it."

He chuckled softly and shook his head. "So, you trained out of spite?"

"It's not rational." I took a deep breath, then let it out. "Before I met you, it made sense. Then I kept training because I hoped it would help keep you safe." Which I had utterly failed to do when it counted. The emotions I'd held in surfaced as my eyes filled with tears and I tried to breath around the knot in my throat.

"Oh Gregor, fuck." When he moved, I felt bereft of his weight until gentle kisses landed on my face, and his hands caressed my cheeks and soaked up my tears. "I fucked up and got in your way. You did nothing wrong. You were handling it, and I should have let you. I let my worry for your safety put me in the wrong place. Don't blame yourself, love, please."

"If you weren't part phoenix, you'd be dead right now," I whispered.

"I know." He wrapped me in his arms, and I went willingly. The solid feel of him helped calm me. "We got lucky. I didn't even know it was possible until I felt it happening. I've never had a phoenix cycle before."

We laid together in silence as I thought about his words. The ring his brother made might be the only thing to save him from me.

"I'll wear it." I surprised myself with how clear my voice sounded.

He didn't ask what I meant. "Why?"

"If I could have stopped what happened to you, I would have. I don't want to go through that again without a chance to change the outcome." The ring wasn't any different from my training. I'd be able to use my inherent magic and my ability to save lives, especially his.

Xavior made a gesture, and the ring box appeared in his hand as if he'd had it all along.

"Should I even ask how you did that?"

"Space-time. It's a dragon thing. I can summon anything in my den, except plants and animals. Something about dimensional magic doesn't let that work. Or I'm not old enough to make that work. Either way, this is yours." He handed over the box.

I opened it and stared at the symbol. That damn white shield with its red cross was an ugly part of me. I was a Knight, but everything that symbol stood for was corrupted by my mother. It reminded me of the pain of being rejected and alone. It stood for the lies I told myself, the secret I never told Keith, the hurt I caused Xavior right before he burst into flames. It was a holy symbol, part of an Order that should protect those that couldn't protect themselves. Instead, it had been reduced to trophy hunting. The ring gave me more than that, it gave me the possibility of a different direction. One I could choose and not regret.

Before I knew what to say, Xavior plucked the ring from the box and took my hand. He looked at my face while he slid the ring onto my left forefinger. For one moment, his hand covered the ring. When he lifted my hand to his lips and kissed my knuckles, the shield symbol on the ring was gone.

"What did you do?"

"I didn't alter it, only added a glamour hiding the part that makes you resent yourself. You're a gift, Gregor, and I'm lucky to have you in my life."

"You sure about that?"

"More than anything," Xavior replied.

THE CONNECTION

XAVIOR

Sometimes I wondered if Greg realized how much he affected me. Elements have mercy, but sometimes the rest of my long life feels like a fever dream because he wasn't in it until now.

I had so many questions for Faith. I understood so much more about her relationship with Trevor than before. I'd always compared it to some horrible burden to be connected via pheromones. They had to deal with each other, whether they wanted to or not. They sensed each other's pain, emotions, and longing, even when they were apart.

The more I picked up from Greg, the more I craved feeling anything from him. To understand him in a way no one else would ever be able to because of the connection we shared. It was one thing to pick up his emotions through his scent. It was another to share a sense of each other and be open and honest about it. While it worked for us now, I also knew it was the reason my sister and her mate took time apart. They needed a break from each other after being connected for so long. Greg and I wouldn't have that kind of time, though I wished with all my heart that we did. Even with all the magic that existed in the world, we'd only have his lifetime, and that had to be enough.

"You're worried." Greg touched my face. "Having regrets?"

"Not about us." I kissed him, trying to chase away the confusion we both felt.

I turned toward him, pressing closer along his side. He immediately responded to the contact. I tested it further with a slight movement that made Greg groan.

I laughed. "Being able to sense each other gives us advantages. For example . . ." I traced my hand down his chest until I reached his cock. As I wrapped my hand around it, Greg's eyes widened, then closed as his lips parted. I picked up on his need and pleasure like an open book.

"But . . ." I couldn't keep my voice even.

"But?" Greg asked with a breathy voice.

"We should work on mental shields . . . later."

"Later," Greg repeated as he thrust his hips to make his cock slide through my hand.

His lust and desire combined with his smell to nearly consume me. I wanted to lick every centimeter of him. I wanted to wrap myself up in him until I didn't know what time it was, or what day, or whether the world existed outside of this bed.

A rational bit in the back of my head knew that was not practical, but practicality could fuck off. If I had been anything with my sex life and relationships, it was practical. No expectations, no requirements, just a good time at metered intervals so as to not create an attachment.

Greg's voice broke through the odd mental track that threatened to derail us again. "If you're thinking about anything other than sucking my dick in the next thirty seconds, I'm going to turn you over and drive those thoughts out of your head."

I blinked. *Fuck me, that was fucking hot.* Greg didn't mind if I took control at times, but when that subtle dominance made an appearance, I wanted nothing more than to bathe in that scent and ask for more. While I was with Naomi, I hadn't looked at it too closely. I wasn't about to right now with Greg.

I weighed a bit more than my size suggested in my bipedal form, but not much, and not anything Greg couldn't handle.

We'd sparred in the gym enough for me to know that. I still yelped in surprise when Greg quickly maneuvered and rolled us so he was on top.

I stared while he took a deep breath and gave me a slow smile. My hands rested on his shoulders while his arms bracketed my body and his cock slid against mine.

"Better," Greg said with a slight growl in his voice. His lips slammed into mine. And he was right, I stopped thinking. I ground against him as we devoured each other's mouths. My hands moved to his neck to keep him close.

He practically wrenched himself free from my lips and gasped for air, intent on something. When he found his voice, it was hoarse with need. "Supplies?" he asked, in a half-question, half-groan, while he continued to slide his dick alongside mine.

"Fuck, um, drawer." I pointed to a nightstand. The loss of his body heat made me feel exposed. When he returned with a condom and lube, I realized I was shaking.

He leaned down and gave me a gentle kiss. "You alright?" he asked as he paused.

"Yes. Very. I'm trying to be patient."

Greg made a silent "Oh" with his mouth, kissed me again, and then covered his dick with the condom.

I fisted my hands in the sheets to keep from reaching. I watched as Greg poured a generous amount of lube onto his fingers, then watched as his hand slipped out of view. His fingers slipped between my ass cheeks and quickly found their target as he gently pushed one digit against my hole. The sensation made me close my eyes as I lost myself to the feeling.

The first finger was nice, the second stretched me a little more, but by the time he got to the third finger, I knew he was being a tease. "Fuck, Greg, please." He found my gland and played with it as I writhed under him. "You're going to make me come if you keep that up."

He eased his fingers out of me, then set himself in the wider opening he'd created. He added more lube and slowly pushed into me. I whimpered as he groaned. He continued until his hips met the back of my thighs. I wrapped my legs around him, and we stayed like that for a moment or two, panting into each other's faces. I noted the tremble in his lip, the slight flex of his thighs as he held himself back.

Now that we were here, connected, mind and body, neither of us wanted it to end. Our kisses were lazy at first. Almost gentle. Greg started with slight movements that teased like his fingers had previously. As I matched his pace, he moved his hips more. Each kiss amped up our need for each other.

Greg's brown eyes were intent on my face. His hands drifted along my neck and shoulders. The friction became intense, and his touches seemed like brands on my sensitive skin. When I felt him caress the hidden scales underneath, I gasped as it caught us by surprise.

I worried Greg might stop or slow down, concerned for me in some way. Instead, his hand snaked into my hair and grasped it, then pulled so that I bared my throat. He drove into me faster as he bit and sucked at my neck and shoulder.

I held onto him as his quick thrusts caused me to come over both of us. As I lay there, slightly befuddled with pleasure, Greg wrapped his arms around my shoulders, then made four long, brutal thrusts into me. I felt his dick throb as he came, groaning into my shoulder.

I had no concept of time or where we were, only that I felt deeply connected to the man in my arms. Eventually, Greg moved his head, and as he did, he pressed soft kisses from my neck to my face, then my lips.

He was still half-hard inside of me. "Tell me when you're ready," he whispered.

"I could just . . ." I waved my fingers, and Greg chuckled.

"Oh no, no magic in the state you're in. I'd like my dick to stay attached to me."

I laughed, and he picked that moment to pull out. The sensation brought on a ghost of an orgasm. I shivered through it for a few moments as Greg held me. I blinked and looked up at him.

Your ex was fucking clueless. I had just enough sense not to say it out loud. It was fair to say that I've had a lot of sex with many species, and it's never been like that. Whatever Keith was chasing obviously had nothing to do with Greg's capabilities in bed.

My expression must have seemed funny because Greg laughed softly and caressed my cheek. I was in awe. How had I ended up this lucky? "Come on, let's clean up so we can get dirty again." He gave me another kiss, then moved. He offered his hand, and I followed.

THAT ONE THING

GREGOR

"Bathroom lights, fifty percent." The bathroom controls responded as expected, only to be given another command moments later.

"Lights, twenty-five percent," Xavior called out.

I chuckled. "Mood lighting?"

"Maybe," he said with a soft laugh. "It's too bright."

I turned to look at him, and that's when I noticed his eyes had changed. "Do they normally do that after sex?"

"Does what do what?" he asked, confusion on his face even though I felt his desire, and slightly sated lust. It was like being near a banked fire that would only need one kiss to bring it back to a roar.

"Your eyes, they look like your dragon form."

"Oh, fuck." He laughed. "That explains why everything is so fucking bright." He followed me into the shower and took a seat on the bench.

"Shower on," I called to the voice-activated system. The shower heads sprang to life. "Do you want to stand or sit for a bit?"

"I'm not sure how long my legs will hold me up. I'm surprised I made it this far."

"You good here for a second while I grab soap?" Xavior nodded as he put his hands on the marble bench to steady himself. I quickly grabbed a bottle and a cloth. I poured soap onto the fabric and started washing him. "You look pretty spaced out."

"Yeah, I feel like it, too."

"Is that normal?" I ran the cloth over his arms and legs as we talked.

"No, not really. I've been tired, but I've never felt this before."

"Is it more pheromone stuff?"

"Maybe. I don't know."

As I moved to his chest, he gave a heady sigh, scales surfacing and disappearing as my hands caressed him. Xavior was still pretty dazed. He had always trusted me, despite my ability. To see him this vulnerable gave me a fierce desire to protect him.

My mate. My love. Mine.

The possessive thoughts gave me a hyper-focus. Details impressed themselves on my brain. Like the feel of his muscles under my fingers and the power of his limbs, even though he was in a relaxed state. The difference between the texture of his hair on his head, arms, and legs and the trimmed pubic hair around his dick and balls. The light dusting of hair and freckles on his ass amused me, and the languid look on his face made my heart feel like it was being squeezed in my chest. His skin was flawless. Not a scar anywhere I could see. If his phoenix episode did that, I was grateful. I didn't want him to have a reminder of what happened.

I finished cleaning us up and wrapped him in a fluffy bathrobe, then wrapped a towel around my waist. As we got back into bed, I put my arms around him and tucked him against me. The longer Xavior was quiet the more worried and out-of-sorts I felt.

While we both had experience, and perhaps Xavior had a lot of experience, to have him not know what was happening was disconcerting. The way I felt concerned me, too. I'd never felt this possessive of anyone before. Touching Xavior cooled an itch just under my skin. I tried not to think too hard about it as we drifted to sleep.

When I woke up later, I walked out to the living area to find Xavior busy eating his way through a small buffet of food.

"Hope you're hungry. I was starving. It feels like I haven't eaten in days."

I smiled as I walked over to join him. He shoved a piece of cheese into his mouth, then grinned. "Um, I think I figured out what happened to me. I mean, why I was so out of it?"

I made myself a plate from the plethora of food options and sat in the chair to the left of his at the end of the table. "Oh?" I dug into an omelet and waited for his explanation.

"Do you happen to know anything about dominance and submission?"

I nearly choked. I coughed and picked up a glass of juice, taking a swallow to clear my throat. "Why?"

"Because, and maybe you haven't realized it, but you have moments when we're together where you're clearly directing things."

"I have?"

"Yes."

"Why didn't you say anything earlier?" I hadn't realized I was doing something he didn't like. That bothered me. This entire conversation bothered me.

"Because I thought you understood what you were doing, and I liked it. Don't you think I would have said something otherwise?" My eyes focused on Xavior's mouth as he wiped it with a napkin.

I moved on from his lips to his eyes. The amusement I sensed from him, mixed with kindness, was a stark contrast to my awkwardness and curiosity. It was all good for him to talk about his biological needs and for me to set boundaries, but now that the table was turned, I understood how hard it was to separate feelings and needs. Had I let my need for boundaries morph into a need to be dominant, or worse, a need to control our relationship? Was that why I was feeling possessive earlier?

I thought about what he said for a moment, then answered him after applying a bit of logic. "Not necessarily," I pointed out. "You've had biological imperatives driving you, driving us both.

I'm still not sure if you can actually be angry with me, or anyone else either for that matter."

"Oh, well, I have. With my brother, for one. Your ex for another. I remember at various points over the year thinking I shouldn't meet him alone. Then I did, and he survived the encounter."

I sat up straight. "When the hell did that happen?"

"My birthday party. He walked into my library naked, with another person. We exchanged some heated words and he left. At the time, I knew he was scared of me, angry, and jealous. I liked it. I wanted him to know I was better than he was, and he couldn't possibly ever measure up. Then I felt like shit after because I knew he'd take it out on you somehow."

We'd stopped referencing Keith by name. Usually, the "ex" or "he" was only mentioned in passing with a slightly less than neutral tone. Xavior was not even near neutral at the moment, and whatever he remembered had sent a heady mix of emotions in my direction.

Xavior continued. "I know what I can do when I'm angry, and it's significantly more damage than a hedge witch."

"Okay, so you aren't angry very often. I can accept that. Still, I think being explicit about boundaries is a far cry from the dynamic you're describing." Or so I thought.

"Some of our experiences together lead me to believe otherwise," Xavior said with a mischievous smile.

"Such as?" I had my doubts, but they were wavering. I remembered the night with Keith at Xavior's house. I'd thought it was just magic influencing me.

"Our first date, the way you laid it out. Maybe not the specifics, but certainly the parameters. The phone call after, and other calls we had. Rewards and punishments around our original boundaries."

"When did I punish you?" That surprised me. Punishment from my mother, Narissa, was more exercise or manual labor. A punishment from Philip, my dad, meant taking on chores at my pace or helping him with the wood shop. Jennifer, my stepmom, would make me write what I felt or help her with tasks. I honestly had no idea what he was talking about.

"Remember when we were hanging out after work right after we started dating, and I tried to kiss you in public?"

"Yeah. Our coworkers were in the bar that night. We'd only been dating a few weeks, and I didn't think it was smart." I shrugged. He might not have had to worry about his career all that much, but I did, at least before the vampire altercation.

"We didn't have our call that night because of it." He smiled as he added butter to a biscuit. "You said I needed to learn patience and made me wait a whole day before we could talk about things other than work."

"Oh. Shit." My hand settled over my eyes. I felt horrible. My need to control our relationship in a way I could handle had clearly impacted Xavior, but he'd been patient with me. "I was trying to figure out how to keep our boundaries. I didn't intend to be an asshole about it."

"Greg, look at me." I turned toward him as he set down his food. "I never said I didn't like it." He moved toward me, reached for my hand, and nudged me to stand as well. He wrapped his arms around me. I couldn't help but mirror him.

"As a matter of fact, I like it a lot. The problem is, you didn't know what you were doing, and I had no idea that you were working on instinct instead of experience or knowledge."

I'm not sure how high my eyebrows were. My emotions felt optimistic, but erratic. The one I landed on was an odd sense of shame. "I . . ." I tried again. Then his words registered as they broke through the multiple feelings and thoughts we shared. "Wait, you like it?"

"Yes." He caressed my back in a way that soothed me. While the conversation made me feel awkward, he never did, and I appreciated that.

"So what happened earlier was in response to what I did?"

"Yes. While I've had some experiences, last night was the first time I've lost myself so completely. Before, it was mostly emotional or physical, not both."

I slowly let go of him. "Do I want to know?"

He smiled. "You're jealous."

"Yes. Why are you smiling?" I shook my head, and I couldn't find it in me to be upset with him. I knew I could be jealous, but it was alright because he was with me, regardless of who he was with before. Xavior and I chose each other.

"Because I think it's all tied together." He stepped away from my embrace and held out his hand. I took it, and he led me to the couch. When we sat, he turned to face me. "You're trying to protect yourself. Which makes sense, because someone you trusted hurt you. I've hurt you. You're not mean about anything you've done, but you've made clear demands, given directions, and set boundaries every step of the way."

"But none of that means I'm a dominant, Xav. It means you're putting up with someone who has a lot of emotional and mental baggage."

"Call it what you want, but I'm not putting up with you. You've always discussed things with me, even when you've made decisions for both of us. I'm not trapped. I've had choices the whole time. Nothing has been an ultimatum or even a burden. There's a difference."

"If you say so."

"I do. I've been in a controlling relationship. When I got out, I spent the next two centuries avoiding anything that even resembled a relationship."

"You've never told me this before." I squeezed his hand. "Do you want to talk about it?"

He nodded. "I met Jordan when I was pretty young, while he was traveling. He was a carpenter then. I didn't find out until recently that he had a partner and children and that she had passed some time before we met. We spent a summer fixing houses and had fantastic sex."

I groaned. Xavior continued. "What I'm saying is, he was my first, but he was also almost a century older, maybe more. I didn't ask. He knew I was young and told me to figure out what I wanted from life, then find him. After the summer was over, he left. I left my family too. I went from Spain to Britain. My sister Faith and her mate Trevor had started a family there. I stayed with them for a while. Traveled around there for a bit, and then met Bianca."

"How old were you when you were with Jordan that first time?"

"Forty-five or fifty. I don't quite remember. Barely an adult by dragon standards. To most people, I wouldn't have looked much older than twenty. Unfortunately, it's also about the time we develop obsessions," he said as he sat back on the couch.

"You've never mentioned Bianca." It was a reminder that we hadn't known each other that long.

"I haven't for good reason. I get enough crap from my family about Bianca, and she's my past."

I sensed regret. A lot of regret. To sit with his emotions was hard sometimes, especially when I wanted to protect him. "What happened?" I wondered how many people outside of his family knew.

"Well, I thought I'd found someone mysterious, exciting, and a little dangerous. It was all rather heady, to be honest." He gave me a bit of a look that seemed to ask, *does that sound familiar?*

"But?" Because it definitely sounded like there was one in the mix.

"She's a vampire."

"You were in a relationship with a vampire?" I was surprised, but I really shouldn't have been. This was Xavior, after all. "How did that work, exactly?"

"Well, when two species are interested in each other . . ."

"Xavior." I shook my head. He added humor to the conversation when he wanted to avoid talking about something serious. "I mean with the pheromones. Vampires aren't, technically speaking, among the living."

"It worked, but it was a false connection." The amount of sadness I felt from him hurt. It mixed with his regret and sat between us. Something went wrong, or he wouldn't have been alone so long.

"I met her before I reached my first aging cycle. We'd shared blood the whole time. I thought nothing of it. I did it for love and I wanted her to be happy. I even removed several scales so she could feed without hurting herself." He absently touched a spot on his neck. It was close to the same place I'd bitten him. He took a deep breath and continued.

"When my aging cycle started, I sensed her, or I thought I did. She claimed she was never able to, though she used that to hold me to her when she figured out that what I was sensing wasn't really her."

"How so?"

"It was a reflection. My blood powered her being. So whatever I picked up from her, it was basically me. My own senses and emotions. At least that's what I eventually figured out. She even smelled a little like me. Though I thought that was because she was, you know, mostly dead."

I held his hand to reassure him as he continued. "My sister found out when I brought Bianca with me to visit. Faith picked up on something that I hadn't and begged me to stop feeding her and told me that if we had a genuine connection, feeding her wouldn't matter."

"Did you?" I gave his hand a squeeze.

"No. We stayed together for another decade. Bianca used me as her private bodyguard. I stayed with her in her home, but we didn't sleep together that often, only when she wanted to feed." He glanced at me, then continued. "Then she made a mistake when I visited my sister for a few weeks. She fed on someone else while I was gone and when I got back, she barely smelled like anything I recognized. I couldn't sense her any longer, either. I often wondered if she did it on purpose. She clearly didn't love me. I realized that what I thought I sensed was really my love for her.

"Her family was a different story. I did a lot of work for them. Especially around finding things. A lot of it was tracking down people and money. Sometimes art and artifacts." He'd told me once that he hadn't always been a public safety officer, and hearing he was involved with a coven family wasn't exactly a surprise, but it shocked me a little. "I liked the challenge of it and made a reputation from it. They weren't happy with either of us when I left."

Vampire covens were notorious for flaunting the law or working just enough inside of it that they got away with a lot. When the Vampire Accord came along, it codified their behavior and justified it, which let them govern themselves. The coalition of covens used the Necromantic War to their advantage. The other part of the deal was that the covens had to stay out of world government and political structures, though it's rarely enforced.

"I left Britain, came to the Americas and wandered around for a bit, then met up with Jordan again."

"Why didn't the two of you ever make that work?" I tried to be neutral with my question, but I didn't quite manage it. Xavior smiled as he explained.

"Um, he's fun. I like him. But he's not you, Greg. Plus, by the time Jordan realized he wanted more than a fuck buddy, it was too late."

I tugged on his hand and pulled him toward me. "His loss," I said as I wrapped my arms around Xavior and gave him a kiss.

"Yeah, he thought so too."

My brain swam with this new information. It put into perspective why Xavior had acted like he did and how much his first century had shaped his life. It occurred to me that I should be grateful for Jordan. If he'd stayed with Xavior, I wouldn't be here with him now. I hoped that at some point, I wouldn't be jealous of Xavior's past. Not when I was part of his future.

THE GRAND TOUR

XAVIOR

I untangled myself from Greg and gently slapped his knee. "Enough of this serious stuff. We have a whole resort to explore. What do you say to some drinks by a pool with a view?"

Greg looked at me and sighed. "Why not?" He shrugged.

"Let's finish eating breakfast, then head out." I went back to the table, and Greg followed. The rest of the conversation was about the food and the varieties of things the resort had available.

I grabbed the complimentary pool bag that had towels, sunscreen, and a couple of ball caps. I also threw in condoms and lube as a bit of wishful thinking. The whole point was to have Greg relax. If I managed that, at least I'd be prepared.

I walked out of the bedroom to see he'd changed into a pair of board shorts, with sunglasses propped on his head and sandals on his feet.

Greg was clearly interested in what he saw. "Fuck." He shook his head. "You can't walk around like that."

"Like what? Everything important is covered," I stated, pretending I didn't know the show I was clearly making with my clothing choice. My shorts were barely on my hips, and the material shifted colors with the light. One minute green, another blue, then translucent. It created a peep show of sorts, which was reasonably modest, especially since clothing was optional throughout the resort.

"Maybe I should bring my shield," he said as he moved closer. "I might have to defend you from unwanted advances."

"I'm pretty capable of defending myself, sir, or haven't you noticed?" I took a few steps toward him. He closed the distance.

"The idea of growling at people as they approach appeals to me," he said as his arms looped around me and tightened. The move brought us close enough to feel his thighs pressed against mine.

"Your growl is pretty sexy." I laid on the sarcasm pretty thick, but in truth, I really liked it.

He narrowed his eyes. "You're doing this on purpose."

"Yes," I admitted as I groped his ass and got the previously mentioned sexy growl.

"Okay." Greg took a tiny step back. "We have to get out of here before we don't." His obvious response brushed against my leg before he moved. I was similarly affected.

"You're right. Besides, we could find another spot to have sex if you wanted." I let go of him and headed toward the door.

"I'm not having sex in public, Xavior."

"You say that now," I teased.

Fifteen minutes later, walking through the resort toward one of my favorite areas, we passed a lot of different sunbathing species, most without clothing. Some were definitely engaged in sexual activity.

"Wow, ents are so, um." Greg hummed as he fished for a word, then sneezed.

"Colorful?" I offered.

"That's, yeah, maybe. I'm still trying not to be grossed out that we inadvertently walked through their spore cloud."

I laughed. "Other species find it to be like an aphrodisiac or good luck. Especially those that are sentient plants. Orgies with plant species are a trip, sometimes literally, because some of them have psychedelic properties. Spore parties are one event they offer here, if you're interested."

"That's a definite no. I prefer my boyfriend's gametes, thanks."

"I promise I'll pollinate you later." Greg snort-laughed, then sneezed again, and I couldn't help laughing. "The spot I want to show you isn't much farther."

"I hope so. I'm thirsty. Why this mysterious pool area rather than the other dozen or more we've already passed?"

"You'll see." I took Greg's hand as we rounded a corner.

We walked for another ten minutes, and when we reached it, I watched the sheer childlike delight appear on Greg's face, like the sun had come out from behind the clouds. "Dragons." That one word from his lips sounded like a benediction.

He squeezed my hand. I felt the ring dig into my palm. Even though the glamour had helped, I realized it also helped him hide in plain sight. Greg wasn't the only one that would have a very negative response to the symbol on his ring.

"Welcome to the dragon pools. Wide and shallow, with a mix of heated and cooled pools and waterfalls. All with enough space, air circulation, and water movement to not trigger territory issues."

"This has to stretch for a kilometer or more!" He took a step forward, then stopped. "Wait, this is like your den."

"How can you tell?"

"I can sense the entrance."

"You can do more than sense it. You see past the barrier. If you didn't have a dragon with you, you would walk right past this and not even know it was here. To anyone else, it would look like a dead end." I gave Greg's hand a tug. "Come on, let's find a spot."

We walked in and wandered around until we found a secluded pool with only one other couple. The smaller wyrm dragons played at the far end from us and waved as they splashed in the water.

"How is this place possible?"

"Dragon magic, mostly. They created it with several pocket dimensions. A family of dragons lived here, and over the years, with fae help, they've combined and expand their space."

"What happens to a place like this if a dragon dies?"

"If no one has the key to a pocket space when the dragon dies, it basically disappears. Sometimes families pass spaces down and can combine them with their own or maintain multiple spaces. Spaces exist because of the energy put into them by dragons. If that exchange stops, the pocket collapses. Or at least that's what Denis said when I asked about it once."

"So you don't get it either?"

"Nope," I said with a laugh. Greg grinned as we found a spot and dropped our stuff.

A pixie dragon appeared as soon as we settled. They were about the size of Greg's forearm. They had a tiny device around their neck that turned into a holo menu that introduced them and let us order our drinks. It was a clever way of communicating since they weren't shifters and have their own language that sounds like growls, barks, and squeaks to everyone else.

"Thank you, T'mony," Greg said as the dragon flew off. "I didn't know they could be that small."

"Yeah. Pixie dragons stick to wild areas or places like this where they have free rein. They also like to pull pranks. Best comparisons are cats and dogs."

"Alright, I admit, this place is pretty amazing." Greg laid back on the lounger, entirely at ease. It made me happy to see him relax.

I pulled the bottle of suntan lotion out of the bag. "This is a fraction of this place. Wait until tonight."

"What's tonight?"

"Parties the likes of which most deities would be envious of."

Greg chuckled. "If you say so."

"Ye of little faith," I said.

P☉OLSIDE

GREGOR

I wasn't sure about the parties, but if I wanted to embrace the idea of this being a vacation, I'd commit to trying. So I laid back on the lounge chair, content to dragon watch.

A moment or two after the pixie dragon disappeared with our orders, Xavior appeared next to me with his half-invisible swim trunks and a bottle of suntan lotion. Thinking about it now, it was obvious Xavior was an exhibitionist. He seemed more himself, more comfortable here than in the city, and it wasn't simply because of the opulence.

Dens were safe places for dragons. To be inside a den with other dragons must be familiar, if not a little dangerous. That fit Xavior to a tee.

"Sit up for me," he said.

I did as he asked. He slipped behind me and slathered my back with lotion. "Am I likely to get sunburnt in a pocket dimension?"

"It's the same sun as outside. They thinned the bubble enough so natural light can enter. Given that you're human, the pocket distortion, and being near the water, a sunburn is more likely. I'd rather you not have to seek medical attention later for something completely avoidable."

"So it's like being on a boat." His hands felt good on my back, firm but gentle.

"Yeah, pretty much. Here." Xavior handed me the bottle, and I applied it to my torso. His hands continued to drift across my back and down my sides. When he eventually stilled, he leaned forward and kissed my skin between my neck and my shoulder on the left side.

"How is it you don't end up with a sunburn even though you have fair skin?" I asked.

"Best guess is my scales, and maybe that I have an affinity for fire twice over because of my phoenix half as well."

"More explanations from Denis?" I joked.

"No. I mean, I'm sure he has his theories, but it doesn't take several science and magical focused degrees to work things out. I'm quite capable of deductive reasoning."

The slight affront in his voice and the swell of pride I sensed made me reach to comfort him. His legs bracketed my hips, and I leaned back a little and caressed what I could touch. "I know." It's not as if I could forget that we worked together. "You have a lot more than a sore spot about your brother, don't you?"

"He's . . ." His frustration was apparent even without my newfound sense. "He's infuriatingly perfect at everything. If my parents requested anything, Denis would dutifully comply." I realized I had struck a nerve when Xavior continued.

"Denis understood his obsession before me. He found a mate before me. He's obtained several degrees and worked with some of the most prominent minds ever known. His mate is one of those minds, by the way, though I've never met them. And he's an insufferable know-it-all, too."

"Wow." My touches seemed to calm him. As quickly as he felt frustrated, it would fade as long as I moved my hands across his skin. "I get it. I mean, it's tough when you have a sibling that your parents compare you to."

"I take it your mother was no better in that category?"

"Worse, she was competitive about it. I remember competitions over trips into town. Toys. Equipment. I was the oldest, so I won a lot, but eventually my younger sibling won as often, if not more. Katie and I were the same height, though I filled out a bit more and had three years on her."

I sighed. Xavior rubbed my back, which helped, so I continued to talk. "When I could, I'd set an example by sharing. She followed suit when she was older and protected our other siblings and cousins from my mother as much as I did."

Xavior's hands caressed my sides while I touched his thigh and calves. We were comforting each other. I felt calm even though talking about my family brought up a lot of emotions for me.

"My mother kicked Katie out like she did me when Katie told my mother she was gay. About a year later, Katie came out as a trans woman. We've talked now and then over the years. She's visited me a couple of times, though she lives further south somewhere between San Diego and Tijuana."

"Maybe when things settle a bit, we can invite her for a visit?"

"Maybe. I don't know how she feels about our family history. We purposefully don't talk about it. She wasn't raised by my father either, and her dad, my stepdad, preferred our mother's money over parenting. Her father is still married to my mother last I knew."

"You think she would feel threatened by me?"

"I don't know." While Katie and I were a lot alike, I knew she was much more ruthless when we were training and eventually more skilled than I was with just about everything. When we talked, we didn't chat about our childhood, her thoughts about The Order, or our ability. I didn't want to put Xavior at more risk without knowing for sure that she'd left that life behind.

We kept up our soothing touches. When Xavior's hands drifted across my torso, then lower, I almost let him go further, until a portal opened and a cheerful fae with a tray of drinks walked out, T'mony flying around them.

"Hello! I have a Hurricane and a Pink Tortoise. Will that be all?" She was barely clothed, and her wings flickered behind her. She changed colors from a dusty rose to a deep red while we thanked her. I'd never seen that happen before. After she opened a portal and left with the pixie dragon following close behind, Xavior got up and returned to his seat.

"That was curious."

"How so?"

"She changed colors. Did you know fae could do that?"

"Yes," he said with a smile. Oh right, Jordan.

"So, are you willing to explain, or do I have to find out on my own?"

"Oh, the pale pink, with some variation depending on melanin, is usually their normal color without the glamour to make themselves look more human. The red, that's lust, passion, desire . . ."

I cut him off. "Okay, okay. But why us?"

"Why not? You have this tall, mysterious, tattooed mystique about you, and I'm a carefree, horny dragon. She could guess at our relationship, but it wouldn't matter. She's free to be herself and not have people look at her oddly for a display of emotions."

"Oh, that's pretty cool." I looked down at my own hands, smiled, and looked back at Xavior. "She didn't expect anything from us, did she?"

"No, she would have said something if that were the case. Verbal consent is important here. It was a compliment, but definitely not an invitation."

That made sense. I turned to look at Xavior as he sipped his frozen pink concoction.

"What are you drinking?"

"It's a Pink Lady, but frozen. It's good. You want to try it?"

Xavior held it out for me and watched as I took a sip. "Not bad, but definitely not a Hurricane."

"I'm surprised you ordered that. You barely drink anything stronger than beer. That's got a bit of a kick to it."

"I'll drink it slowly. You wanted me to relax. I'm trying to kickstart it a little."

Xavior chuckled. "That's the spirit."

I adjusted my sunglasses and leaned back in the lounge chair. The sun felt good on my skin. When I looked over at Xavior again, I noticed his scales. The reflection from the pool touched his skin, and the iridescent properties I'd seen in the shower showed as the light bounced off them. I was in a bit of a trance when Xavior spoke up.

"See something you like, Greg?"

I grinned. "Everything. I really like everything."

He chuckled. "You've had three sips and you're already tipsy."

"I'm not. I swear!"

"Sure, lightweight."

"Not all of us have the constitution of a dragon."

Xavior shrugged, then seemed to think of something. "How about a toast?"

I turned toward him. "Sure. You have something?"

"To a wonderful partner two times over. To vacationing in grand style, and to next steps, whatever those may be." He nodded toward me.

"To more adventures and hopefully a life well lived, together."

We touched our glasses, then took a drink. This vacation marked the beginning of our relationship beyond dating. With any luck, the rest would come in time.

THE DRAGON'S GROVE

XAVIOR

It was because of Dragon's Grove that I continued to maintain a membership here. There were more dragons of various types in this one place than any other I'd ever seen, so it didn't surprise me that Greg thought it was special, too.

Every decade, the resort hosts would open this place up to dragons from all over the world. They weren't required to have a membership and only paid a small fee to stay and use the resort. Dragons would share knowledge, obsessions, and hope to find mates or show off their own mates. It was the original function of the resort before they expanded it to other species that needed more accommodating spaces to be themselves from time to time.

"You know what's amazing about this place?" I looked over at Greg as he waved his hand around. It was nice to see him relax, even if he had a little liquid help.

"Do tell," I said, wholly amused.

"Until I met you and knew about your family, I was pretty sure there weren't that many dragons left in the world. Even with your family, there are still not that many. Now, I'm sitting in a place where there are more dragons than most have ever seen in centuries. How is this possible?"

"It's possible because it's necessary. Dragons, like unicorns, were hunted. Long before your family line became famous, people would hunt dragons for all kinds of reasons. It's said that we developed our bipedal form as a guise, a skin that makes us look human enough so we could hide in plain sight. We passed that trait to our descendants. But some, like the pixie dragons, aren't capable of it."

"That's depressing," Greg said as he took another drink. "With the Magical Species Pact in place, it's safer, isn't it?"

The pact was one of the last gifts from the unicorns and other elder magical species before they disappeared. Together, they created a geas that made supernatural beings magically inert upon death. It was carefully done so magical beings could still offer things in trade, or as gifts, like dragon scales, and they would retain their magical properties until the giver died.

What that council of elders hadn't counted on was the discovery of another part of the planet with unique magic, or magic involving death and the undead. If they had any idea how the populations of the Americas, the Caribbean, and parts of Asia would be colonized and nearly eradicated in some fools' rush for new world magic, gold, and enslaved people, I wonder if they would have hesitated. As it was, the MSP held up better if your particular magical species originated in Europe versus anywhere else on the planet.

History said Joseph Florentine's reason for going to war was the MSP. Many believe the real reason was that while he had a great deal of power as a necromancer, if he could gain the magical powers of the newly dead, he would have been unstoppable. As it was, his control of zombies and vampires with their own powers had proven how little the MSP protected anyone.

"Might be slightly safer, but if you've been around for a thousand years and watched other species prey on your kind, you tend to be cautious. Unfortunately, humans aren't the only danger to us."

"What else could possibly take on a dragon?"

"Well, unicorns, for one. They were the main species that enforced the MSP to begin with, and they had enough magic to do it. Some deities might have enough magic, along with necromancers and giants."

"Giants?"

I nodded. "I haven't seen a full-sized one in a while, but they would often thrive in the spaces other species couldn't, like deserts, mountains, and tundras. Most of them were as large as or larger than dragons. I saw one when I was much younger. I don't know how long they live. They are very solitary creatures, and they don't like dragons. I'm not sure why that is either."

"My education feels very inadequate."

"Cut yourself some slack. You haven't had almost four hundred years to learn things. Mostly by living it. Some I truly wished I had read about instead of venturing off to find."

"Are there any other species that don't like dragons?"

"Whales."

"Why's that?"

"It's mostly because of water dragons. In some areas of the world, they used to hunt each other. There were stories about water dragons and orcas fighting for territories and feeding grounds. It's been hundreds of years since that's been the case. Likely because both their numbers are so small now."

"Whales hunted dragons?"

"Before the merfolk disappeared, one of them wrote about it. It's in my den."

Greg looked astonished. I chuckled. "You said it yourself. I have lifetimes of knowledge, but some of that knowledge isn't only about my life."

I left Greg with that thought and walked to the edge of the shallow pool.

"Are you going to get in?"

"Yeah. It'll feel good on my scales." I sat on the edge, swung my legs over, and dropped in. The water line hit me a little higher than my waist. I stripped off my swim trunks and waited until I got Greg's attention, then tossed them at his head.

A bright blush bloomed on his face as he held them in his hands. A moment later, I shifted and displaced a good bit of water in the process. I rolled in the water to coat my scales, then remembered another part of the grove had trees and rocks you could sunbathe and scratch your scales on. I made a mental note to take Greg there later.

When I lifted my head, I noticed Greg at the pool's edge. I moved to nuzzle him and rub my scent along his skin. He sensed what I was doing.

"Possessive much?"

I gave him an affirmative response. Greg laughed.

"I get it, me too." He kissed my snout and ran his hands along the scales under my jaw.

"You're even more spectacular in the light of day," Greg said. "Are the feathers on your wings and tail because of your phoenix half?" I gave another affirmative response.

Greg's scent was a heady mixture of attraction, adoration, and delight. I sniffed at it like a fine wine. Mixed with the scent that my brain called 'Greg,' I couldn't help but be a little turned on. When astonishment mixed in with it, I looked at Greg and noticed what had drawn his attention.

"Xav, that's as big as my leg." I made an amused noise in response. "Seeing it in real life is a lot different from seeing it on anatomy charts."

I nudged my snout into his side. I gave him one tap, then another, to see if Greg would be a little adventurous and get into the pool with me.

"I'm sensing something like mischief from you." I made a light noise to convey my surprise. Greg's voice dropped to a whisper. "Xavior, are you seriously trying to get me into the water so I can touch your dick?"

I adjusted my head so I could see him better. When I gave a soft affirmative sound, he chuckled. "You're such a fucking hornball."

His curiosity got the better of him. He slipped into the water and moved toward me slowly. I tried to be still and make as few waves as possible. I had no idea what his hands would feel like, but I was curious to find out.

As Greg approached my side and ran his hands along my stomach, I stifled a shiver. It didn't quite tickle, but it felt nice. Then he ran his finger through the feathers on my wings. I shook them out in response. Greg laughed as drops of water fell on him. When he glanced down into the water, I tried not to move as I watched as his hand dip below the surface, then caressed me. The mixed growl and moan I vocalized in response surprised us both.

"It feels soft, like velvet. I wasn't expecting that," Greg said.

I wasn't aware my stimulation follicles could be so sensitive. His soft touch made me want to move my hips. I barely kept control, shivering with the effort. In response, Greg moved his hand away. I vocalized my disappointment as he chuckled.

"Not in public, Xav. Besides, I can only imagine what the pool would look like afterward. And I'm not the asshole to make someone clean that up."

I chuffed in response as he patted my belly. Greg kept a hand on me as he walked toward my chest, then caressed the curve of my neck until he reached my jaw. The mood shifted slightly, and the question Greg asked caught me off guard.

"Have you been with another dragon, Xav? Sexually, I mean."

That was another sore point with my family. While Denis wasn't with another dragon, he was mated to a shifter, and my family accepted that. I had been with other shifters, but I was never really drawn to them. When I was younger, I think my father sought to remedy the problem by bringing me here. The resort, and especially the grove, held plenty of options for mates. It's why they gathered every decade and made it a big party. What he hadn't expected, and neither had I until I was confronted with it, was that my hybrid nature was a detractor.

I was smaller and faster than other dragons. The smaller dragons, like the wyrms, admired my feathers, but I was too large, too loud, and too slow for them. In our bipedal forms, we all got along, but dragons were very picky.

I moved my head away from Greg's hands.

Greg followed and touched one of my horns. "Hey, it's okay. I'm sorry." I nuzzled him and he kissed the top of my snout again. After a while, I nudged him back toward the edge of the pool. He took the hint and moved until he could lever himself out of the water. I didn't miss how his swim trunks framed his ass as he twisted to sit on the edge of the pool.

As I rolled in the water to my feet, the wave I created splashed Greg's legs. I shook myself, fluttering my wings like a bird until most of the water was out of my feathers. Greg laughed, and that sound was one of the best things I'd ever heard. I moved out of the pool and motioned for him to follow. He grabbed our bag, the towels, grinning and curious as he followed.

"What are you up to, Xav?" Greg asked as he walked beside me down the wide walkway that branched off to different areas of the cove.

I conveyed a sense of patience to him, and he smiled. "Alright, Mr. Mysterious. I'll follow your lead."

Maybe the trees and sunning rocks would inspire a little more mischief in my mate.

THE TONGUE THING

GREGOR

We spent the whole day in Dragon's Grove. While we had intended to head back out after the sun set to find some evening activities, we got a little sidetracked after our shower.

I was drying my hair when Xavior came up behind me and reached under the towel wrapped around my waist. "We have time. Do you want a blowjob?"

With his hand around my dick, I struggled to think, let alone say no. Though if I told him no, he'd stop. "What would you like?"

"Um, I'll think of something later." He turned me around to face him. His hand continued to work me over as he backed me up to the bed and had me sit.

Xavior pressed his lips to mine, and we teased each other with panting alacrity. I put my hands on his hips, intending to place them elsewhere until he stopped what he was doing and reached for my hands.

"You relax," he said. "This is my show." He moved my hands back to the bed.

I chuckled. "Are you sure that's where you want my hands?"

"I'll let you know otherwise." I grinned as he kissed me again, opened my towel, and dropped to his knees.

His hand gently worked me into a solid state as I grabbed fistfuls of the bedding under me. He glanced up as he opened his mouth and sank the tip of me into all that wet warmth. I let out a soft groan from the feel of his mouth as he sucked and .. . licked?

My eyes flew open as I felt something wet and flat wrap around my cock. It slithered down the length of my dick and back up into Xavior's mouth before I could even comprehend what had happened. When he looked up, his eyes had changed to those of his dragon form.

He did it again without moving his head. I fell back onto the bed and tried to breathe as my brain processed the sensations. Once I had that under control so I wouldn't blow in the next thirty seconds, he changed it up.

Instead of wrapping his tongue around me, he pushed my cock to the back of his throat as his tongue snaked out and slid along my dick, past my balls, to touch my rim. I couldn't get a full breath while the sensations lit me like holiday lights.

"Holy. Fuck. Xavior."

Xavior's teasing chuckle only made it worse while he sucked and licked more places at once than was humanly possible. I shook from the stimulation, and he didn't let up amid my curses, gasps, and moans.

"Xav. Oh shit. Xavior!" I came with a loud grunt.

He didn't pull away and instead did something with his finger, then his tongue, to my hole. He teased until I gasped for air, then he pressed his finger back in. I came again and laid there as stars danced in my vision.

"Please, mercy. Fuck. Please." The words tumbled out of my mouth as Xavior's soft laughter tickled my pubic hair.

"Did you like it?"

"Did I like it?" I said with a shaky voice. "I'm wondering how you don't have everyone throwing themselves at your feet."

"Well," he started.

"No, no, don't answer that. I'm all too aware."

I felt him laugh, and it went straight to my dick, which decided I wasn't done yet. "It appears someone would like an encore."

"Oh no, no, not yet. Fuck, please. Give me a few minutes, regardless of what my dick is saying."

He kept contact with a very gentle handjob as I slowly got my breathing under control. I propped myself up on my elbows to look down at him. "Was that, in fact, the tongue thing?" I asked.

His grin threatened to split his face while he nodded. "Yes, however, I barely managed a fraction of what I could do before you came."

"Fraction? Holy shit, Xav." I laughed and shook my head. "Just be nice when I return the favor."

"Oh, I'm sure you'll do fine. You've kept my interest so far." His hand went back to gently caressing my half-hard dick, and I blew a breath through my teeth.

I watched his eyes and noticed him blink an internal eyelid. If I remember my anatomy classes, it was a nictitating membrane similar to frogs. He focused on something near my groin. I squeezed my eyes shut because I knew what he saw before he even opened his mouth. It surprised me he hadn't seen it before, but it was half-covered by pubic hair.

"Is this a tat, next to your penis? Fuck, Greg. You've been holding out on me." His hand stopped as he read the small letters. The next thing I knew, his face was buried in my groin, his laughter making my dick jump in his hand.

"Xavior. Shit!" I groaned.

"Sorry, sorry. 'Let's get dangerous?' Greg, what on earth made you get that?"

"A bet. Someone I was seeing at the time bet me a semester's worth of books that I would never get a tattoo." I smiled at him. "It was my first one, and it hurt like hell."

"Why didn't you do something on your leg or back?"

"Needed it some place I could hide it. My parents really would have lost their shit over me having a tattoo. Most guys never noticed. But every once in a while, someone would see it and it would catch them off guard."

"I can only imagine." His hand resumed working at my dick, since our conversation had reduced its mass. "Dragon tattoos are more complicated and painful. But they are easiest to get after molting, and use a scarring technique."

"Ever think about getting one?" It hadn't occurred to me that dragons would have to do something different to get a tattoo, but it made sense.

"Nah, not really. Most of the ones I've seen are of mating knots. There are pictures all over the manor of couples in our family showing them off. Simple enough patterns to burn into skin and scale. I figured if that was the only kind I could get permanently, forget it." He gave me a soft smile. "But maybe you're giving me ideas."

"I'm not burning anything into my skin," I protested.

"Oh, that's for me, not you. You can use needles if you like," Xavior said.

I shook my head. I reached for him, grasped his arm, and urged him up. He came without protest and settled next to me on the bed. He moaned softly as I kissed him.

We moved toward the center of the bed. Xavior laid on top of me as we touched and kissed each other. When he was more than ready, I reached over to the nightstand, grabbed the bottle of lube, and handed it to him.

"You sure?"

"You said you'd pollinate me." I couldn't help the twitch at the corner of my mouth as I tried to play it off as a casual suggestion.

"I did, didn't I?" He grinned, then stopped as he opened the lube. "Don't you want protection?"

"I'm not the one that can get pregnant. So unless you want to use it, I'm okay to skip it. I got myself tested when we started dating." I smiled. "Everything is good."

"I had myself checked back when we first started dating, just in case." That made me smile. "I won't go into details, but I will say that everything came back normal."

Something occurred to me as he teased and kissed his way down my body with that dragon-like tongue of his. "How do you talk so well with all that tongue in your mouth?"

"Practice."

I snickered until it was choked off as he put his mouth on me. I felt his fingers tease and probe my crease as he continued to torment me with his mouth.

The marked contrast in his approach to what I'd experienced with others was like a sunrise to my senses. While I'd always tried to be patient and careful, that wasn't often reciprocated. Xavior watched my face as he teased, then pushed a finger into me. I relaxed as he worked in more lube and caressed my body.

That first night at my parent's house sharing my old room, when Xavior talked about reverence, came to mind. He was determined, in his own way, to make this experience more about me than him. It put me in a very vulnerable place mentally. I gasped softly as he added another finger into the mix while playing with my cock, then leaned up for a couple of soft kisses. When he pulled his fingers out, I made a desperate noise.

"Shhh, love, give me a moment. I won't leave you, promise." Xavior smoothed his hand over my left leg and slowly brought it over his shoulder, even as he used his other hand to toy with my dick. When he let go of me, he positioned himself at my hole and pushed. I bit my lower lip at how hot he felt and how good it was to feel him slowly push inside of me.

The position opened me wider as he pressed in. When I felt his hips meet my thighs, I realized how close to the edge I was before he'd even started moving. My heart raced and I made little gasping breaths as he leaned in further to kiss a desperate moan from my mouth.

I tried to focus my eyes on his face, centimeters from mine. His beautiful jeweled eyes seem to glow in the low light. I touched his face and traced my thumb across his cheekbone. He moved slightly, and a zipline of pleasure raced up my spine and back down again before he moved his hips.

"Fuck," he said. "I don't think I'm going to last. You feel too fucking good. I'm having a hard time holding back." The movement of his hips punctuated each sentence, and I couldn't voice a response as he continued his slow, pleasurable thrusts into me.

The only word that fell out of my mouth was, "Don't." My hand slipped from his face to his neck, with my thumb under his chin. I didn't squeeze, just held my hand there. Something felt right about it. "Is this okay?"

"Mmm hmm," he moaned as he thrust a little faster. He mirrored me as his left hand moved to the space between my neck and shoulder. He used his hold as leverage to push himself deeper into me. I let out a gasp as Xavior slowly thrust a few more times, then came so hard that only a strangled cry escaped his throat.

On the verge of an orgasm, the feel of his body pressed into me, and my trapped cock between us urged me to thrust my hips back on him and squeeze his flagging dick.

"Oh shit, Greg. Fuck." He thrust a few more times, then created enough space to put his hand between us to grab my dick.

My mouth was dry as he jerked me while he thrust into my ass. When I came, it felt like all the moisture I had left my body. Every bit of friction felt like seductive sandpaper creating an edge between pleasure and pain leaving me drained and sated.

Xavior eased my leg down and laid on top of me as I groaned from the feel of my overly stretched limb, pins and needles shooting up my leg. When he tried to move, I wrapped my arms around him to keep him in place.

A comfortable silence grew between us. We laid in that calm bubble until I realized we'd need to clean up again if we wanted to go back out. "We're going to miss the parties," I said.

"Yeah. I'm good with that. Are you?"

"I'm pretty content right here."

"Good," Xavior said as he kissed me. We didn't stop until the first rays of sunlight splashed across the marble floor of the bedroom.

FALLOUT

GREGOR

The following day, we kept our hands off each other long enough to make a call to Captain Lang.

We stood in front of the holovid together, wearing more clothes than we had in the last three days. The call connected, and Lang's face materialized in the light stream. His gaze shifted from me to Xavior, then back to me.

"Good morning, detectives."

"Morning, Captain," we said in near unison.

I was the senior of the two of us, so I went first. "We're reporting as requested, Captain. Have there been any developments?"

"None that are positive. The Hargrove Coven is filing for damages to their holding. They weren't aware of anyone working for them by the name of Larry Jackson and suggest it might be another coven or faction that's trying to subvert them somehow. The coven also disavowed the three candidates. We haven't found evidence of transfer-of-life paperwork for the vampires we still have in custody. The only connection so far is the flophouse."

I nodded. "No one's been able to track down the lawyer?"

"Not yet. We found receipts for regional transports to the east coast. However, we are still working on verification as to whether Jackson took any of those transports."

The Captain switched focus and zeroed in on Xavior. "Have you fully recovered from your phoenix episode, Brantley?"

"Ah, yes, Captain. Fully recovered. Thank you." We glanced at each other. The look between us conveyed concern and worry in a split second. I doubt Lang missed it but he continued.

"Good," Lang said. "Then let's talk about the final issue at hand." He cleared his throat. "We reviewed the imager footage. The department did a spectral and magical analysis of the incident and what no one can figure out is how, you," Lang looked right at me, "Lyndon, suddenly generated magic."

The worry shifted to alarm bells. I had not disclosed my magical ability because it was limited to a specific action which did not meet the need to disclose. However, since my co-worker was, in fact, what could trigger my magic, I should have disclosed it when we started working together.

"While Brantley's misjudgment put him in harm's way, no one can figure out how a knife with no magical properties injured Brantley. Would you care to offer an explanation?"

Fuck. This was not good. Xavior fidgeted, hands balled up at his sides. If I didn't speak up, he'd try to fix this. It was my fault to begin with. I reached out to touch Xavior's arm, and he settled, hopefully sensing the resolve I had to see this through. I had exposed the department to liability. It was my job to take responsibility. Hopefully, they would let Xav keep his job so he could manage his obsession.

"I have genetic ties to an Order called the Saint George Knights which have historically hunted, and now legally executes, dragons under judicial orders. We have a particular magic that can activate under the right circumstances. While they disavowed me when I was nineteen, I still retain the magical ability passed genetically to family members."

Lang was silent for what seemed like forever. Finally, he said, "You didn't think to disclose this information when Brantley was assigned as your partner?"

"I thought it posed little risk given our usual work assignments in General Support." I saw Xavior wince. It was half a lie; it wasn't me that thought there was little risk, it was Xavior. Though I had gone along with it since I didn't want to be associated with The Order at work. The last thing I wanted was to draw any kind of attention because of who my mother was, and my ability.

"That's unacceptable, Lyndon. You put your fellow officer and members of the public at risk. It was your job as the senior officer to come to me with this, not decide for yourself that it was an acceptable risk."

When Xavior opened his mouth, I tried to stop him with a glare, but he was undeterred. "With all due respect, Captain, he's been with the service for ten years. He had no reason to believe he'd be a danger to the public or me. He disclosed his status when we met, and I deemed it an acceptable risk."

"You deemed it?" Lang didn't yell, but his tone implied Xavior had overreached his authority. "You knew about Lyndon's ability this entire time?"

"Yes, Captain," Xavior said. He had to know that admission doomed us both. When we started dating, I wondered if this relationship could cost me my career. I had decided that Xavior was worth it, though I hadn't expected it to be so soon.

"You weren't in any position to deem anything acceptable, Brantley. And furthermore, the implications of the two of you in a relationship make the situation even worse. The coven could, justifiably so, see your partnership as some kind of vendetta or vigilante action."

Lang sighed. "In light of this information, I have no choice but to release you both from service. This was not a simple decision to make, given both your records. The public's trust is important. You must have known that working together created a risk which needed oversight."

"I did." Lang nodded in response to my admission. He seemed to accept that at least I was taking responsibility for my actions.

If I had told Lang the day he assigned me as Xavior's partner instead of keeping my secret, we'd still have our jobs. I would have kept my distance and never known Xavior. I'd be alone and still hiding who I was, even from myself. While I knew that logically, losing my career was still a blow I felt in my gut. Glancing at Xavior, he was shocked and a little concerned. He caught my gaze and the full weight of his concern made sense. It wasn't for himself; it was for me. He understood what my career meant to me. For him, it was one more experience on his long list of things he's done over several lifetimes. Lang cleared his throat, bringing our attention back to the holovid.

"Is there something I could have done differently which would have encouraged you to bring this to me once you were aware of the risk?"

"What would you have done if you had known, Captain?" Xavior asked.

"At minimum, I would have assigned you other partners and minimized the risk initially, but I might have had one of you reassigned to another headquarters to reduce it completely."

I glanced at Xavior, and he smiled. "Working with Gregor has been one of the most exhilarating and rewarding experiences of my life. I can tell you that regardless of what you did, I would have sought him out."

My imagination tried to picture what it would have been like without Xavior as a partner, and instead, him pursuing me in an effort to understand me and my ability. If I was more like my mother, I would have outright rejected him, maybe even threatened him. My career was important to me, but not as much as being near him. He was my dream brought to life. Over the last year we had worked together, I was more myself than I had been in the last decade. Still, losing my job hurt more than I wanted to admit.

Lang shrugged. "Even so, Brantley, at least the department would have had some forewarning." He paused a moment before he continued. "Considering your collective contributions to the service, I've negotiated two weeks' leave before the service files severance papers. Expect that you'll both be on the public service registry with do-not-hire status. It was the best I could do with the review committee, given the circumstances. Some diplomatic representatives of the community wanted more severe actions taken because of the non-disclosure of Lyndon's magical ability, and the fact that you both failed to report the risk once you knew about it."

His words hung in the air between us. With the diplomatic representatives involved, Xavior and me disclosing my ability was only a formality. They knew, somehow, about me and The Order, and in that light, Lang's decision wasn't a surprise.

Do not hire. That was it. There were appeal processes and other options for civil service, private operations, or volunteering. Still, I'd devoted ten years of my life to being a public safety officer. Now it was over, just like that. I only had myself to blame.

"Understood, Captain," I said. I could feel Xavior's eyes on me. He wanted to fight, to protest, but we were in the wrong. We'd been in the wrong the whole time. Especially me.

"Good day, gentlemen," Lang said.

"Captain." Xavior reached out and, with a hand swipe, ended the call.

As large as the suite was, I felt like it was closing in on me. I needed some time to process everything. I needed space.

"Please, Greg. Talk with me." It was barely a whisper. He didn't try to touch me. I was relieved and disappointed at the same time.

"Xav." I sighed. "I can't, not right now. Let me get my head around this. Okay?"

He nodded. I stepped toward him. He stood still as I touched his shoulders, kissed his cheek, then moved past him toward the door. My heart raced, and with each step, my breathing turned ragged as if I'd run a kilometer flat out.

I remembered the signage that led to a lake and hiking trails. I found it pretty quickly once I was out of the building. The trails were well maintained, and when I reached the lake, I slowed down and took in the view.

I had left a message with my parents apologizing for missing our regular dinner, saying that Xavior and I were working. I needed to catch up with them. I took out my phone. I had enough bandwidth for a voice call. It was close to midday, so there was a chance they were both home for lunch.

"Greg?" Jennifer answered. "Honey, there isn't a vid feed. Are you alright?"

"I'm out in the middle of nowhere. I don't have enough bandwidth for video. How are you and Dad?"

"Hey, son, we're fine. We had a few calls from the press asking about you and Xavior. We didn't comment since we do not know what's going on. Are you two alright?"

"We're fine. We went to a place Xavior knew that's pretty secluded, hoping you would be left out of the mess."

"Do you want to explain it to us?" Jennifer asked.

"It's a bit of a story, so you might want to get comfortable." I rehashed everything that had happened so far. I explained Lang's decision to fire Xavior and me, with a do-not-hire status on our records.

"That's somewhat extreme, isn't it?" Jennifer asked.

"Not really, if you look at it from the committee's perspective. For ten years I've lied about an ability I knew I had. Then Xavior knew and didn't report it. That alone is enough. If Lang had known, I would have been assigned somewhere else in the department, or at the very least, Xavior and I wouldn't have been partners.

"I knew I should have said something from the start, but Xavior was fine with it, and I hid my ability for so long that I was . . . relieved. Technically, we don't have to disclose abilities unless they can endanger the public. There weren't reports of dragons anywhere near our service area. So I thought it was safe."

"Greg, son, I feel horrible for you and what you are going through," Philip said. "But you had to have known that eventually, with or without Xavior there, it would come out."

"I knew it was a risk." My emotions stuck in my throat. In some ways, this was like being thrown out of The Order all over again. Maybe even worse, since being a public safety officer was a much more worthwhile endeavor, with better goals. "I was afraid people would look at me differently. The Order has a reputation. I wanted a chance to live out from under that shadow. After a while, I believed I had." I rubbed a hand across my face.

Everything had happened so fucking fast. All I had left was Xavior, and I'd left him standing alone in our room, probably wondering if he would ever see me again. I hoped he would forgive me.

"When will the two of you be back?" Jennifer asked.

"It might be a while. We're here for two weeks, but Xavior mentioned visiting his family in Spain." The breeze by the lake was barely a whisper. The only sound was my feet crunching against the gravel path.

"When you decide to see his family, let us know. We worry about you both. Where is he, by the way?" Philip asked.

"Back in our room. I came outside to get some air."

"That makes sense, honey. Make sure you talk with Xavior too, alright?" Jennifer suggested.

"I promise." I paused for a moment and gathered my wits a little. "Love you both."

"Love you, Greg, be safe," Philip said.

"Love you," Jennifer said.

"I'll message you as soon as I know anything else."

"Okay, son. Take care." Philip's voice echoed the sadness I felt.

"You too." I disconnected the call. While the weight of several emotions had lifted, the one that settled the most was regret. I needed to get back to Xavior.

FAMILY CONCERN

XAVIOR

I stood there for a long time, staring at the door. Greg left. It took all my self-control not to go after him and be his shadow while he sorted things out in his head.

I flopped down on the couch and looked around the room. Any way of fixing our predicament eluded me. I thought the Captain had been too severe, though, given the circumstances, I understood.

While I'd have to figure out how to deal with my obsession, I was most worried about Greg. It was his life's work. I pushed him into working together. Would he resent me for it? Waiting for him to come back was going to drive me bonkers. Though if I left, and he came back, would he think I abandoned him again?

No, staying put was the best option. Greg waited for me. I can wait for him. Simple as that. I played some holo games, and tried to keep my mind off where Greg might be and what would happen when he came back.

My phone vibrated in my pocket. Faith. I stood and made a hand motion that tossed the call onto the holo display in front of me. But it wasn't just Faith. She had my parents, and Denis conferenced in as well.

"Xavior." Faith's brisk version of hello was always fun. Since she took over as head of the family, it was hard to talk with her. She felt responsible for me and everything that happened. We always had a good relationship based on mutual respect. This was very much her pulling rank, especially in front of everyone else. It was expected of her to deal with these things. Part of me felt sorry for her, and another part wished she would break with tradition and not set up this dynamic of family figure head and wayward family member. But since she went there, I followed suit.

"Faith. Mother. Father. Denis."

"Well, Brother, you certainly made a name for yourself this time," Denis said, speaking out of turn. Faith didn't say anything to stop him. It reinforced where I was in the order of things. "Though I have to say I'm surprised you only took out a house and not the entire block."

"Denis, be civil," Corley, my mother, chided. "We called to see how you were doing, Xavior. Faith thought it would be best if we all spoke with you at once."

"Well, that saves me explaining myself four times over."

"We were concerned when news reports indicated you and your partner were in an altercation and you nearly died. Why didn't you let us know you were alright?" My mother's concern softened me a little. If anyone understood, she did. She'd been through what I experienced several times.

"I sent Faith a message. I thought that was sufficient."

"Then you didn't call or send another message after that. What did you expect us to do?" Faith asked, clearly annoyed.

"How's the whelp?" Trevor and Faith hatched their egg not that long ago. Faith had sent pictures.

"Lena's fine. She's sleeping. Quit trying to change the subject, Xavior. Are you alright?"

"Well, yes, for the most part. My memories are still intact as far as I can tell. In the meantime, I've gained a mate and lost my job. Not just lost it, but I'm banned from any public safety position."

Everyone stared at me, stunned into silence. Then they all started talking at once. I glanced around the suite and waited for the din to subside.

"Your memories are intact?" Denis asked.

I nodded. "From what I can tell yes. There was some disorientation at first. Then I sensed Greg and my pheromones on him and things quickly snapped into place."

Denis frowned, but I wasn't sure why.

"Who's your mate, Xavior?" Ransford, my father, asked. Faith hadn't told him. Well, this might be a bit of a shock then.

Before I could open my mouth, Greg walked in.

His face was a little red, and so were his eyes, but I sensed calm from him. That alone made me happy. He tilted his head and glanced around the room as the door closed behind him. "Am I interrupting something?" Greg asked.

I shook my head. "Not really. I'm glad you're here, actually." I held out my hand. "Do you want to say hello to my family?"

His eyes brightened, and he smiled as he walked toward me and took my hand. I pointed to the holo display. "My sister Faith, my mother Corley, my father Ransford, and my brother Denis." I looked at him and couldn't help but feel warmth from his presence. "This is Gregor Lyndon. My mate."

"Wait," Denis said. "You're mated to the Saint George Knight? Maybe you lost your common sense instead of your memory after your phoenix resurrection."

"Denis. That's uncalled for," Corley said. "You didn't say you were interested in him when you spoke with us, Xavior. I rather thought you'd end up with Jordan."

"I don't know that the fae would have been any better than the Knight, but Xavior has never made safe choices when it came to his partners," Ransford said. My mother gave him a very pointed look, and my father cleared his throat.

A squeeze of my hand gave me all the reassurance I needed. "Greg and I have worked together for over a year, and in that time, we've grown to care about each other. It developed into more, especially since my aging cycle came early."

Questions poured out of the holo, and I turned toward Greg. "Sorry about this," I whispered.

"It's alright," Greg whispered back. I sensed relief and a scant bit of enjoyment from the ruckus my family made. I felt better knowing he could take it all in stride, even after this morning's call.

I whistled to grab everyone's attention. "I know it's late where you all are. Message me with questions if you need to, but it's already been a long day for us, and we need to talk. I promise I'll call in a few days. I love you all. Be well." I made a slashing hand gesture that dropped us from the call.

"So, that was your family." Greg sat on the couch. I followed, keeping hold of his hand. "You're sister takes after your father. And you and Denis look a lot like your mother."

"Yep, and they're all taller than Denis and me for some reason." I laughed a little. "And that was only a small taste of what it's like around them since Trevor wasn't present and he and my sister have ten whelps now. Plus Denis's mate." I sighed. "Still think you'd be up to visiting them?"

He nodded. "Given that we'll have more than two weeks off now, sure, why not?"

"Fuck, Greg, I'm sorry. Truly." I wiped a hand over my face, then looked at him again. It struck me how calm he was despite everything.

"It's alright. I made the potential for this to happen long before you showed up. I'm sorry you lost your job, too."

"Well, I didn't need the job. Though it was convenient, whatever happens, we'll figure it out. We have each other."

"Yeah." It was the first time his facade of strength broke as tears ran down his face.

I sensed and smelled the regret Greg felt. Maybe I was wrong, and it wasn't calm but resolve, or a combination of both. I gently pulled him toward me and wrapped my arms around him. "I know we're going through some shit right now, but in a couple of weeks or months, we'll look back and laugh. Or be grateful that this happened."

He leaned back and looked at me with narrowed eyes and a slight frown. He wasn't buying it, and I barely believed what I'd said myself, so I tried a different tack.

"When's the last time you've taken a vacation at all?" I rubbed his back as I spoke. "Or traveled anywhere without your parents? Or your ex, for that matter."

"It's been a while."

"Exactly. Let's travel, see things, and enjoy developing our connection. Maybe we'll come up with new ideas, or new jobs, or both. We've got this, you and me."

We held each other for a while, then dozed on the couch as the emotional roller coaster took its toll. When we woke, it was to gorgeous afternoon sunlight full of promise.

TRUST & FRENCH FRIES

GREGOR

The hotel couch was more comfortable than one might think. The artful decorative pillows were supportive while my boyfriend laid across my body, asleep, his drool soaking into my shirt.

It was so fucking domestic and oddly comforting. I didn't want to wake him. The morning had been hard on both of us. My choices, and the ones we'd made together, brought consequences we'd thought were possible but unlikely. I could make all the excuses I wanted for our decisions, but we knew the potential outcomes.

I had weighed my career against my relationship with Xavior and at some point, I calculated that life without him, no matter what I was doing, wouldn't be worth it. For the first time in my life, I was completely myself. He'd given that to me and saw who I was when no one else did. It was liberating and terrifying. If I said I knew what to do with it, I'd be lying.

His breathing changed. I kissed the top of his head and ran my fingers through his hair. Fuck, I loved this dragon. I wanted a home, children, a life with him in the worst possible way. Everything I dreamed I'd have with Keith, I hoped for with Xavior. But I also knew, whatever our life was, whether or not we settled down, or had kids, it would be terrific. Not because of his wealth or connections, but because we'd continue to have moments like this one.

"Hey, handsome," Xavior said before he moved his head so I could see his jewel-green eyes.

"Hey." I bent slightly to give him a proper peck on the lips. He shifted a little to reach up and kiss me back. It was not the chaste version I'd planted on him a moment before, and his body let me know it as his clothed hardness brushed my half-sleeping dick and brought it fully awake in short order.

Xavior's body pressed to mine as I wrapped my arms around him. "Did you sleep alright?"

"Yeah, I must have. I drooled all over you." His face split into a huge grin as he chuckled. "You have a good nap?"

"One of the best in a while." I let a soft sigh escape. "I actually feel a lot lighter. You know? As if my past has stopped haunting me."

Xavior nodded. "Keeping a secret like that, even with good intentions, can weigh on you." He drew a heart on my chest as he glanced at me.

"Sounds like that's spoken from experience."

"Somewhat. I don't broadcast what I am. Life is easier when I don't."

"We screwed that up, didn't we."

"Ah well," he said. "Given the whole circumstance, I think it turned out alright." He smiled and touched my face. I leaned into that touch.

"So," I wondered. "Do you have any thoughts on what you'd like to do for the rest of the day?" I turned my head slightly and nipped at Xavior's fingers.

"Uh," he blinked as he tried to regain his focus.

"Yes?" I went a little further and encouraged him to slide a finger into my mouth. He watched, eyes wide, as I moved my head slightly. Each small movement pushing his digit further into my mouth, as I sucked and rolled my tongue around it.

All Xavior did was breathe, and he barely did that. I liked that I could make him lose his words. Without talking, I had him move so that he straddled my chest. I reached for his pants and looked up. He gave a silent nod, and I opened them to pull his cock out. The second my hand wrapped around him, he groaned as my hand mirrored what I was doing with my mouth to his finger.

We adjusted a bit as I encouraged him forward a little more. I let go of his dick and put my hands on his ass. His finger slipped out of my mouth as I pushed him forward slowly until my mouth wrapped around his cock.

"Fuck, Greg." I got a sharp gasp as I prompted his hips to move, and he sunk further into my mouth.

We started slowly, with deep thrusts. I controlled Xavior's movements with my hands on his hips. It was heady, as I worked him into nearly coming, only to stop short of the last bit of friction or suction he needed. By the fifth time I edged him, he begged.

"Please," he whispered.

"Please, what?" I asked, loving every moment of his vulnerability. It was something I craved, and now I knew it was something he wanted, too. This was something we both enjoyed. However, after our talk the other day, I realized I might need to learn more instead of being so instinctual about it.

"Please, can I come?" His eyes closed and his head fell back as I sucked and teased more pre-cum out of his dick.

He slid out of my mouth as I pushed his hips back and asked, "Where would you like to come, Xav?" I licked the tip, and he shivered before he could respond.

"In your mouth. I want to come in your mouth." He sighed softly as I let him thrust forward again, slowly, then back, until his dick rested on my chin.

"You have my permission to come in my mouth." Xavior slowly rocked forward again, as I maintained his movements to set the pace. When he tried to alter it, I'd slow him down again to the point that he made a growling-whining sound. Once I was sure he would maintain the pace I set, I got my dick out and fisted it. With my free hand, I prompted him to take off his shirt.

His hand carded through my hair as he plunged in and out of my mouth. "Elements, I'm close. Shit."

I gave his hip a squeeze to let him know I heard him as I found a sensitive spot and teased it with the tip of my tongue. His hand tightened in my hair, and I felt his legs spasm first before his dick throbbed in my mouth and unloaded. I swallowed and sucked until he sighed above me. I wasn't far behind him as I lifted my hips slightly and my balls tightened with pleasure. The groan I made around Xavior's dick made him shudder above me as I creamed all over my hand.

We breathed heavily for a few moments, then Xavior eased out of my mouth. He moved a little to lean down. As we kissed, I took my covered hand and smeared the contents on his back, then blindly drew a heart in my spunk. It gave me a perverse thrill to mark him, however temporary.

When he caught on, he broke away from our kiss. "You're fucking dirty minded, Greg," he grinned. "And I love that about you." His eyes narrowed slightly as he spoke softly. "No one had a clue, did they?"

"No one made me feel safe enough to try." I hid so many things for so long. Now, everything was different. I didn't have to hide any longer. Not with Xavior.

Xav kissed me again, then levered himself off my chest. He held out his hand, and I took it. "Let's have a soak in the tub and order room service."

I hesitated to follow, worried about someone coming into our suite while we were so vulnerable.

"Trust me." He pulled my hand to his lips. "It'll be fine."

I did trust him, so I let him lead me to the bathroom, and we stripped, showered, ordered food, and then plunked ourselves into a tub full of bubbles with hot swirling water. When the food showed up, I was so much of a noodle that Xavior dealt with the kind staff person who was nice enough to bring the cart into the bathroom.

After the staff person left, Xavior grabbed a couple of fries from a plate and brought them to me. He sat in my lap and fed them to me like they were grapes. If I hadn't already been in love with this dragon, that would have clinched it.

SPA DAY

GREGOR

After the week we had, a trip to the spa sounded exactly like what we needed. Xavior had set up everything, and when we walked into the spa area, we were given an overview of the schedule for the day while sipping on some fruity concoction designed to enhance the spa experience.

"At your request, you have a private steam room with the scents you selected. After you spend time there, the next area is the pools, which feature several temperatures and aeration choices. You also requested the couple's massage package, which includes private dining for lunch and dinner with your choice of available chefs."

Our guide, Quinn, was fae, tall, well-muscled, and very poised. As if elegance was part of his very being. I had met other fae, and I had never seen one so . . . regal, for lack of a better word. His skin was the color of a sunset, displaying a blend of yellow, orange, and hints of pink.

When we reached a door marked with Xavior's last name on a gold leaf placard no less, our guide opened it. The light turned on, and it looked very much like the bathroom in our suite.

"This is your changing room for the day. You'll find everything you need here. All the sessions will be conducted at your pace. If you should desire anything while you're with us, don't hesitate to ask. I would be more than happy to provide anything you desire."

"Thank you, Quinn." Xavior gave him a friendly smile, and I did the same. Something about the fae set me at ease. I didn't know if that was innate or if that was an ability he had. Either way, I felt fairly calm, which meant the whole spa thing was working already.

Quinn shut the door, and Xavior sat down for a moment and closed his eyes. I sensed a calm around him, too. I hadn't realized how much Xavior operated in a high energy state until I experienced the opposite. He could be calm, but there was always that buzz of energy under the surface. That buzz was hushed now. I didn't know whether or not to be worried.

"You alright?" I touched his shoulder as I sat next to him and dropped our bag to the floor.

He nodded. "Yeah," he said in a dreamy voice.

I looked at Xavior, glanced at the door, and wondered if I should be jealous. I could get Xavior to relax, but not this much. Well, not without a lot of bedroom gymnastics. "Did I miss something?"

"Pheromones. Our friend Quinn apparently has some kind of calming pheromone or ability. Fae have unique abilities, though I've never met a fae that could do that without magic. It makes me wonder if he has more than fae in his lineage." Xavior opened one eye to glance at me, then smiled. "I can't tell if you're jealous because of what Quinn did or because it didn't affect you as much."

I chuckled. "Can't it be both? I feel calm, but not as mellowed out as you." Xavior smiled. "I'm guessing his coloring was friendliness or something of that sort?"

Xavior nodded. "He likes us."

"What would he look like if he didn't?"

"Something like a green-blue combination, or he'd put up a glamour and hide his colors altogether or project warm colors, though, for the fae, that would be lying, and there are very few that would use that kind of deception. Most would rather omit the truth."

"How would you know the difference?"

"Glamour has a smell, like cheap potpourri." He tapped his nose.

"Of course it does," I said with a chuckle as I slipped off my sandals and bent to reach for our bag. We'd brought swim trunks, though we could go nude. I wasn't comfortable with that unless we were in private spaces. However, when I reached into the bag, what I found weren't my board shorts.

"Xav, what are these?" I held up a pair of men's bikinis, one purple, one blue. He blinked, and the lazy smile already on his face grew wider as he reached over and plucked the purple pair out of my hand. "No, Xav, seriously?" I pleaded.

He leaned over and whispered, as if we weren't alone in the room, "I love you." Then he blinked and somehow gave me the most adorable moonbeam eyes. It was threatening to become an adorable pout the longer I made him wait for my answer.

We'd be alone most of the time, so I took a deep breath and let it out. There were some public areas, but not many. Plus, was I going to ruin a whole day of relaxation because of a clothing choice? I sighed. "Fine." Xavior practically beamed with delight.

I went to a locker to change, and once I had the suit on, I grumbled. "It barely covers everything." I had hair in a lot of places Xavior didn't, which made for a glaring contrast. It's why I wore board shorts in the first place. Manscaping wasn't my thing. My ex did it. Xavior had little in the way of body hair to begin with. The only time I bothered is if it seemed a bit unruly.

Xavior peeked around his locker door. "I know," he said with a sultry voice and a grin.

I shook my head and closed the locker door. Xavior did the same and turned toward the main door, and that's when I realized our suits were not the same. His was a G-string, and his ass looked perfect.

"I don't know if that suit is any better than the color-shifting invisible one."

"Why? Don't you like what you see?"

"Oh, yes, I like it very much. However," I moved up behind Xavior, "it makes me wonder if you're showing off or trying to tempt me." I caressed his ass and felt him shiver.

"Maybe it's both?" Xavior let me fondle him a few moments more, then stepped away and went for the robes hanging near the door. We left our changing room with robes in place to find Quinn waiting for us at the entrance.

"If you follow me, I'll escort you to your steam room."

When Quinn let us inside, I wondered for a moment if we were still at the resort. The room was bigger than the one at Xavior's estate. There were massive rocks big enough to hold a dragon and various other large beings. It had a natural geyser in the center. A stoneware bowl nearby, full of a herbal mixture, invoked memories of old-growth forests and mountain streams.

"There are hooks here next to the door for your clothing. I'll set the timer for thirty minutes. After a ten-minute break, if you'd like to stay for another thirty minutes, I can arrange it. If you need anything else, use the panel outside the sauna for your request. I'll be notified immediately."

We gave our thanks and took off our robes. Xavior stripped down completely, then shifted and went to one of the larger rocks. He made a kind of chuffing noise as he settled. I moved toward him, and he kept his gaze on me. I settled on a rock right below him and leaned back. The stones were warm and cool in turns. The small geyser went off every few minutes and released more scent and steam into the room.

Xavior moved his head so that his snout was on my shoulder. His deep breathing relaxed me as much as the steam did. I had nearly dozed off when Xavior's tongue flicked out and licked my neck. I flinched and turned to look at him. He was being playful.

"You have me at a disadvantage, sir," I said playfully, and it was clear Xavior didn't care as his tongue flicked out, then swept down across my chest to find a nipple. The teasing licks were a pleasurable torture. My swimsuit did a horrible job containing my hard-on, and before I could do anything about it, a chime sounded and announced it was time to exit the steam room.

My naughty dragon shifted and climbed down from his perch without a second glance at what he'd done to me. I moved slowly and willed myself into a half-normal state by thinking about how Tina Colt ambushed me with a kiss at one of the holiday gatherings my mother, Narissa, had when I was sixteen. That moment solidified my sexual identity better than anything else could have at the time. It always worked in situations like these. By the time I had my robe on, my dick was no longer threatening to make a surprise appearance.

"That was an odd sensation. Gratifying and unpleasant? Was my tongue that bad?" he asked with a laugh.

"No, it was actually that good." He gave me a curious look. "I'll explain after we reach the pools." I took his hand and led us out of the steam room to find Quinn ready to take us to our next location.

The pools were semi-private, but Xavior's voice seemed to carry, or my embarrassment thought it did. "So, your first kiss was a disaster?"

"Shhh, yes. I think Tina meant well, and I knew she liked me. I was still indulging my mother then. So when I asked her to dance, I was trying to be nice, and while I didn't have feelings for her, I did like her as a friend." I twirled my fingers in the water as Xavior sipped the juice he'd requested for us.

"Growing up in the families we did, none of us were ones to wait for opportunities. When we talked about it later, she understood better than I thought. Tina was pansexual but kept it from her parents. Right before my mother kicked me out of the family, I heard that Tina started dating a woman, which her parents were fine with right up until they found out the woman was a wolf shifter and the leader of a local pack, then they lost their shit. Her parents not minding she was in a same-sex relationship was slightly more progressive than my mother."

We chuckled, and it felt good to talk about it.

"You rarely talk about anything from your childhood. I'm glad you have some memories you want to tell me about."

I touched his face. "I've hidden everything for so long, the good and the bad. The only way we move forward is if I'm honest."

Xavior had a curious look on his face. "That statement feels funny, like you think you've lied."

"Haven't I? I've lied about who I was for a long time. It came naturally at some point because every other person I've been with never knew me, not really. It was so much part of my persona that a hedge witch couldn't tell. I wouldn't have told you if you'd been anything other than a dragon. My lie wouldn't protect you, so I had to say something."

"Do you regret it?" Xavior drew closer, and I sensed he was bracing himself. I'd stabbed him, but never in the heart, and I'm glad I didn't have to now.

"No. I thought I would. But after everything we've been through, I realized living with the truth is much better. I can't change who and what I am. It's part of me, and it turns out, I like being me, not a persona that thinks that if I do all the right things, then I'll have the life people expect of me."

"That sounds like someone has internalized some therapy lessons."

"Maybe." I smirked as I leaned close and gave him a soft kiss. "You've been highly motivating in a lot of ways."

"I could say that about you, too, my knight."

"That's the first time you've given me any kind of nickname." My hands moved to his torso and I pulled him closer. It was better than Gregie.

"And you liked it. I can tell." His nose nuzzled mine.

I caressed his back, feeling his scales under my fingertips. "I rather like the notion that, for once, the knight protects the dragon rather than royalty."

He nodded as he continued to nuzzle, and I caressed. It wasn't sexual, though it could have turned that direction. Instead, in the warm, bubbling water, it was comforting to be at peace with each other.

A soft chime sounded, and another bipedal being entered the pool area, though they went for the waterfall feature instead of the warm bubbling caldron we sat in.

"Wanna stay here longer or go play in some mud?"

"Is it large enough for you to be in your dragon form, like in the sauna?"

Xavior nodded. "There are other pools large enough." He tilted his head a little. "You want me to shift?"

"We have a whole day in a place where you don't have to make yourself human-sized all the time. You should take advantage of that."

He kissed me rather soundly, then hopped out of the pool. I watched as he walked to a panel, and within moments Quinn appeared. They had a short conversation I couldn't hear but saw Quinn give a slight nod. After the fae left, Xavior came back and held out a hand to me.

"The dragon-sized pools are not far. Would you like to come with me?"

"I'd be delighted to." I took his hand and let him haul me out of the pool like I was nothing more than a leaf. In the timespan of a blink, he shifted and made hardly any noise at all as we moved to the pools that would accommodate him.

COUPLE'S MASSAGE

XAVIOR

There were memorable moments in my life with lovers I've had over the long years, but none of them were interested in every part of me. Sure, I could do tricks with my tongue and flash some teeth if that's what they liked, but never did anyone ask to spend a whole day with me as a dragon.

The hallways that Quinn moved us through were designed for larger guests, and when we arrived for lunch, I took Greg at his word. The room was designed for me and accommodated Greg as well. A lot of fast magical arranging likely went into play to set this up since I'd initially booked for two bipeds.

The room featured a large, flat rock with a small table-like structure built into it. My food would be laid out on the rock while Greg would be treated to his usual dining experience, at least where plates and utensils were concerned.

The first course was a salad. When the salads arrived, the quantities and differences in the presentation were amusing. Greg had mixed greens tossed with fruit and nuts. In contrast, I had a large platter of whole vegetables that included heads of different kinds of lettuce, tomatoes, pears, walnuts still in their shells, sweet onions, zucchinis, squash, and a couple of pumpkins.

I dug in and crunched away at all the delicious produce. Greg chuckled, and I stopped to look at him. He cleared his throat and tried to compose himself. I gave him a querying noise.

"You're adorable when you eat. Your eyes narrow to slits when you like something, and you even chew with your mouth closed, which I wasn't expecting at all. I figured you'd swallow things whole."

I picked up a pumpkin and tossed it into my mouth. The crunch and squish were very satisfactory. Greg stared. It was amusing and also made me self-conscious at the same time. He must have sensed it and returned to eating his salad.

"Sorry, Xav. I'm only staring because I appreciate the view." He took another bite while I let him sense my amusement.

After lunch, Quinn escorted us to our couple's massage, where two orcs were waiting for us. Orcs were a species created from the combination of ogres, fae, and humans. They were the usual species height of around two and a half meters, along with bluish-green skin.

Of the fae, the orcs, Greg and myself, I was the tallest in my dragon form. Greg looked up at me. He likely caught the amusement at my own observation, or the smugness I felt from being the tallest and the largest in the room for once. He reached up to pat my shoulder as Quinn made introductions.

"Charles and Chuck are certified massage professionals with knowledge of several species and their muscular skeleton structure. Mr. Brantley, if you follow Chuck, and Mr. Lyndon, if you follow Charles, they will explain what will happen next," Quinn said.

As Quinn left, Greg and I followed our massage therapists to the massage room. I don't know how a being managed to be lanky and bulky at the same time, but these fellows were exactly that. Their eyes were a dull gray, but not unkind. Chuck had tusks protruding from his lower jaw, with closely shaved black hair on his scalp. Charles had rare upper jaw tusks, and his black hair was styled a little longer on top, but closely shaved on the sides. Another distinct difference was that Chuck had several piercings while Charles did not. Piercings like Chuck's usually indicated he was a magic user, or possibly a cleric. It was rumored that orcs used piercings to help focus different kinds of magical energy. It was rare to see pierced orcs outside of their communities. I wasn't versed in the specifics, and the orc who gave me a brief history once a long time ago, was more like Charles. It piqued my curiosity.

As we entered the massage room, I noticed one side contained a large stone slab, which I hoped was heated, while the other had a human-sized table for Greg. "If you'll follow me and arrange yourself on the stone, we can discuss where you'd like me to start," Chuck said. His voice was deep, but soothing. It made me wonder, not for the first time, if that was part of the spa's training—to help calm guests—or a talent the resort specifically hired for this area. Everyone seemed to have a gentle, reassuring touch or voice.

I nodded and moved toward the stone and was delighted when I felt warmth seep in from the pads of my feet. I was distracted from the tantalizing sensation when Chuck began to detail a rather impressive list of places to start my massage. I indicated with my tail that I'd like him to begin with my back. He immediately went to work with an oil and salt scrub that soothed and made my scales sing with a gentle chiming sound.

When I looked over at Greg, Charles seemed to handle him like he was glass while Greg made moaning noises that amused me.

"You're laughing at me. I can't help it. Charles has magic fingers." I inadvertently growled, and Charles stopped. So did Chuck. Greg lifted himself off the massage table to look at me. "Xavior, if you're not okay with this, we can stop."

I hadn't expected Greg's joke to set off some protective instinct. Nor had I realized that someone else touching Greg would bother me.

"Do you want to leave?" Greg asked. I thought about it for a moment, then shook my head. Greg laid back down.

"Good. Just relax. I'm right here, we're both safe, and after this, we'll both be so relaxed we could probably sleep the rest of the week."

I huffed out my agreement with that statement as Chuck went back to work finding spots along my scales that he coaxed into relaxing. After the massages were over, Greg and I were left in the room alone. Greg slowly moved to my side.

"You alright, big guy?" I moved my head to see him, and he leaned over to kiss me on my snout. I sighed with contentment. "Good. Your scales look amazing. They're practically glowing. Do you think Chuck and Charles are related?"

Though I couldn't say I've met many orcs, they smelled similar. Either it was a mark of their species, or they were related. I wasn't sure, though. So I made a questioning sound, and Greg nodded.

Greg relaxed against me and I curled myself around him, enjoying the quiet. It reminded me of my den, and I suddenly wished we were there instead of here. The smells were pleasant enough, but I missed the scent of leather and paper and the faint traces of ink made from various substances. I contented myself with gently rubbing my cheeks along Greg's body, careful to avoid hurting him with my horns.

A chime sounded, and Quinn entered the room but stayed near the door. "I hope you are feeling relaxed and well-rested. Would you like me to bring you refreshments? Or if you'd like, I can lead you into the garden area."

"Hmm, I could use some water. Xav?"

I nodded. Water sounded good, then maybe we could move along. Quinn brought a refilling glass for Greg and a device I hadn't seen since I was young. The beverage device looked like a giant marble bigger than my head on a stand with a spout. With a press of the spout, the marble dispensed a beverage. I wouldn't have to lap at a bowl, which was usual in most circumstances, given the length of my face. Greg watched me use it and seemed delighted.

"I wonder why these aren't more common across the resort?"

It was a good question. I hadn't seen any, even in Dragon's Grove. Maybe they were out of fashion. On the other hand, I tended to use my biped form more often, especially when dealing with food and drink.

"Could it be that crafting something like this is much harder than a refilling water glass?"

It could be that as well. Definitely, a mystery that could probably be solved with a few questions and research. We were of like mind, always asking questions and being curious. I think that was the first thing I admired about Greg. He was ever the detective, regardless of the circumstance.

Eventually, Quinn led us to the garden room. It was similar to the sauna but not as hot and filled with plants and other guests. We found a private spot and curled up for a nap until they offered us dinner.

We could choose between a simple or complex dinner, and we both decided simple would be better. Neither of us wanted to sit through six courses. I imagine it brought up memories of Greg's childhood. He'd mentioned before that the long fancy dinners had been a bit traumatic.

Greg ordered a steak and fries, and I had a side of beef. All replicated, of course. Greg's steak was presented beautifully on a plate. At the same time, my selection was brought out on a platter, sliced, and arranged for me to pick up without much difficulty.

As we began to eat, I realized Greg was watching me again. I looked at him and made a pointed look at his plate as I ate a raw slice of beef. He smiled and grabbed a handful of fries, then walked over to me.

"Care for some garnish with your beef?"

I opened my mouth, and he gently set the potatoes in the middle of my tongue. The salt was lovely, and the crunch was short-lived, but Greg's adoration grew. As I reached for another piece, he took it and offered it with his open hand. I slipped my tongue out and took it from him with little effort.

Before I could even sense it, he reached for me and caressed my face. "You are the most wondrous being I have ever met in my whole life. If all I do for the rest of my days is be your mate, it will be my absolute honor. I love you, Xavior."

As did I, though I did not have the vocal cords to express such things just then. Dragons spoke in emotional scents and tones. I let him know that I loved him as well and that he was cherished with all my being, then brought my tail to his chest and, with the feathery point, drew a heart right above his.

He grinned then gave my snout a kiss. I licked his face, much to his delight. "After dinner, we can go back to your den and make another mess."

If I could have taken us directly back to my den, I would have. As it was, I shoveled and chewed as quickly as I dared, while Greg chuckled and begged me to slow down so I wouldn't choke.

EXPLORATION

Gregor

Watching Xavior leap off the balcony for the second time in a week was less terrifying and more interesting as he shifted in mid-air then caught a draft that sent him skyward in all his feathered dragon glory.

Earlier, when I found him standing at the open balcony door watching the sun come up, I knew, whether it was from his body language or the sense of longing I felt through our budding connection, that he wanted to fly. The morning was perfect for it, and the only thing holding him back was me.

I walked up beside him in the open doorway. "We're as safe as we're ever going to be here. You should take advantage of it." The sensation of conflict between longing and attraction he expressed hurt. Not because he wanted to hurt me but because he was clearly being pulled in two directions. "Xav. I love you. Go."

"But . . ." He turned to look at me.

"What could you possibly say as an excuse not to do what I see plainly written on your face?"

"What are you going to do while I'm out?"

At least I had convinced him to go. Now it was only a matter of settling his worry. "I'm going to explore the resort. It's massive.

My boyfriend said I could buy anything I wanted. Maybe I'll find someone to give me a basic lecture on dominance and submission."

I was half-joking, but Xavior's face brightened. "Guest services can help. They do have a few people on staff. If I remember right, one of them is a yoga instructor too."

"Okay, wow." I chuckled. "This really is a full-service resort."

Xavior grinned. "While you're out exploring, make sure we have the latest event schedule in our room. You did say something about dancing."

"I did, didn't I?" I walked up behind him and ran my hands over his bare skin. His scales flickered in the sunlight under my touch. "I don't think I'll ever get over seeing that."

"I like how it feels." He leaned against me.

I wrapped my arms around him then gave him a quick kiss on the temple. "Go spread your wings. We can meet back here around lunchtime, and maybe I'll have learned a thing or two by the time you get back."

He turned in my arms and gave me a very memorable kiss. Then he stepped back, turned, jogged to the end of the balcony, then leapt off as I watched from the doorway. I'd imagine that the sight of him as he flew off into the morning light would never be dull no matter how many times I saw it. I hoped that I'd see it for a long time to come.

I found clothes to wear, which felt odd after barely wearing anything most of the week. I opted for a very touristy look with a T-shirt, cargo shorts, and sandals. The hotel's interior was quiet for a Sunday morning as I walked down the hall and took the lift to the lobby.

When I found the concierge desk, they verified that we had the latest schedule and access to the VIP schedule via our holo.

Felven, the concierge, wore a tailored resort uniform which allowed their tentacles to move freely. I'm not exactly sure what they were. They had too many arms to be a squid or an octopus. It's possible that they were related to some kind of mollusk or jellyfish though that was a guess. They had a large eyes and something that resembled a mouth, but with no lips. When they spoke, it was through a translator amulet that changed their tones and clicks into words in the guest's preferred language.

As we talked about the resort's different options, I was told we could easily set reminders for any event from the holo, and if we'd like to host one ourselves, they would help us arrange it. It made me wonder if Xavior had stolen some of his staff for his estate from this place at one point because it sounded like a very familiar model.

"Is there anything else we can provide for you or Mr. Brantley's stay?" Felven asked.

"Uh, I . . . need some help with a very delicate subject." I paused and then rushed to explain as the back of my neck heated. "I need an instructor that specializes in dominance and submission techniques. Someone that would be willing to teach the basics to begin with, and maybe more." There would be a lot to talk about with my therapist later.

While their tentacles moved, their face didn't betray any surprise. I couldn't tell if that was because they were used to such questions or if they didn't have analogous human facial queues or emotional responses.

"Certainly, Mr. Lyndon. We have several instructors on staff, and we have an area of the resort specializing in such things. Let me have someone escort you. I've already set an appointment for you with Ms. Eilidh. She'll meet you in fifteen minutes." They paused. "Is there anything else you require?"

I blinked, surprised at how fast they had organized the meeting, and realized I might not be ready for what I was about to embark upon. But I did say I would learn a few things. I shook my head. "Thank you, Felven. I think that's all for now."

"Excellent. If you follow the individual behind you, they will lead you to the correct area. Good morning, Mr. Lyndon."

I followed the staff member down a series of hallways I had no hope of remembering before we arrived in a cozy space with mood lighting and a large lobby. It looked more like a comfortable living room than a place specializing in BDSM. The only difference was the furniture. It was all different sizes and types to accommodate various guests.

Ms. Eilidh found me nervously tapping my fingers on the arms of my chair. I shot up as she approached. She was a larger woman, dressed in comfortable slacks, heels, a half corset, and a flowing blouse in a combination of red and black that accented her tan skin. Her golden hair was pulled back into an elaborate braid, and her face had a glow to it that instantly set me at ease, but only if I avoided her dark brown eyes. Those, if I stared too hard, looked dangerous.

"Mr. Lyndon." She held out her hand, and I reached for hers.

"Please, call me Greg." My intention was to shake her hand and let go, but she held fast, much to my surprise.

"Greg, then. I understand you are looking for some instruction."

"Yes, ma'am."

"You can refer to me as Ms. Eilidh or Mistress."

"Yes, Ms. Eilidh," I said as her hand warmed. She patted my hand with her other then let go.

"And that was your first lesson," she said as she pointed at the chairs, and I watched her curl up in a chair next to mine as I retook my seat. "Regardless of whether you know someone or not, you always start off any interaction by setting the boundaries for that interaction."

"That is surprisingly useful and not an obvious place to start."

"It becomes more familiar as you practice. It's vital, though, especially in the beginning. Even before exchanging preferences and safe words, establishing who you are relative to the other individuals in the room is important. Being vague with boundaries can lead to problems."

"I think I understand." She held up a finger, and I stopped talking.

"You think you understand what, Greg?"

I caught on and realized where some of my tendencies toward these kinds of interactions came from. To be trained at a young age in a boot camp-like environment, along with my public safety officer training, mentally, everything added up. "I think I understand why it's important, Ms. Eilidh."

With anything in life, there are structures or systems built around how to do things. In structures and systems with a leader-follower dynamic, there's an immediate understanding of the power dynamic being created. In BDSM, while the structure could be up for debate, once it was established between two or more people, along with boundaries, it was only a matter of following the leader, or the dominant in this case. Xavior and I had inadvertently followed a pattern we were already familiar with, as I was the senior officer in our partnership even before we had decided to be in a relationship. The power dynamic was already there. That thought alone meant I had more to think about later, and would probably need another therapy session to work out.

"Excellent, Greg." She smiled, and it warmed me from the inside out. I blinked. That was an unusual response for me, especially toward a woman I didn't know. Ms. Eilidh picked up on my confusion immediately.

"Explain to me what you felt just now, if you can, please."

I shook my head trying to put it in words. "Pleasure, from your approval. As if you were my mom, Ms. Eilidh."

"How do you feel about it that, Greg?"

"Odd. I've never had that experience with a woman I didn't know or wasn't friends with, Ms. Eilidh." Gina, my old work partner before Xavior, had worked with me for five years, and I liked helping her. Her approval meant a lot while we were coworkers. So did my mom Jennifer's approval.

"Well, I do have a slight advantage. I'm a descendant of a goddess, and there are some individuals, especially humans, that are inclined to please me or purposefully disobey depending on what they desire."

"That must be helpful in your line of work, Ms. Eilidh."

"Yes, I find it so." She paused for a moment. "Now, Greg, let's talk about your experiences and how I can help you."

After talking for nearly two hours, I learned that as long as Xavior and I had understanding, consent, and set boundaries between each other, then what we did and how formal we were about it was up to us.

After that, I wandered around for a bit before I'd found a cute open-air café to stop for coffee and a pastry. When I thought about Ms. Eilidh's advice, it made me feel better about some of the things we'd done already. I looked forward to talking with Xavior about it when he returned from his flight. I chuckled to myself as I realized I was a bit envious of him being able to fly. To have wings and just take off wherever it seemed suitable.

When one of the waitstaff came by to fill my coffee mug a second time, she asked, "Are you finding everything to your satisfaction?"

"Yes," I replied. "It's been a pretty informative morning."

"I'm glad, but I can't help but be a bit curious." She tapped her carafe of coffee. I looked up at her and realized something about her manner seemed familiar. She was dressed in the waitstaff uniform of white button-up, black slacks, and a matching apron. Her brown, natural hair was in a ponytail, and her light brown skin looked like it shimmered in the sunlight, along with her golden-brown eyes.

"Oh?" I set my pastry down and brushed my hands together to dust off the crumbs.

"Why are you sitting here by yourself? You're rather good looking. There must be any number of guests you could strike up a conversation with or enjoy their company."

"Oh!" I laughed. "I'm here with my partner, but he's currently out flying in the desert, so I took the morning to explore."

"Ah! Shifter then?"

I nodded. "He's a dragon."

"And you're human, which explains the bit of envy I smelled." That made me sit up straight in my chair. This interaction was not the standard experience I'd received from the rest of the staff, and I wondered about her intentions.

"Let me guess," I said. "You're also a dragon?"

"Yes." She laughed softly. "It was the emotional smell, wasn't it?"

"That, and your curiosity." I smiled and took a sip of my coffee as she sat in the chair across from me.

"Are you here for a vacation then?"

"Of sorts, yes," I nodded. "My name is Greg, by the way." I held out my hand, and she took it.

"Oh, elements, my parents would clobber me for my manners. My name's Francesca, but most people call me Freddie." We shook hands as she gave me a big grin.

"Nice to meet you, Freddie." We were silent for a moment, enjoying the view, when she shook her head as if to wake herself.

"Sorry, I nearly forgot." She stood, suddenly animated. "The envy you felt, was that because you wanted to fly with your significant dragon?"

"Uh, yeah, I mean, who wouldn't?" I was curious as to where this was going. It made me wonder about her obsession.

"Good, good. When you're finished here, you should find the apothecary. It's a small shop that smells to the moon and back, but I think you might be able to find what you're looking for there."

"What am I supposed to be looking for?" Freddie had my attention now.

"Wings," she said with a smile and walked away, only to come back and grab the coffee pot from the table, fill my cup again, then waved as she wandered off.

"Wings," I murmured to myself.

WINGS

The apothecary wasn't hard to find. Like Freddie said, the place sorta stunk, but in a good way. Like someone burning sage and boiling flowers at the same time. When I walked in, the individual behind the counter was busy with another customer. Something about a hair tonic. I wandered around the tiny shop until they concluded their transaction.

The shopkeeper spoke as I picked up a crystal. "Hello, can I help you?"

I looked over at the counter, then looked down. While the shopkeeper had lizard-like features, they had appeared to be the same height as the person they were working with at the counter until now. They climbed part of the shelving to reach my eye level while their tail gently reached out, plucked the crystal I was holding, and put it back on the shelf.

I watched, wide-eyed, and then cleared my throat. "Yes, thank you. Someone told me you could possibly help me with wings." I tried not to fidget as the shopkeeper flipped around and lowered themselves to the floor, then scuttled across the short distance back to the counter. It wasn't uncommon to see lizard folks near the desert. The ones I've previously encountered were taller and shifters. If I had to guess, the shopkeeper probably wasn't a shifter.

"Wings? Oh, well, that's fairly easy. Do you have them already, or do you need them?" They asked as they flipped through a book.

"Need, actually." I walked over to the counter and looked at their book. It held a variety of wing types, from feathers to fae to insects.

"Are they for aesthetics, or should they be functional?" the shopkeeper asked.

"Functional. My boyfriend is a dragon. I'd like to be able to fly with him once or twice while we're on vacation."

"Ah! Well, we have several nice options then." They pointed to one image, which was basic bat-like wings. "These are good for gliding and function much like dragon wings. Can easily attach to the clavicles, and cause minimal pain and muscle fatigue in the growth process." They wrote down a number. From the look of it, I guessed it was the price, which wasn't too bad.

"These are more whimsical and operate more on a magical system than biomechanics. The learning curve is decreased, but side effects are somewhat troublesome, even if they are rare." The wings were feathered and artistic, like a bird's but human-sized.

"What are the side effects?" I asked.

"Scarring, feathers growing in odd places for a while. But like I said, rare." They wrote down another price, and while it was more expensive than the previous option, it wasn't too horrible. At least not for Xavior. For me, it would have been a month's salary.

The shopkeeper flipped to another page with vague shapes and two or three numbers next to that. "Now, there is a third option, which requires some components from you and your partner, but I think you might be delighted with the results."

"What's that exactly?" I was almost afraid to ask. The other two options were fairly pricey already.

"Full transformation. You would become a dragon yourself. The formula would give you the ability to shift and be broken by a specific trigger. With dragons, it's mostly elements. Water or fire work nicely."

I let what the shopkeeper said sink in. A dragon. A full dragon, like Xavior. To be able to fly with him, soar over the desert together. I could picture it and nearly felt the wind on my face from my imagination alone. My face heated as a lewd image of touching Xavior like I had in the Dragon's Grove, except as a dragon, sprung to mind. I cleared my throat. "How much?"

The shopkeeper added the number to the list, then added the zeros, likely to make a point. My mouth went dry as I tried to swallow. "That's quite a lot compared to the others."

"Yes, but it's a tailor-made transfiguration potion. Very tricky to do, make safely, and reduce the risks to you. This is complex magic. It can have side effects."

"Right, you mentioned that. So what's the downside to this one?"

"You don't shift back to being fully human. You're stuck as a dragon, and the trigger doesn't work. You turn into a pile of goo rather than shifting."

"That's some serious downsides," I said, becoming less enamored with the idea.

"I'm legally required to tell you these things, but they are all very rare. They become more likely, for instance, if you are a heavy magic user, cross multiple kinds of magic, or you are a shifter already."

"Well, I recently discovered I am a latent magic user." Maybe I should think about the bat wings and leave it at that. Then at least I could fly, which was the whole point of seeking out the shop.

"Most dragon magic is elemental. Do you know if your dragon has an elemental affinity?"

"Yes, it's fire. Twice over, so my partner told me."

"Twice over? Explain, please."

"He's a hybrid. A phoenix dragon."

"AH! Well then, that does explain it. Then, to reduce the risks to you, all I would need to do is test your latent magic for its affinity, which is a small fee with a regular transfiguration spell. For this one, I throw it in at no extra cost. I'd also require a scale, or if he has feathers, that will do as well. In this instance, I would recommend collecting both."

"That should be fairly easy to do, I think."

"Good. Excellent. So to explain the process. First, I'll test you, then once I have the materials from your partner, I can create a potion that should give you the general shape and size of your partner, along with any inherent properties he has, and possibly his magical abilities, too."

"You mean I could breathe fire?"

". . . yesssss. Quite possibly. We can also set the trigger for water, specifically creating a threshold for how much. That way, if you are caught in a rainstorm, unless it's a hurricane or a torrential downpour, you shouldn't shift immediately."

"We have a pool on the balcony of our suite."

"Oh, very nice. That would do nicely. Might leave a bit of a mess, but if you are looking at this option, you can likely afford the cleaning bill." They took a deep breath and exhaled through their nose slits. "What do you think?"

I didn't take long to decide. I was afraid I'd back out if I thought about the cost, which was more than a small apartment back home.

When Mr. Uluke tested my magic affinity, it came up as elemental. I had the same magic class as most dragons. It made sense, since my whole family line was engineered to kill them. He indicated that the test couldn't specify what element, but having the same class of magic would be helpful.

Once I'd signed the paperwork and promised to have someone bring him the materials, I left the shop excited about the surprise. I was so lost in thought about what Xavior might think that I bumped into another person as he entered. "Excuse me, I'm sorry."

He glowered at me and continued into the shop. I shrugged and went to find a kiosk map that would lead me back to our suite from the shopping area. Xavior hadn't returned yet. I ordered us lunch, went to his den, and found a couple of scales and a feather he'd shed in the mess of nest bedding. I sent those items off in the container Mr. Uluke gave to me, grabbed a beer from the fridge, and activated the holo to see the schedule for the evening.

"I don't know if Xavior is going to love this or break up with me," I mumbled to myself as I sifted through the different events.

"Break up with you for what?" I spun around and watched as Xavior walked into our suite from the balcony completely nude.

FANTASIES & WISHES

XAVIOR

"You couldn't possibly think I'd break up with you for wanting to go dancing." I noticed Greg was looking through the schedule for the resort and had marked several events already.

"No, no, not that." He waved the schedule away and set down his beer as he came over and wrapped his arms around me. "Mmmm, you're warm and smell like sunshine."

"I wasn't aware that sunshine had a smell," I said with a chuckle.

Greg nodded as he pulled me closer. "It does. Like baking clay."

I laughed again. "So, what on earth could you have possibly done that you'd think I'd break up with you?" He was nervous but excited, and gave me a kiss, which I melted into before pulling away to look at him. He seemed on the verge of saying something. All I sensed was trepidation and excitement. "Greg?"

"I spent your money," he blurted out.

"Okay." I shook my head. "I said that was alright."

"Yeah, but I spent a lot of it."

I gave him a curious look. "Maybe you should start from the beginning."

"Sure. Uh, could you put on a robe or something first, or talking isn't going to happen."

"Oh?" I teased as I pulled him into another kiss. He groaned as his body responded to mine.

He pulled away. "No, no, talking first, lunch, then sex, then dancing."

"I didn't realize you were going to plan out the rest of the afternoon," I laughed.

He shrugged. "I learned things," he said with a sly grin. I'm not sure what my face looked like, but he laughed as he pulled me into another hug and gave me gentle kisses. "Christ, your face is adorably sweet with that odd, clever grin of yours."

"You had me at 'learned things.' I want to hear about your morning."

"I want to hear about yours, too." A chime from the door distracted us. Greg went to answer it. Room service put things on the main dining table as I threw on a robe. The smell of food hit me, and I realized I was hungry for more than Greg.

We sat down to eat, and Greg started talking between bites of his grilled chicken salad. All the while, I shoveled several large pieces of chicken, pasta, and roasted vegetables into my mouth as he explained his meeting with the BDSM club's mistress.

"I have an invite to The Playground. I think Ms. Eilidh wants to meet you."

"She sounds intriguing. I'm surprised you took a liking to her so quickly."

"Even without the goddess aspect, I think I would have liked her. She definitely has a presence. I think you would like her too."

I took another bite of my veg and waited for Greg to continue. There was something else he wanted to talk about because, while it excited him to learn a few things, he hadn't hesitated to talk about meeting Ms. Eilidh. When he talked about dancing later that night, I knew he was trying to figure out how to talk about what he'd done.

"Greg."

"Hmm?" he said around a bite of food.

"Why are you so nervous? Whatever happened, it's okay. We can talk about it."

He nodded and set down his fork. "I met another dragon today."

"And?"

"Her name was Francesca, but she likes to be called Freddie. She works at the café where I had breakfast at this morning. She was concerned about me sitting by myself until I explained I was here with you. Then she suggested something that I followed up on."

"What suggestion did she give you?" Now I was really curious because I was pretty sure he'd spoken to my grandniece without knowing it.

Freddie was one of the best social manipulators I'd ever seen. If at a party, she could broker any number of deals or tear entities apart with a few key conversations. Gavin, my nephew, one of Faith and Trevor's whelps, had mentioned she was working at the resort. Something about exploring other options or paths for her talents. Unless they had talked with her recently, I doubt she knew Greg was specifically with me. Though it was rare for dragons to have human partners. Or she might have learned, and my family was using her to check up on us.

"Wings."

"Wings?" I repeated. Freddie, what were you up to? Were you trying to be helpful or testing our connection?

"I was eating breakfast and felt rather envious that I couldn't fly with you. Freddie picked up on that, and her suggestion was wings."

"Well, that's not a horrible suggestion. There's more or you wouldn't be nervous."

"You're right. Initially, that was the plan. Talk to the apothecary, get some wings, learn to fly so we could fly together."

"But that's not what happened?" He shook his head. Then he picked up his glass of water and swallowed half of it. "What happened, Greg?"

"I, um, was presented with another option." I gestured for him to continue. "It cost quite a bit, and I took you at your word that I could buy anything I wanted."

"I did say that." I smiled. "Do we own an island now or something? What did you buy that has you so flustered?"

His words came out in a rush. "A transfiguration potion that will turn me into a dragon until the removal trigger is used."

I blinked. I hadn't expected that, though it made sense. If I'd been with Greg, I might have suggested it myself instead of looking at simple wing augmentation. "Did the apothecary tell you that full transformations are risky?"

"Mr. Uluke did, yes. It also required some samples from us. Blood from me, scales and feathers from you. It'll take about a week before it's ready."

"That's about the time we are supposed to leave the resort and head to Spain."

He nodded. "I thought, if we didn't use it here, we could use it in Spain. I could fly with you and your family."

"Oh." It was a nice thought, but there were definitely some downsides to that plan. I reached for his hand and squeezed it.

"Are you mad?"

"No. You can sense that, right?"

He nodded and frowned. "Yes, but you're worried."

"That's true." I sighed softly. "I love that you want to be inclusive of my family. It's one of the most beautiful aspects about you, Greg. Family is important to you, and it's important to me too, but dragons can be territorial. It's somewhat of a game to test a connection between new mates."

"Really?"

I nodded. "It makes us competitive. As a human, you wouldn't really be subjected to that. My family might tease us, but I wouldn't need to put up much of a fight."

"Wait, you're talking about a literal fight. In your dragon form?"

I nodded again. "It's one reason we don't bring our mates home unless we are fairly sure the connection is well established, or there are special circumstances."

Greg tilted his head and looked at me. "So your decision to mate with me wasn't noteworthy since I'm a human and also a special circumstance since I'm a Saint George Knight."

"Somewhat, yes."

"And if I transformed into a dragon?" Concern was evident on his face, likely mirroring mine. My thoughtful, kind partner hadn't known the consequences.

"All bets would be off. They'd sense you as too young. Basically, prepubescent, because you've never had an aging cycle. While we are a rational species in general, we act on instinct in our dragon forms. Especially with family groups. So, if we identified as mates and both of us were dragons, it could trigger them to do more than make a couple of scratches."

"More, like what? Kill you?"

"Maybe. Or maim me in a way that would indicate to other dragons what they perceived I had done to a minor."

Greg shook his head. "But it wouldn't be true." He knew better than most people that the truth is more subjective than any of us like it to be.

"Doesn't matter. Smells for a dragon are the truth or a version of it. It's what keeps us safe to some degree."

"It's also why you've never been with another dragon, isn't it?" he asked quietly.

I nodded slowly. "Hybrids aren't exactly shunned, but in our dragon form, we're somewhat outsiders. There's something slightly off about how we smell."

"What about Trevor and Faith?"

I chuckled. "Trevor and Faith were betrothed initially. Back then, different families would assure their bloodlines and continued peace by creating alliances with marriage. They hated each other when they first met, so I was told. By the time Denis and I came along, they had developed this quasi-open relationship and decided they were madly in love." I shook my head and shrugged.

"It worked out. And since Trevor is a full dragon, their children fare better. For instance, Gavin, their son, is mated to a lovely fellow named Brice who's from a red dragon family." They were also Freddie's parents.

Greg's pained look made me reach for his face to try and smooth it away. "Hey, it's still a really great idea. I don't care how much it costs. Even if we have to wait until we are back at my estate, we'll make use of it. I promise." He gave me a small smile and leaned his face into my hand.

I got up from the table, let my hand slide from his face, down his arm, to his hand. I took it in mine and gave it a gentle tug until he came into my arms. "You had an agenda for this afternoon, didn't you?"

He laughed, and it was the best sound I'd heard all day.

TWO LEFT FEET

GREGOR

Xavior insisted we dress up. Linen button-ups, ties, vests, slacks, and dress shoes. Everything was themed to Xavior's house colors, and while I felt a little ridiculous about matching, he looked delighted. It was our first official night out after committing to each other. He wanted to show off, and that was fine with me.

When I asked him when he had the clothes made, he waved his hand and distracted me with a kiss while we finished dressing. Either he'd planned this some time ago or had them made on short notice. Whichever it was, it was still a bit mind-boggling to think about. Though it shouldn't have surprised me since he'd done a similar thing for his birthday party.

I'd picked a couple of parties that featured dancing I knew, like salsa, swing, and tango. The tango party was first, and when we arrived, the music was sultry with a mild beat. I thought it would be an excellent warm-up since swing could be pretty intense.

We found a table to stand at, ordered drinks, and watched as the dancers moved to a live band playing on a small stage to the side of the dance floor. When I finished my drink I offered my hand to Xavior. "Shall we?"

His hand bypassed my offered one and landed on my hip as if to give me a little push. "Maybe I could watch you for a bit?"

It took a few moments, but when his nervousness reached me, I turned toward him fully and asked, "What's wrong?"

"Nothing," he replied, and the strength of the wrong sensation grew. Then a sharpness in that sensation hit my gut, and I knew he was lying to me.

"Wanna tell me why you're trying to make me feel better when clearly you don't, and you lied about it?" I took both his hands in mine and held them in front of us, and pulling them to my chest. We were nose to nose. He relaxed slightly and looked me in the eye, then looked down.

"I didn't know you wanted me to dance with you."

"Of course I do. Why wouldn't I?"

He glanced around. "I want you to have fun. If I danced with you, it wouldn't be."

"What do you mean?" Xavior's embarrassment was heavy between us, and it confused me. I vaguely remembered what Vanessa said about dancing in public. Still, I assumed it had more to do with his choice of dance partners than anything else.

"I can't dance, Greg."

"Bullshit." I snorted. "Of course you can."

"No, I really can't."

I knew he was telling the truth from our connection. The deep embarrassment I sensed from him made me gentle my tone. Until now, I couldn't have imagined Xavior being embarrassed. "Have you ever tried?"

"Once, at a party my parents had, and it was horrible. I was horrible. I didn't know which way to turn and I kept messing up the other dancers. This style looks even more complicated than the dances we did when I was young."

When he was young? I knew some historical context around dancing in Europe, and he was right. Those were less complex in movement, but the beat was mostly the same. Maybe all he needed was a teacher.

I looked around and noticed an empty balcony to one side of the dance floor and led us there. The floor-to-ceiling windows were open to let in some air. I was thankful that the breeze was cool, but not cold, as it could be in the desert. Once we were alone, Xavior relaxed, then tensed again when I maneuvered us into a common couple's position to start.

"I'm sure you could find someone to dance with other than me. I'll foul up the steps." His excuses were interesting, along with what I sensed. There was insecurity for certain, then an intense desire to please, along with lust. I didn't want to think about it too hard, but I noted it and continued.

"Don't think about the steps." I whispered in his ear. "Don't think about what people will see." I brought him closer and started with a swaying motion. A simple rocking step in time to the music. "Feel the music and let your body move with mine."

Xavior sighed and relaxed into me. From there, we added another step and then another. He had a basic pattern down by the end of the third song. It wasn't flashy, and he stopped stepping on my feet. While he wasn't confident, he kept trying, which was definitely Xavior. Some combination of our desire to be near each other and his curiosity overcame his insecurity, paired with the undercurrent of lust and pleasure.

"See, you've already made progress." The pleasure I felt from him intensified slightly.

"Maybe. I feel like I'm slowing you down."

"Never." I kissed his brow. "It's like anything else; it takes practice." I smiled, then leaned down to kiss him. He leaned against me, his hands on my back, holding me close. The insecurity I sensed from him melted away in the face of pleasure and our connection.

We walked back inside and watched the other dancers for a bit. I took his hand and tugged him a little. "Let's see what you think about salsa."

It turned out that Xavior thought salsa was pretty intimidating. We stood on the edge of the dance floor for a long time before he spoke up. "Listen, you find someone you can dance with, and I'll get us drinks. I wanna see what it looks like when my two left feet aren't holding you back."

I sighed. "Xavior—" He cut me off.

"Greg, I'm serious. You've proven I can learn, and I'll learn, but tonight should be fun. You spending the entire night teaching me to dance, while quite gratifying, it feels selfish."

"Who said?" I protested, having found it to be not only gratifying but also stimulating, since I could sense his reaction to it.

"Me. Now go be your charming self while I grab us drinks." I watched as he walked away, glancing over his shoulder. I'd pushed his insecurity enough, and he'd been vulnerable with me. It was something he didn't do easily in public.

Even though I was easily embarrassed about things, especially relating to sex and relationships, Xavior wasn't. How often, I wondered, had he felt awkward? To look at him, you would have never known. I imagine he wouldn't have told me or would have talked his way out of it otherwise. I smiled as I looked at the floor. It was nice to know that I could still teach him a few things.

I looked around to see if anyone wanted a partner and felt a tap on my shoulder. When I turned, a gorgeous woman in a floor-length red and black dress with slits up either side almost to her torso smiled at me. She had pale cream skin. I couldn't tell if that was because of the contrast of her nearly black hair and red dress to her skin or something else. When she offered her gloved hand, I took it, and she led me to the dance floor.

I struggled to keep up with her. Even though I led, she pushed me. It's not uncommon in salsa. Her movements felt aggressive as we moved across the dance floor. Her posture was exacting as we made tight circles near the center of the floor as the tempo picked up. I was out of breath by the fourth song, then noticed we had become the center of attention. When the music stopped, we bowed to a crowd of people clapping.

As we walked toward the edge of the dance floor, I looked for Xavior. When I saw him, he had an expression on his face I couldn't read, and I altered my path to meet him. My dance partner followed, to my surprise. When I reached him, he grabbed my hand.

I picked up on his fear immediately. "Are you alright?" What could he possibly be afraid of here? The woman stopped a short distance from us as Xavior stared at her. "Xavior, this is . . ."

I held out my hand, palm up. "Sorry, I didn't ask your name earlier."

"Her name is Bianca Cooper," Xavior said. "Why are you here, Bianca?" His greeting was even colder than the ones he'd given Keith.

"You're that Bianca?" I looked between them.

"Why yes, if you mean I was his betrothed at one point, then I'm that Bianca." She smiled, and this time, her fangs were visible. "Hello, pet, how have you been?"

I ground my teeth together. *Who the fuck was she calling pet?* I started forward, and Xavior's other hand landed on my forearm to stop me.

"Bianca, what are you doing here?"

She feigned an innocent look. "Same as you. I needed a holiday. I was in the Americas on some business for my family, so I thought I would stay here a week or two."

"You knew," he stated.

"It was hard to miss, pet. You and your partner made a big splash in the regional news. Though I don't think the news realized that 'partner' had a double meaning in this case."

I cursed myself for not catching on that she didn't have a pulse or barely needed to breathe. My pulse had been rapid enough for both of us on the dance floor.

In a show of strength that Xavior rarely ever made, he pushed me behind him and stepped to her. They exchanged words I couldn't hear over the music, but I could sense the anger from him like it was a physical thing.

When he finished speaking, he turned toward me, took my hand, and pulled us toward the door. I went with him, startled, and upset enough for both of us.

ANGER MANAGEMENT

XAVIOR

"If you ever come near him again, I'll kill you."

I'd never threatened anyone like that before, not even for Bianca. I was close enough to smell her mint-laced breath. She loved mints or gum, especially after she fed. She said it kept her mouth from drying, since vampires didn't breathe all that often. I'd forgotten how much I disliked that smell.

"Ah, pet, you've mated, haven't you?" She smiled. "You were never this fierce when we were together. Then again, our connection was mostly one-sided, much to my regret."

"Bianca, whatever you are doing here, forget it."

"Does he know that even after we split up, you would run to me like you would run to Jordan?"

She still knew what buttons to press. She had threatened Jordan once, too. When I told Jordan, he laughed it off. He had magic he'd never shown me. I hoped it was enough to keep him safe. Greg had no such luxury. Vampires were not Greg's forte, though he had proved he could hold his own.

"I told you the last time, never again."

"Did you tell Jordan the same?"

"I didn't have to. Jordan would never hurt me." He, in fact, loved me. Loved me enough to not interfere with my relationship. I was still a little confused about that one, but definitely not about where I stood with Bianca.

"Maybe." She looked me over, and I fought to stand my ground. "What if I turned your little plaything, Xavior? Would you come to me then, for his sake?"

"Bianca." My anger was on a knife's edge. My scales brushed against the inside of my skin. I wanted to burn her down where she stood. "You hurt him, I *will* kill you, and anyone else who gets in my way."

She held up her hands in a placating gesture. "If you change your mind, I'm in room 2305."

"Fuck off." I turned to leave and brought Greg with me.

We made it as far as a supply closet before I pulled Greg inside, threw him up against the door, and kissed him. He seemed surprised but went with it. When I finally had more control over my senses, I pulled away to look at him.

The light was stark, and Greg's shirt and vest were rumpled from my rough handling. I almost backed away, scared of what I'd done, until I saw something shift in Greg's gaze.

He caught me by the back of the neck and pulled me close, then kissed me slow and hard. A moment later, he'd spun me like we were on the dance floor and switched our positions, except my face was pressed to the door, and his mouth was pressed to my neck.

"Red? Yellow? Or green?" Greg asked quietly.

I was breathing hard, but answered, "Green."

Greg pressed kisses into my neck while his hands opened my pants. The moment his fingers wrapped around my cock, he bit my neck. When his teeth let go of my skin, I finally took a full breath. As my brain adjusted, I felt a cool liquid drip onto my ass while my slacks and boxers fell to my feet. It warmed quickly as Greg slid a finger inside me and continued to pump my dick.

His lips were in my ear, whispering, "You're mine. And she can't ever have you again. Not in this lifetime or the next."

A gasp tumbled from my lips as he pressed another finger into me and massaged my gland. I fidgeted until the pressure was somewhere between frustrating and maddening. "I need you."

"I know." Then he removed his hands. Bereft of the contact, I stifled a whimper until Greg's left hand wrapped around my throat, his right hand around my dick, while his covered cock pressed into my ass. "You're mine, Xavior. You'll always be mine."

In some less addled part of my brain, I wondered if Greg had always been this possessive, or if our connection had brought it out. He had moments where he needed control, and we both knew that, but this was different. His left hand drifted from my neck to my shoulder as he held me to the door and thrust hard, and we grunted at the impact. He dragged himself out slowly, then slammed into me again.

My hand reached for his bare hip as he pulled out again and pressed in. He let go of my dick and pressed me to the door. His left hand wrapped around my neck again as his right landed on my shoulder. His thrusts were quick and demanding. All I heard in my ears was the rattle of the door on its hinges, and Greg as he whispered "mine" repeatedly until he came.

When he pulled out, he turned me around and wrapped his hand around my dick and his. That less addled part of my brain was concerned about something, but I ignored it as I reached for him. He pressed his forehead to mine. "I love you . . . I love you," he repeated as he worked me over and kissed my face. I held onto him and screamed his name into his shoulder as I came in his hand. We stood there panting, sated by the intensity of what happened. Greg moved first, letting go of my dick. I sighed, feeling bereft of his touch.

"Feel better?" he asked as he wiped his hands off on a towel he'd retrieved from somewhere.

"We're a mess." I laughed a little as he pulled me into his arms.

"Maybe." Greg kissed me. "But we're each other's mess, and that's all that matters."

There must have been an odd smile on my face, because Greg gave me another kiss and let me go. I swayed slightly until he caught me. We put each other back together enough that at least we appeared decent, even if we didn't smell like it.

We walked with our arms wrapped around each other's waists for a measure of balance. As we made our way back to our suite, my pheromone brain finally connected with my rational one. "Did we use protection?"

"Huh?" Greg looked at me. He paused, and I stopped. "Of course."

"What did you do with it?"

"It's in my pocket. I didn't want to leave it for staff to find." He grinned at me.

I nudged us forward and gave his waist a squeeze. "When did you start carrying supplies with you?" I asked with a pleased smile on my face as we entered the lift.

"When you said we should use protection." He gave me a smirk. "Given our habits, I wanted to be prepared."

I laughed. "I did the same thing when we went to the Grove."

Greg grinned and kissed my forehead as we exited the lift and slowly walked toward our room. "Are you alright?" His concern was tempered with desire. He'd been rough with me. While we'd talked about having those kinds of interactions, it wasn't planned. Neither was running into Bianca.

"Yes." I squeezed his hip. "She knows how to get under my scales. I could have handled it better."

He caressed my right side as we turned down the hall to our room. "Maybe. I sensed your anger. Then, when we were in the supply room, it felt like a physical thing between us. It gave me this overwhelming need to mark you," he said.

As we reached our door and thumbed it open, I made a contemplative noise.

"Should we be worried? That was a lot more aggressive than I've ever been with you." Greg held the door as I walked in first.

"It's possible that you're more territorial than I am. It might not have been apparent until we became connected."

"Should we expect any more surprises from our connection?" He went to the bathroom while I sat on the bed and unbuttoned my shirt.

I paused for a moment and thought about it. "I'm not sure. This is my first time, too." He laughed, and it made me smile as we continued to talk. "It's responding much differently than I expected."

"Well, whatever happens, I'm sure we'll be able to handle it," Greg said as he came out of the bathroom with a towel wrapped around his waist. "You didn't see it, but your back had shifted to scales, and anywhere I'd touched, it stayed that way until you came."

His words drew my gaze away from his waist to his eyes. "That didn't stop you?" The feel of him caressing my scales through my bipedal form was usually very pleasant. Powerful emotions sometimes caused shifters to lose control of their changes. I've never heard of a partner being able to affect another like that. It should scare me, and might have if it had happened with anyone else.

He shook his head. "Why would it?" He walked toward me and gave me a kiss. "Who you are doesn't scare me, Xavior." He kissed me again and walked back toward the bathroom, then casually dropped his towel. His toned body was framed in the doorway with an obvious invitation before he disappeared. As I heard him give commands for the shower, I finished stripping off my clothes to join him.

MOTIVES

GREGOR

Later, when we were tucked into bed together, I couldn't help but ask the question. "Why is Bianca here?"

"I don't know." He grit his teeth as he spoke. I knew he wasn't upset or frustrated with me. Her showing up here was very much a surprise. "Vampire motives are tricky. She could be here on behalf of her family, or she could have her own ideas."

"She knew about this place. Did you bring her here before?"

He winced. "I wouldn't have guessed Bianca knew about it. They have similar places in Europe. Maybe she found out about this one somehow."

"Oh." I lay there as I tried to sort through my feelings and couldn't. "Am I disappointed, or is that you? I don't know why I would be."

Xavior shook his head. "I'm sorry, Greg." His hand came up to cover his face, then he rolled away from me and buried his head in a pillow.

His regret hit me in waves. I wrapped my arms around him and pulled him closer. He moved his head to the crook of my shoulder as if it was the most natural thing in the world and he'd done it a million times. "Look, you couldn't have known. You said it yourself when you brought us here that it was safer than any other place you could think of, so why do you feel regret?" I brushed my hand through his hair. It was oddly soothing for us both, I think.

"The last thing I wanted to do was shove my past in your face."

"You have a long past, Xav. It's not fair for me to be upset about who you were. I know a lot more than most, probably more than your ex." I tilted his head to look at me. "You dealt with Keith. Plus, you know about my past. So it's not like either of us has a boring history."

"That's an interesting perspective." He frowned slightly. "You're being very gracious."

"We're both different people. You're different from when you knew Bianca. I've changed a lot too. Nothing is perfect, life isn't perfect. We have to accept each other for who we are now."

This wouldn't be a onetime thing. We'd have to work through this as things came up about our lives that neither of us were comfortable with, like our exes, family, and overly familiar friends like Jordan. "We talked about our past, about what we did before. We'll have fights and misunderstandings, but remember your promise," I said as I held him tight. "You said you would do what you think is in my best interest and try not to be a bonehead. So, I'll promise the same and try not to be a bonehead either." I kissed the side of his neck. He made a pleased sigh and relaxed in my arms.

I paused, but only for a moment, then put the thought out there, because it was itching in my brain. "Do you think she's here because she had something to do with the coven house ambush?"

Xavior didn't flinch when I accused his ex of being involved.

"It's possible. Seems more like a coincidence than anything else. The news went pretty wide. If she was in the area, she could have taken an interest and tracked me down. Though the way she approached you first was clearly meant to test me, or us. I'm not sure which. If you had asked me before tonight, I would have assumed I was just an afterthought to her."

"I don't know how you could even think that. Oh, he who solves world problems in his backyard. I'm a jobless nobody."

Xavior turned in my arms and gave me a light slap on my chest, then met my gaze. "You aren't a nobody!" I laughed, but he frowned. "I'm serious. I've been thinking about how we might start over." His fingers reached up and traced my shoulder. "We can start a private company. Protection, bodyguard work, security . . . meet interesting people and see interesting places."

"Once we're on the restricted list, would anyone seriously hire us?"

"There is a branch of your family in Europe that works for a lot of royalty."

"You have a very broad definition of family, Xav."

He went on, undeterred. "Listen, one of them even married a royal, was thrown out of the organization, and still does security work for his partner and others."

"That would mean telling people who I am."

"Yes, that's true, but the advantage—"

"I don't know, Xav," I interrupted. "Let me think about it. I've kept that part of myself secret for so long it feels weird to put it out there. Also, I've never worked for royalty, so who'd hire me?"

"You have specialized training. If it's anything similar to what the other parts of your extended family know and exhibit, then people will find that desirable. Or at the very least, recognize it as valuable."

"What about the part where the family on this side of the world is known for being a cult rather than an elite protective detail?"

He sighed. "You're right. But maybe if you meet the European half, things could be different."

"Maybe." My hands wandered and caressed his sides and back. I felt scales under my fingertips again. I didn't know what exactly caused it. The pheromones were likely, sure, but the response I had when I felt or saw his scales was visceral. A longing and satisfaction so deep welled up that the words were inadequate to describe it.

"Yeah. We have time. No rush, really. Unless you buy a couple more expensive potions," he said with a teasing tone in his voice.

"Hey, you said . . ." I didn't finish my sentence as he kissed me.

The next morning, we went back to the café where I'd talked to the other dragon. Xavior mentioned wanting to meet her, and I thought nothing of it when he asked. I mostly sensed curiosity about him where she was concerned. Besides his family, he never mentioned being friends with any other dragons. Maybe there was a reason for that, or it was by choice. I wasn't sure and made a mental note to ask later.

"Good morning, Freddie." I gave her a warm smile as she filled my cup. Xavior's response was a surprise, but Freddie wasn't caught off guard.

"Freddie!" He stood and gave her a hug while I sat with my mouth open. When he finally glanced at me, he grinned, and I tried really hard not to be the confused one in the group. "Greg, this is my grandniece, Freddie." He gestured at me. "Freddie, this is Gregor Lyndon, my mate."

"Charmed," Freddie said as she offered her hand, making a show of the introduction even though we already knew each other. We shook hands as Freddie stood there, all smiles, with a carafe of coffee. "I feel like someone played a prank on me," I said. "Did you know who I was before we talked?"

"No," she said with a grin. "But it explains why you smelled so familiar."

Xavior smiled as she poured him a cup of coffee, too. "Are you here for the season?" Xavior asked.

"Yeah. If I like it, I'll probably sign up for next year. Everyone seems to be worried about my prospects these days."

Xavior shook his head as he sat. "For a moment, I half wondered if our family was keeping tabs on me." He ate another bite of omelet, and Freddie burst his bubble.

"Oh, they had me do that too once they knew you were here." She grinned. Xavior sighed, and I tried not to laugh.

"Does your family worry about you that much?" I glanced between the two of them, not sure who I was addressing the question to exactly. I had my hand wrapped around my coffee cup, wondering if I needed to spike it with something. If Xavior's family was that protective, it might be harder to win their trust than I thought.

"It's equal parts protectiveness and possibly Faith being nosy because I've only messaged her a few times to let them know we're alright. It's natural for families to worry about newly mated pairs, though this seems excessive."

Freddie shrugged. "I think worry is their natural state of being sometimes. I've been here for almost a month, and your partner was the only interesting individual I've smelled."

Xavior responded with a great deal of sympathy, which I understood, given his history. "Freddie, be patient. If it happens, it'll happen."

Xavior reached for my hand, and I gave it to him. I brushed my thumb across his knuckles, prompting his scales to flash in the morning light. I glanced up at Freddie and gave her an encouraging smile.

"Aww!" She grinned. "You must have an excellent connection with each other for Uncle Xavior's scales to flash like that."

Xavior glanced at me as he quizzed his niece. "You've seen this before?"

"Sure, my parents do it all the time. When I asked, they told me once that it was because their connection was so strong it couldn't help but show itself. Isn't that romantic?" She sighed, then continued. "Anyway, I don't understand why everyone is freaking out. Since my aging cycle, the first thing out of their mouths is: meet anyone yet? They don't like it when I bring up that others in our family didn't have a mate for a really long time, and you're perfectly fine."

Xavior sighed. "I know." He tried to continue eating as Freddie spoke. I gave his hand a squeeze and let go.

"Then there's Aunt Dawn. Supposedly she has a mate, but no one's ever seen her, and Dawn comes to gatherings by herself. Granma-ma worries about her and thinks she's becoming more like you every day. But she isn't lying when she says she has a mate." She shrugged. "And everyone wonders why I spend most of my time in libraries."

"Who's Granma-ma?" I wasn't exactly sure where Freddie was in the family tree.

"My sister, Faith," Xavior replied, then he looked up at Freddie again. "We should let you get back to work, Freddie. We don't want to get you in trouble." Though Xavior sympathized with Freddie's plight, he didn't seem in the mood to talk about it. Running into Bianca last night did more to his mental state than I think either of us realized.

Freddie's smile dimmed slightly, but she leaned over to give Xavior a peck on the cheek. Then she turned toward me and gave me a quick kiss on the cheek, too. Xavior smiled at my surprise. "Nice to see you again, Uncle Greg! Bye Uncle Xavior!" she said as she walked away with a little wave for both of us.

"Uncle Greg?" I glanced at Freddie, who was already busy with another table, then looked at Xavior.

"With dragons, mating automatically makes you part of the family. Especially since it's nearly impossible to separate afterward. In some ways, you'll be family no matter what happens." He tried to look me in the eye but couldn't.

"Hey, I knew what I was getting myself into. I don't have any regrets. Do you?" I offered my hand again, and he slipped his into mine as we laced our fingers together.

He shook his head. "None." He looked at me and smiled.

"Good." I finally took a drink of my lukewarm coffee. I decided that was fine, as I didn't want to take up more of Freddie's time. "Why don't you tell me about the rest of your extended family?" It was better to have a rundown now than when I was face to face with them.

"Ever the detective, I see." He grinned. "Alright. Where would you like me to start?"

"How about with your siblings?" I took a sip of my coffee and watched as he took a few more bites of his breakfast.

"Ah, well, Denis and I are polar opposites. And he has a mate that everyone's met but me. Faith thinks they are a horse shifter, possibly, but no one has ever asked the few times that Denis has brought them around the family."

He spent the rest of the morning talking about his family. I longed to meet all of them and find out what it was like to be surrounded by dragons.

THE PLAYGROUND

XAVIOR

When we left the café, it was mid afternoon. I hadn't thought of how we'd spend the rest of the day, but Greg had ideas.

"I think you would really like her. Ms. Eilidh, that is. She has a very warm personality and is quite the teacher."

I couldn't help but smirk. "If I didn't know any better, I might be jealous." Greg wrapped his arm around my waist, and I mirrored him as we walked toward the BDSM club in the resort called The Playground.

"But I know you're not. How come?"

"Because I trust you, and if a woman could actually turn your head, that's someone I definitely want to meet."

"So it would be another mystery for you?" Greg wiggled his eyebrows.

"You're my greatest mystery, Gregor, or haven't you figured that out yet?" We stopped for a moment, and Greg pulled me to the side of the hall, where he wrapped his arms around me. I looked up at him, and he leaned down to kiss me. The complex desire and satisfaction I sensed from Greg made me weak, and the kiss was just a precursor. I sensed he had plans.

Before I could completely melt into him, he pulled us away from the wall, and we continued to our destination, obvious hard-ons be damned. I tried to clear my throat to talk. "You know, I've come to this resort a few times, and I've never been to this particular club."

"Enough going on elsewhere to keep your interest?" Greg glanced at me. He smelled confident, and he liked leading me somewhere I hadn't been before. It was the same the night he taught me how to dance.

"Something like that. I've always enjoyed sex and as long as my partners were happy, I was happy. I never thought about any deeper connection or wanting someone to understand me enough to assert their dominance."

"What about Jordan?"

That was a fair question, and understandable. There was a hint of jealousy in it, but I didn't mind. "Oddly enough, no. We had adventures together, which consisted of how many orgasms we could bring out of each other or our partners. He has some kinks, though being in control isn't really one of them. Which is odd given how he runs our companies."

While I talked about Jordan, Greg's emotions took an interesting roller coaster of jealousy and self-doubt before he came back to jealousy and confidence. While I was curious as to the thoughts which caused it, I didn't stop our conversation to ask. Through all that, he still smelled really confident, which fascinated me.

"Not even with Bianca?" He hadn't asked to be cruel. I could sense that. Nor did he try to compare himself to her. It was genuine curiosity. It was clear to me that Greg considered Jordan more competition than Bianca. I debated bringing up my experience with Naomi. He knew some things. If he asked, I'd tell him. Though what she and I did together barely scratched the surface and ultimately led me to him.

"Ah, no. It was enough that Bianca wanted me back then, and when she didn't, I had free rein to do what I liked. The gentlemen's clubs were entertaining enough, and Bianca kept me in pocket change until I came into my own."

"So you weren't a trust fund kid, then?" Greg asked with a chuckle.

I laughed. "No, of course not. Our families support most of us during the first fifty years or so. We always have a place to stay, of course, but we wander, we make names for ourselves, we work. Take Freddie, for example. This is her first job. She's very headstrong. If her parents hadn't pushed her out of the house, she would have stayed in their library reading into her second century. As it was, she left their house and went to my parents' house and lived there for a good decade, still reading."

"Maybe that's her obsession."

"It might be. Gavin thinks she'd be skilled at medicine or law if she'd go to school." Even if Gavin and Brice, her parents, wanted Freddie to attend school, it was clear Freddie didn't feel the same way. She'd always had her nose in a book. My guess was that once she spread her wings, she'd look for adventures, or become a writer.

"But she didn't want to leave home?"

"Precisely. Freddie knows ten languages but hasn't used them. She's read most of the great works on the planet but hasn't seen the places they were created. Her memory is astounding, but she hasn't used it for more than cleverly manipulating people at parties. Though Gavin blames that on Brice. No one could resist a young whelp chatting about any topic she could get her hands on."

"Are we talking about the same dragon? Your Francesca?" Greg chuckled.

I nodded and shrugged. "I think that's why Freddie's parents and my sister are worried about her."

"I'm surprised they talked her into working here. It seems like she would be better suited as a librarian." Greg continued down another hallway like he knew where he was going, and I talked. To have a partner lead me around in public was new. Where most of my partners were concerned, I did the leading. I liked this reversal of roles.

"It was a bargain, from what I understand. Freddie spends the season here, working, interacting with people, and they let her come home again for the rest of the year and spend it in the library. To be honest, I think they are hoping something, or someone, turns her head enough that she leaves the nest for good."

"So her response to me wasn't normal, I take it?" Greg smelled concerned, but we continued to walk.

"Oh, that was normal." He cringed, and I tried to explain. "That's the pheromones at play. While they somewhat tell others I've claimed you, it also sets a challenge because it makes you more desirable. You might find that people will pay attention to you more."

"Will your whole family respond like that?" The concern in his scent grew.

"Not the mated ones. And the unmated might be curious, but not enough to cross any lines or initiate something that isn't welcome. As I explained before, dragons are very big on consent and permission. They might challenge me over you, but that's part playfulness and part tradition."

"To make sure you're worthy of me?" Greg asked, as his scent spiked with something like pride, along with a dose of possessiveness. He liked that our roles were reversed. While he might be the knight, in reality, I was the one that would have to prove myself.

"Something like that," I offered with a grin. We turned a corner, and the hallway ended with a gradual dimming of lights until we entered a space that looked like someone's huge, very chic living room. At the other end was a set of double doors with a spotlight on them.

Greg led me to a couch, and one of the waitstaff came over to take our drink order.

"When will the doors open?" Greg leaned forward. His anticipation was palpable.

"The current floor show is finishing up. You'll be able to enter again in fifteen minutes." The staff member nodded, then left to fill our order.

"What do we do in the meantime?" I asked, playfully leaning into him as we waited.

"Ms. Eilidh said this area is mostly a place to relax or discuss what might happen behind the doors. Establish boundaries, rules, etcetera." The server returned with our drinks and placed them in front of us, then disappeared again.

"Okay, so what do we want to happen?" My nervousness surprised me. I didn't mind sex in public, but it's one thing to be submissive to someone in the comfort of your room; it was another to be vulnerable in a way that was more than being naked.

"Well, this time, I think we'll mostly watch." Greg picked up his drink and took a sip. "I know you're comfortable kissing in front of others. What else would you want to try?"

"Wait. What else are you suggesting?" I didn't move to pick up my drink. There was something in Greg's gaze that I'd say was predator-like, but I'd never seen him look quite like that. My brain screamed that it was a trap, but I knew Greg. He preferred choices, not snares.

I watched as he set his drink down and reached for my hands. "It's not a trap, Xavior. I promise. No one touches you here but me, and even then, you can tell me to stop."

My relief was instantaneous, and weird. Had I really worked myself into thinking Greg would make me participate in something to only shun me for doing it? He was here too, but he wasn't afraid of what I would think. Why had I assumed that?

"Why did you think I was trying to trap you? I sensed your instinct to flee. Not that you were scared of me, but scared of what might happen. Are you still worried about pheromones?"

His hands felt good in mine, and I knew if he asked, I'd do anything for him. Anything for the connection we shared, and the feeling of knowing absolutely that I wasn't alone any longer. If he had rejected me a few months ago, at my age, it likely would have killed me. But I would have died happy knowing that there was someone that I had a genuine connection with, even if he didn't want it. Because while I ran from it for most of my life after Bianca, it's all I had really wanted.

"I think . . ." I paused because I hadn't talked about this with anyone, not even my therapist yet. "I think my time with Bianca had a lot more influence on me than I realized." The knot in my throat made it hard to swallow. "While I didn't wear a leash and collar, she certainly had one around my neck. Even though it was false, she used our connection to keep me tied to her until she rejected me."

Greg looked concerned. "What happened?"

"She fed from someone else as a way to make me pay for visiting my family. When I realized our connection wasn't there, I offered to let her feed from me again. She refused and threw me out. We'd been together for almost forty years. Even if it was a false connection, physiologically and mentally, I was desperate for it. After it worked out of my system, I was determined not to fall into the same trap."

"I'm kinda thankful I can sense you at the moment. I can't mistake what you're feeling, and I know you don't think our connection is a trap. However, something about this situation made you think of that." Greg pulled me toward him, and I settled into his arms.

"Running into her the other night has surfaced a lot of things I never talk about." I sighed. "So much of my time was spent arranging my life so I'd never end up in the place Bianca left me. I resented Faith and my family for how they treated her and blamed them for a long time. It seems ridiculous now, but when I came to my senses, I was pretty angry at them for being right. I thought she loved me." I tried to breathe through the knot in my throat as Greg held me more tightly. "When we met, I was scared. I fought our connection for a lot of reasons. And I wanted it for a lot of reasons, too."

"I love you." Greg kissed my forehead. "Your family might not accept me at first either, but I would never stop you from seeing them, and I wouldn't dream of leaving you because you wanted to see your family." He rocked us a little in an effort to soothe each other.

"It's that, and wondering if you'll leave me or find a way to reject me somehow. I know you need your space from time to time, but it's not hard to think that you could leave, and that would be the last time I would see you."

We sat on the couch curled up together until the lights blinked and voices indicated that the doors to the main room had opened.

"Maybe we're not ready for this yet." Greg's voice caressed my ear, and I shivered slightly. I wanted to please him and give him everything he wanted. The disappointment that welled in my throat threatened to spill over into a sob. "You have boundaries too, Xavior. We'll give this another try when we're ready. Promise."

Greg likely didn't know how much what he said and the timber of his voice soothed that disappointed, panicked part in my brain. He didn't have to touch me to establish control or display dominance. He took care of me in ways I'd never even considered were important, which made me love him all the more. I'm not a frail creature, though I have vulnerabilities. Greg knew the physical ones, and he was quickly learning ones I'd never even considered.

Greg pulled me up from the couch and turned us to leave. He put his arm around my waist and kissed the side of my head as we walked away from The Playground. When we made it back to our room, he opened the door, then walked us to bed, closing the sliding door behind us.

I stood there until he sat me on the edge, then bent down to take off my sandals. I watched, fascinated. Had I ever been undressed like this before? Sure, there were moments with partners where hands were grabby and clothes disappeared, but this? It was so different. I didn't know what to do with myself.

Greg stood and reached for my shirt. "On or off?" he asked.

"Off?" My voice had an odd lilt to it. I wasn't sure where this was going, even though I liked the direction.

He lifted my arms and took off my shirt. I watched him kick off his sandals and remove his shirt, too.

We were both in shorts as he leaned over to give me a kiss. "Pants or no pants?"

You'd think that I would have been able to give a straightforward answer to that question. Greg waited, didn't rush, and I thought about it. "Why?"

"I want you to be comfortable."

"Comfortable?"

He smiled, then touched my face. I leaned into that. "You're tired, aren't you?"

I was. I hadn't really noticed since I was so focused on Greg. "Yeah."

He stripped and tossed his shorts and boxers with the rest of our clothes. "Did you decide?" he asked. His voice was so soft and strong, his scent so confident and comforting, it prompted me to take deep breaths. I reached for him and pressed my nose into his navel in an effort to smell nothing else but him. He held me like that until I cried. Then continued to hold me and touch my face and hair until I calmed down again.

He touched my shoulder, and I eased my hold. It let him move enough to reach over and pick up his shirt from the pile. Greg then cleaned my face with it, then wiped his stomach off because it was covered in tears and snot. It was funny, sort of. I might have laughed if I wasn't so drained.

"No pants," I breathed. He worked them off my hips, along with my boxers, and tossed them with the rest. He pulled back the covers, then directed me to lay down. Once I was comfortable, he got into bed with me. In bed, our height difference was an advantage. I moved to put my head on his shoulder and bury my nose in his neck, just to the side of his jaw.

We settled next to each other, and I drifted off. When I woke up, it was dark, and Greg was still there.

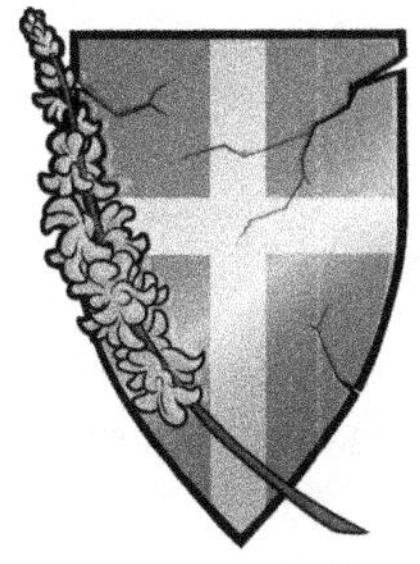

Needs & Wants

Gregor

"Did you have a good nap?" I smiled at him as I watched his eyes change, then return to their human-looking irises.

"You're here." He blinked as if he was trying to make sure it wasn't a dream.

"Of course I am." I touched his face. "You were scared and hurt. If you had told me to leave, I would have, but I got the impression that you needed me."

Xavior wrapped his arms around me and gave me a hug. "I did. I do." We were quiet for a while before he spoke again. "I'm sorry I ruined your plans."

"You didn't ruin anything." I caressed his back. "We've had a lot happen recently. Sometimes you have to recognize when to slow down a bit, you know? You'll always be more important than any plans."

"Thank you." We held each other for a while, then he shifted in my arms and looked up at me. "Though. . . I don't want to spend the rest of the night in the room. We only have a few more nights. We should go out and do something fun."

"What did you have in mind?"

Turns out, Xavior knew about a party in the Dragon's Grove. It sounded perfect. Have some cocktails, watch acrobats and fire breathers entertain the crowds, meet other couples, and have a fun, relaxing evening.

When we arrived, it was anything but my idea of relaxing. It was half theme park and half street carnival. Dragons were everywhere in all shapes, sizes, and with various parts shifted. Some were even flying around, performing in one visual spectacle or another.

Fire-breathing dragons melted things into patterns while an ice-breathing dragon reshaped and topped them off with snow. Pixy dragons were in full force, delivering drinks and taking orders. Others had curled up with various guests or roamed and played as they pleased. With so many dragons and their partners present, it was breathtaking.

Most were with other dragons, but a few here and there had non-dragon partners. While I was at the bar ordering drinks, Xavior walked over with two women.

"Greg." He reached for my hand, and I took his. "This is Delilah and Bonnie." Xavior pointed to Delilah, a very tall woman—maybe ten or twelve centimeters taller than me—with dark brown skin and long black wavy hair that ended around her waist. Her eyes were a striking shade of light blue. Bonnie had a lighter skin tone, dark brown eyes, and natural black hair that showed off her pointed ears. "Delilah is a water dragon, and Bonnie is a mage." Xavior grinned. "We were just talking about the show with the fire and ice dragons across the way, and I wanted to introduce you." They were dressed in the latest fashions appropriate for a warm night, which meant that they barely wore anything at all.

"You're human," Bonnie said with some surprise as she shook my hand. "Don't see many of you in the Grove. Are you a mage as well?"

I chuckled, "No. I'm a latent user at best, though Xavior thinks I can learn." Xavior left me to introduce myself as he grabbed our order from the bar.

"There must be more to it than that. You have a fascinating scent," Delilah said. I shrugged and suddenly felt I lacked enough social skills for the situation.

"How long have the two of you been together?" I asked in a somewhat desperate attempt to shift the focus off me. Xavior was no help when he returned, watching me flounder while he drank his beer.

"About twenty years now? I think. Is that right, Dee?" Bonnie asked her partner.

Delilah shrugged. "Something like that." Then she gave me a smile with a once-over like she was sizing me up to eat me. That's when Xavior took notice. He handed me my drink, then took my hand.

"Delilah was telling me that in Jamaica, there's a whole resort specifically for magic users. Like this one somewhat, but everyone uses magic for just about everything."

She nodded and caressed Bonnie's shoulder. "Yes. Lovely place. Not as big as this one, but it's right on the water, and the sunsets are amazing."

"With that much magic in the atmosphere, it's not surprising," Bonnie said with a soft laugh. She glanced at her partner and then across to me and Xavior, her gaze assessing us. "You two are newly mated, aren't you?" Her tone made it sound like a rhetorical question instead of curiosity.

"Is it that obvious?" I asked.

Delilah sighed, and Bonnie laughed. "Normally, no, but my love here is more sensitive than most to new pheromone connections. It's like catnip to her."

"Should I be worried?" Xavior asked.

Delilah smiled, and Bonnie shook her head. "Not unless you're me, or you both want to join us in our room later." She glanced at Delilah, then at us with a smile. "Delilah likes the, um, stamina newly connected couples exhibit."

I laughed. "Oh, that makes complete sense." I glanced at Xavior, and his eyes were wide with surprise. I don't think he expected me to gossip. For once, I felt like bragging. "Once we connected, we haven't been able to keep our hands off each other. Even before that, it was hard to resist. We waited for a bit to be sure it was what we wanted." The ladies nodded, and Xavior gave me a sly smile.

"It's amazing. Best high on the planet, if you ask me," Delilah said.

"She's not wrong." Bonnie smiled at her mate. "It gives me a pretty good magical boost as well. Newly mated couples radiate a lot of magic. It gives a whole new meaning to that honeymoon period, you know?"

"I'd never thought of it like that," Xavior admitted. "Do you often share with others that are mated?"

"When the mood strikes us," Delilah practically purred as she caressed Bonnie. "Your combined pheromone signature is quite enticing. I've smelled nothing like it before."

"Oh? I hope that's a good thing." I'd hate to think we walked around offending people. Though on second thought, maybe that would make some situations easier.

"Very," Delilah said as she moved behind Bonnie and appeared on the other side of her, closer to me. "It's intoxicating." She took a deep breath. "Like something dark and rich that would melt on your tongue."

Bonnie grinned at her partner, then turned that smile toward us. "So, gentlemen, would you be interested?" It was evident what she asked for, and I was flattered. I'd had women make a pass at me before, though not exactly like this.

I glanced at Xavior, and his eyes were so round that it made me laugh. "I think we have enough on our plate at the moment, ladies. But thank you for the offer." I watched as Delilah whispered to Bonnie, and she giggled. "I hope we didn't offend you."

"No, of course not," Bonnie said. "We understand, but we were wondering if there's a favor we could ask of you."

Five minutes later, we were wandering around the Grove shirtless. "Should we have given them our shirts?"

"Least we could do since we turned them down." Xavior grinned. "A gallant gesture and all that."

"You're imagining them rolling around in your scent." I shook my head. Xavior turned to look at me.

"No, I'm imagining them rolling around in yours and how much they'll get off on it. And how they'll envy me because you're all mine." I couldn't keep the grin from my face. It was nice to know we were both possessive of each other. I stepped in a little closer and pressed my lips to his ear.

"I'd love nothing more than to spend the rest of my days making everyone envious of us." He shivered slightly, and his hard nipples pressed into my chest. The next thing I knew, we'd found some random closet, and I was on my knees with Xavior groaning above me.

I started off with quick strokes and sloppy licks, which quickly devolved into full-on mouth fucking. I grabbed Xavior's hips and let him have my mouth until I got the bright idea to slip a digit into his ass.

"Fuck! Greg, oh shit." He came, and I nearly choked as it caught me by surprise. Xavior's cock popped free of my mouth as he slid down the door he'd been holding up. I pulled him to me and spilled Xavior's seed back into his mouth in an all-consuming kiss.

PARTY FOUL

XAVIOR

The aftermath of my orgasm felt like the world had stopped, and it only moved forward one breath, one beat at a time. I couldn't do much but stare at Greg as he played his fingers across my chest. My scales responded as they always did to Greg's touch.

"You alright?" I worried that I'd hurt him somehow. We hadn't been gentle. I reached out to wipe the sheen of saliva from his lips.

Greg smiled, then leaned forward to kiss me. "I'm fine." His voice sounded like he'd eaten gravel, but other than that, he seemed fine, even by his scent.

"I didn't know that would happen."

"That they would be attracted to us or want to fuck us?" Greg was amused. His hand pressed to my chest, caressing my nipple, which made my dick twitch. I had my back to the closet door, with Greg pressed to my right side. Knees bent enough that his left arm was resting on top. It reminded me of how we would do our sit-ups together for our morning workouts, facing each other while we did reps.

"Both! They seemed fun, and I thought we'd have things in common."

Greg laughed. "You know what I just realized?" he grinned, as he continued to caress me. He was so casual about touching me and I loved the contact. At some point, we had overcome our hesitation to touch each other, afraid of what it might cause. He was right earlier when he said we couldn't keep our hands off each other. It made me ridiculously happy that Greg craved the contact as much as I did. That wasn't always the case for some mates.

"What's that?"

"You don't have some suave rogue thing where you seduce anyone that walks by. You really are this wide-eyed adventurer that is more than happy to be charmed by those around you into just about any situation." Greg caressed my face. "Tell me, if I wasn't in the picture, would you be with them right now?"

My happiness turned to worry when he asked his question, but I trusted him. "Yes, more than likely. Though I doubt they would have found me all that interesting without you."

Greg closed his eyes and smiled. It baffled me. "That's the truth, and I sensed it. Do you realize how comforting it is to know exactly how you feel? To talk about it?"

I nodded because I could only imagine how confusing it was without it. It had been confusing enough before the connection. "Does it bother you I felt that way about them?"

"No." Greg paused and watched me. "You'll always be attracted to others. I knew that. The difference is that you don't feel you have to hide it from me. That even as you're aroused and tempted, you look to me to help you."

My face felt hot, and so did the rest of me. Greg's scent still radiated some combination of desire and dominance. I swallowed hard in an effort to resist my own urges for the moment. Greg had no such compunction.

"Would you like it if I let you imagine what would have happened with that couple?" He whispered in my ear, and I shook my head. "Why not?" His hand never stopped caressing me, and I clung to him, if only to ground myself amid all the sensations and smells.

"Because they're not you, and it's you I want."

He nodded and kissed me. It started slowly, then escalated until Greg took out his cock and I climbed into his lap. Amid our heated lip-lock, Greg's hand wrapped around my dick as he fisted us both. The friction was delightful torture. Each stroke matched his tongue as it thrust into my mouth. We teased each other until Greg's mouth drifted away from my lips, down my jaw, and then my neck. Each stop along the way he painted a path with momentary hickeys which he sucked into my skin while his hand motions sped up. When his hand slowed, he would move to another spot, work us over harder, and then slow down again.

I lost track of how many hickeys he'd made or how close I'd been so many times. I could see stars behind my eyelids from the sexual tension. Our precum was thick on his hand when I leaned forward and wrapped my arms around his shoulders, burying his face in my chest. I moved my hips to encourage him to stop teasing. His lips landed on my nipple and I bucked and moaned in his lap until I came. As I caught my breath, I looked into his eyes, then glanced down to watch as he continued, using my cum as lube, while his tight fist stayed wrapped around his dick.

His grunts and moans were seductive music while maintaining eye contact with Greg until the last moment when his orgasm took him and he unloaded across my chest. Our foreheads came together like two magnets as we panted, breathing each other's air as our lust came back down to a light simmer.

"Did we just make ourselves walking targets?" Greg chuckled. "I didn't think about the fact that we'd have to walk back through the party."

I laughed. "Well, kind of, though, we won't be approached unless we indicate we're open to it." I lifted myself off him slowly and looked around the closet to see what we could clean up with. I found towels and tossed one to Greg.

"Wait, we're near the pools, aren't we? There are showers next to those." I liked that idea much better. We grabbed a few more towels, left the closet, and found the poolside showers. The outdoor shower stalls were large enough for a decent-sized dragon or several bipeds. Once we stripped down and turned on the tap, we took our time. Heated kisses became pleading pants as I returned the favor and treated Greg to a thorough tonguing.

He braced his hands on my shoulders, and I held onto his legs to keep him from collapsing. We shared a quiet laugh, and then he bent down to kiss me. "At this rate, we won't make it back to the room tonight," he said, pressing another kiss into my swollen lips.

"Would that be such a horrible thing?" I said, as my lips brushed his.

"Not really," Greg said, then grinned as he offered a hand and helped me up. More soap and water later, we finished cleaning up and dried off, then put what clothes we had left back on and went to find some food and drinks. The party was still crowded, and as the night went on, people lost more and more clothing. As the mood shifted from party to orgy, we grabbed some drinks to go for the hike back across the resort to our room.

"Has there ever been an instance where dragons opt to have children without a mate?" After our small fuck fest in Dragon's Grove, I hadn't expected the serious question. It was easy enough to answer.

"Sure," I said with a shrug. "It's up to the dragon, really. Aging cycles biologically gear us toward finding a mate. And usually, we don't want to procreate with someone unless they're our mates. However, we're prone to accidents like any other species, especially if a non-dragon species is involved."

"And in all this time, you've never had an accident?"

I reached for Greg's hand and brought us to a stop in the hallway, set the drinks we had on a convenient table, then wrapped my arms around his neck. "As far as I know, and as far as anyone has ever told me, I've never had a child with anyone and I've always been careful. I might not have a canine nose, but most species have a slight smell when they're fertile. Plus, there were prophylactic spells and then condoms. So it was pretty easy to avoid an issue."

Greg leaned down for a kiss. "I only asked because I didn't want you to think I wouldn't accept . . . "

The pause was odd. "Wouldn't accept what, Greg?" He didn't blink or respond but still held onto me. When his eyes clouded slightly, gaze locking on to something behind me, I turned just enough to see my fears realized.

"Hello, pet." Bianca stood a few steps back. Greg's arms tightened. She slowly walked into my peripheral vision as I tried to push myself out of Greg's arms, but he wrapped them around me tighter, making it hard to breathe.

"Tsk, tsk, love. Try that again and you'll either break his arms or hurt him, and we don't want that now, do we?"

"Bianca! Elements, so help me, if you hurt him, I'll kill you."

She caressed my shoulder, then Greg's. It made me sick to my stomach that she even touched him. "Hurt him? Now, why would I hurt the only dragon I've ever loved and his boyfriend?" She leaned in close and whispered in my ear. "A boyfriend who's a Saint George Knight, no less." She kissed my earlobe, and I flinched.

"What do you want?" I kept my tone even so we wouldn't attract attention. Greg seemed oblivious to everything, which meant she'd used magic on him or a vampiric power. I wasn't sure which.

"Why don't we take this to someplace more private? The hallway isn't made for these discussions. Greg, follow." I don't know what I expected to happen. I certainly didn't think Greg would pick me up and follow Bianca into a public restroom. It was one of the few places around the resort that didn't have some kind of surveillance, besides the hotel rooms.

Bianca's day watcher followed us inside as well. "Mark, be a dear and lock the door. I'll make sure we're not disturbed." It looked like she cast a silencing ward into the walls, but I wasn't sure, and Greg's hold hurt. He was much stronger than he looked. "Greg, you can let him go now."

Greg dropped his arms to his sides. I took a breath and looked him over to make sure he was alright.

"Xavior, he's fine. You needn't worry, pet."

I spun to face her, determined to end this. As I took a step toward her, she held up her hand. "Now, Xavior, I said he was fine, but that can change, love. So don't do anything hasty."

Greg made a gasping noise as I turned to look at him. His hands were on his throat as he tried to breathe.

"Okay! Okay, you made your point. Stop it, Bianca." Greg gasped, and his breathing returned to normal, but his face remained slack and unresponsive while he panted for air. I slowly turned to face my ex.

"I'm glad you can be reasoned with."

"Bianca, why are you doing this? We have nothing you could possibly want."

She smiled, and the tip of her tongue played along one of her fangs. At one point in my life, I had found that unbelievably sexy. Now I only wanted to make sure Greg was safe, and if I had to, I'd figure out a way to end Bianca to be sure of it.

"But pet, you do." She walked closer to me. "I need you for a job."

"What?" When I knew her, she never cared about anything her family was involved in. I had worked for them to keep them happy. For her to propose this meant something had changed.

"I know you're about to be, shall we say, in a career transition, and I thought, what a wonderful time to renew our family partnership. You can come back to work with us, and we'll take care of you. Of course, you can bring your boyfriend too, if you'd like. It's very much a win-win for everyone. Wouldn't you agree?"

"No, absolutely not." I couldn't even imagine how she thought that idea would ever work. "First of all, I don't need you or your family. Second, how in all the world could you have possibly thought I would ever work for you again?"

She sighed and walked toward me. "Oh, Xavior, I do miss that fire of yours. Always so passionate." She reached out to touch my face, and I tried not to flinch. "It was a mistake on my part to let you go. Now that I'm in charge of a large portion of the family's interests, I want to rectify that. Don't you miss me?"

A twist of her fingers and a few words, and her smell changed from practically nothing to something that pulled at my senses and screamed *mate* to my dragon brain. Each breath I drew was labored as I took a step back from her. "No. Bianca. I don't miss you." Though apparently my body did, and my reaction to her made my heart race. I took another step back and found myself between Bianca and Greg. Her gaze went to him, and before I could turn around, he grabbed me again.

"Xavior, please stop being difficult. How hard would it be to do what I ask? You'd have everything you'd ever wanted. Mysteries, your boyfriend, a girlfriend, hell, a whole troupe at your beck and call. I'll even throw in the fae business partner." She gestured to her companion. "Mark, what's his name again?"

"Jordan, ma'am," her oh-so-helpful bodyguard offered. I was like Mark once. I knew how these kinds of things could end if an individual didn't cooperate. It's not like she needed Jordan's name. She knew it. The point was to tell me that Mark was a threat.

"That's right, Jordan." She sighed again. "Fae are trickier to subdue, but I'm sure I could manage it for you."

"If you think I would stand by and let you harm people I care about, you're out of your mind." I tried to feel for a gap in Greg's hold, but he would only tighten or twist to compensate. To break it might hurt him, and I couldn't bring myself to do that.

Bianca's smell assaulted my senses. It might have given her some measure of control if I didn't have a genuine connection with Greg. I had a fleeting moment to wonder if my original connection with Bianca was never created by me to begin with.

"My, my, pet. There was a time you'd gleefully smash someone's nose at my whim." She traced my face with the tips of her fingers. "You've changed."

"Some of us grow up, Bianca."

"So I take it your answer is no, then?" I didn't answer and stared at her instead. "Very well. I guess we'll have to go with plan B, Mark." I didn't have time to wonder what plan B was as Mark drew a knife from his pocket and flipped it open. Bianca backed off, and Mark walked up to Greg and forced the blade into his hand. As Mark stepped back, I went still in Greg's arms.

"We'll leave the two of you alone. I know you have a lot to work out. Greg, let him go." He did, and I moved away from him. She turned to walk out of the restroom and then turned back. "Oh, and Greg, you have ten minutes to wound him. If you can't manage that, I want you to slit your wrists." She blew a kiss at me. "It was lovely to catch up, pet."

"Fuck you."

She cackled as she left.

I sensed that the silence ward was still in place, and when I tested the door, I found it locked. I could break the door down, but it would take more time than I had before Greg acted on the command. A wound from him would either kill me outright or cause a phoenix cycle and kill him, which would eventually kill me. Or Greg would harm himself in a way I couldn't possibly fix, which would ultimately kill me, too.

Greg lunged for me, and I barely avoided a slash to my mid-section.

"Gregor, fight it. I know you don't want to do this." We circled each other. Assessing the situation, I knew shifting wouldn't do any good. Maybe fire was the answer.

We kept circling, and I sucked in a huge breath and blew out a burst of fire that rolled along the ceiling, which made Greg duck. Depending on the magic, water might break it. It was the universal solvent, after all. A moment later, alarms blared, and the sprinkler system activated. Greg looked up, distracted by the water.

"Greg, you don't have to do what she said." I tried to get his attention, but he stared at the ceiling. "It's magic. You can fight it. Gregor, can you hear me?"

He dropped his gaze from the ceiling to me, and I thought for one moment that I saw the man I knew in his eyes. Instead, he let out a yell and lunged for me again, and I made a choice.

It didn't hurt any less the second time, and I dropped to my knees as the cold crept through my body. I only hoped that the water would slow or stop my phoenix cycle if it happened. Blood dripped from the wound and mixed with the small pond the sprinklers had created. It became hard to breathe. "Fuck, that hurts." I chuckled as I tried to suck in another breath.

"Xavior?"

Ah, fuck, no. Damn magic. Either Bianca's command wore off because Greg stabbed me, or the water finally did the job. It was hard to tell. I had kind of hoped he wouldn't remember. The withdrawal would be bad enough for him. He didn't need the memory of my actual death during our last moments together.

Greg dropped to a crouch in front of me and came to a quick conclusion. "No, no, not again."

I watched as he jumped up and went for the door. Unfortunately, it was still magically locked. He banged on it, but it didn't budge, and I doubted anyone heard him. I shook my head and tried to tell him about the wards, but coughed blood instead. The knife must have punctured a lung this time.

"Xavior, please, not again. I can't get out. Hang on. Please hang on." I don't remember laying down, but I was in his arms with his hand pressed to the wound. The creeping cold was nearly done. The pain was gone, and I didn't feel warm any longer.

The accumulated pool we sat in that made me feel cold as the water rained down on us. The warmth I felt before from the phoenix cycle wasn't there. I wondered if I didn't have another one. Or it was too soon after the last one. It didn't matter. Greg would be safe and I wouldn't risk losing my memories of him. That's all that mattered to me now.

I used my last bit of energy to pat his hand and felt something on his finger. The ring. I grabbed his hand and wrapped my fingers around his forefinger with all the strength I had left. If the damn thing worked as Denis said, now would be an excellent time to find out.

KNIGHT FALL

GREGOR

Xavior squeezed my fingers, and I wanted to kick myself the moment I felt the bite of metal. He closed his eyes, and I knew I didn't have much longer before he died and burst into flame, killing us both.

"Okay, okay. If my power lets me kill and heal, then similar to how I would use a weapon to focus, I'll use the ring the same way." Or at least that's what Denis had indicated.

How does one heal when all they were ever taught to do was kill? I'd only ever learned basic triage at work, to look for signs of shock, immobilize patients, that sort of thing. What the fuck did I know about healing anything? I closed my eyes and pulled the knife out of his chest, and pressed my hand over the wound.

In my mind, an image formed. I didn't know why, but I saw my dad in his woodshop, asking a piece of wood what it would like to be. He would sit with it for a time. I'd watch him put pieces back on the pile when they didn't speak to him. I had always thought it was weird.

"Greg, you have to respect life, all life, even at the end, when it seems like there's nothing left. The spirit is there, waiting for renewal or to move on. You need to ask, from your heart, what the spirit wants. If you're open to it, it will answer you."

By Philip's logic, I couldn't heal Xavior if he didn't want it. We both had to hope for it. I lifted his head and pressed my lips to his ear. "Xavior, I love you. I want you to come back to me. I want to heal you. Tell me; show me you want the same thing." I placed my hand over the wound and focused on listening for the spirit, or whatever it was my dad always seemed to hear.

A hum began between my ears, and then it turned into a buzzing noise in my head. I sighed from the warmth that enveloped me, which was odd because the sprinklers hadn't stopped. I opened my eyes to a light that had surrounded us. A burning warmth started at my hand and radiated up my arm. It shifted from comforting to painful as the intensity of the heat grew. I screamed as I tried to remain focused. I didn't know if the pain was from what I was doing or Xavior's phoenix rising.

Xavior gasped, and I watched as he took a breath, then another. Eventually, he opened his eyes, and the light and pain receded. I looked at the wound, which appeared as a pink scar. His scales surfaced as I touched him. The minute he was aware of me, we clung to each other.

"You had me worried for a minute," Xavior said after he kissed me.

"Me?" I pushed him back so I could see his face. "I worried you?!" I shook my head. "That was too fucking close, Xav."

We pressed our heads together. The waterworks finally shut off, and I regretted my lack of shirt. I kissed Xavior all over his face until he laughed, then my mood shifted. Either because I caught his anger, or it was mine. It didn't matter. Bianca tried to kill us.

"We have to turn her in. It was attempted murder!"

"Greg, that would mean we'd have to explain who you are, and then it would cause all kinds of legal problems."

"Why? She manipulated me to use my power against you! The Vampire Accords govern their interactions. They aren't allowed to force living individuals to do things against their will."

"And I threatened her life. She could say it was self-defense."

"You did?" I was surprised. Xavior didn't make threats. "Because of me?"

"Yes. Twice. And one of those times was in the hallway before she brought us in here, which means it's on record somewhere. If we try to go after her the covens will make life really hard for both of us. What happened back home had to be part of her plan. She knew we'd been fired, and that you're a Saint George Knight. Neither of those things are public knowledge yet as far as I know. She did this to convince me to work for her again."

"Did she say why?" It would have made more sense to try to recruit Xavior while he was still employed with public safety. Unless she already had people working for her in one of the departments, which would explain how she knew about things she shouldn't.

"No, not in so many words. She threatened you, and Jordan, and promised me anything I wanted if I would come back to work for her. When that didn't work, she tried to kill us. The more I think about it, it doesn't make sense." His color looked better and his anger shifted into frustration and curiosity.

All of it left me frustrated and cold. "Are we really going to let Bianca walk away?" I reached for his hand, and he let me weave our fingers together. He sat next to me as the drains made loud sucking noises, pulling away the last of the water.

"Well, she tried to kill us both and failed. I think that's a win for now. Our next step is to keep us both from getting bronchitis or worse until they get the door open. Come here." He drew me to him and leaned against a wall while I pressed my back into his chest. He was really warm, which immediately made me shiver.

Xavior held me until an ax came through the door and split it open, breaking the wards with a loud pop. Xavior grabbed the knife from the floor and pocketed it as we stood. When the fire rescue team came inside, all we had were sheepish grins and apologies.

Xavior spun some story about me trying a drug and his magic going haywire because of it. When he told the hotel he would pay for the damages, everyone seemed satisfied and let us go back to our room.

"If anyone stops for five minutes to collect evidence, they'll figure out it was vampire magic. That shit leaves a signature, like any other magical being," I half-whispered as we walked back to our room.

"They won't. I gave the hotel management something plausible, even if they don't think it's the truth. And I offered to pay for repairs and expenses. That's all they care about, anyway. There wasn't a body, so no need to call the local public safety."

I shook my head. "It doesn't sit right with me, Xav." He thumbed the door open to our room and pulled me inside.

Xavior wrapped me in his arms and gave me a soft kiss. "I know it doesn't, but we're not officers any longer. And as much as I hate to say it, money fixes things. The resort will probably use a magical clean-up crew, and it will be like nothing ever happened."

"Right, shit. I don't know if I'll ever get used to that."

Xavior grinned. "I'm okay if you don't. One of us needs to be a voice of reason sometimes."

"Now that's a scary thought." I pulled him through the open bedroom doors toward the bathroom so we could change and dry off. "I vote for room service and using the pool on the balcony. Maybe if we stay out of the way, we can enjoy the rest of our time here in peace."

"I like the sound of that," he said as he grabbed my ass.

Once we were in bed, I had a moment to think about everything that happened while my dragon snored softly at my side. I remembered everything up to the hallway, and when I asked Xavior about whether he had children. Then bits and pieces from the restroom.

Flashes came to me about how Xavior struggled, the knife's weight, the water cascading down from the sprinklers. Then I remembered finding him on the floor, the blade sticking out of him, and blood dripping out of his chest. Except this time, it wasn't an accident. It couldn't have been. Either I had bested him, or he had let me stab him. Both ideas threatened to break me. That's when Xavior touched my face.

"You saved me. No matter what you're thinking, you did that too. Remember?" I couldn't help but curl into him. He held me as I worked through my emotions, kissed me, and caressed my back. "We'll get through this like we have everything else. No one can keep us apart, Gregor."

"Promise?"

"Promise."

A HELPING HAND

GREGOR

The morning brought room service with an order large enough that we could have fed a half-dozen people. Instead, most of it went into Xavior's stomach.

"I'm glad you have your own finances. I'm not sure I could afford to keep you in food."

"Oh, you think this is bad? Wait until I go into heat. I end up eating twice this amount."

"Do you have cravings?"

Xavior smiled. "Sometimes. I remember one cycle that all I wanted was pork. Then another was hot peppers. I ate those like grapes. The hotter, the better."

"Wow." I took a bite of eggs and wondered about something else. "How do you know when it's over?"

"Like anyone else with a uterus, there's some blood, then that's it. After that, it's another twenty-five years or so before the next one."

"So, I'd be fifty-nine before we might have another chance to try?" I put down my fork. Xavior nodded, but he stayed quiet. There were other options, of course. "What are the chances of having a dragon?"

"I don't know, to be honest. I was never interested in having offspring before."

"Are you interested now?" I'd asked him before, but we'd tabled the question somewhat. The protection we used seemed to have slowed things and given us more time to think. But maybe that wasn't enough time since the silence stretched a little too long, and I knew I'd made a mistake asking again. "It's okay. Like you said, we have time."

"No, it's not okay. You deserve an answer." He wiped his mouth and set his napkin down. "If and when it happens," he reached his hand toward me, and I took it, "I want us to try. I want us to have a chance. But I don't want you to get your hopes up in case it doesn't work."

"Because of genetics?"

"That, or any number of things. I'm a hybrid. Outside of mating with another dragon, I'm not sure what will work."

I nodded. It made sense. "What about adoption?"

"Once we've figured out where we want to live, and things have settled a little, I don't see why we couldn't try."

I thought about that for a minute. "Right, our work records." I sighed.

"Hey." Xavior shook my hand a little, then squeezed it. "Don't give up. We'll figure it out, one obstacle at a time." I nodded. "So, after breakfast, wanna go for a swim?" He grinned at his own suggestion. It only meant he was up to something. If it kept me from replaying the night before through my head, I was okay with the distraction.

The balcony pool outside our suite was less than two meters deep and wide enough that it looked like an enormous bathtub for Xavior in his dragon form. Xavior floated on his back, limbs tucked up along with his wings, with his tongue hanging out of his mouth. I sat on the side, wrapped in a towel.

When he bumped into me, I gently pushed him with my feet to the other side of the pool. Not that he went that far before he bounced back. We made a game out of it for a while as we enjoyed the sun.

"Who would have guessed you liked floating. I'm surprised your den doesn't have a pool. Though I suppose you'd have to come up with a way to fill it and clean it since you don't have plumbing in there."

My dragon gave an amused huff, and I chuckled. He was happy, and so was I, even after everything from the night before. Learning I could counter my curse and protect him was all I ever wanted from the moment we met. It was funny how life could give you so much more than you bargained for.

I heard a scrape of a claw on concrete. I lifted my sunglasses off my head and noticed that Xavior had one of his wing claws hooked onto the side of the pool. "Are you stuck? You could shift, you know."

He tapped his upper chest with a front paw. I tried to puzzle out what he wanted as he kicked out his limbs a bit, then tapped his chest again. I couldn't help but chuckle since he resembled a turtle stuck on its back. "Xavior, I don't understand what you want. All I'm sensing is your frustration, but that doesn't help me any."

His tail came for me, wrapping around me slowly, then gently shoved me into the pool. "Okay, I'm in the pool. What now?" I said as I thumbed water from my eyes and treaded water. I liked that he didn't try to make this easy for me. He could have shifted or used a spell, but we needed to learn how to communicate while he was in his dragon form.

My mind wandered to the transfiguration potion. I imagined what it would be like when we were both dragons. What sensations would be new? How would we communicate? What might it be like to have sex? Though maybe that last part was wishful thinking.

He slapped his belly with the flat of his tail, then swiveled his head and neck trying to see me. I moved toward his head, and his tail moved to knock me into him. He slapped his belly again, and I made a wild guess. "You want me to sit on your stomach?"

An affirmative noise rumbled out of Xavior, and I chuckled. It's difficult to climb up on a dragon, regardless of whether they're on land or floating in a pool. I managed to half lay on him, legs still in the water. He held out his tail. I grabbed it, and he pulled me the rest of the way onto his stomach. Though the scales on his stomach were smooth, it felt somewhat odd to sit on him, so I laid down.

If Xavior wanted to play pool lounger, I wouldn't argue. I rested my head on my arms and was almost asleep until something tickled my backside. I glanced up and noticed his tail. He moved it again and patted my back, then made patterns. I caught on after he'd repeated a heart shape a few times.

"Very clever. I love you too." Xavior continued, and I focused my attention on what he tried to communicate. The next message was XAV, then another heart shape, then GREG. "You're very talented with your tail. It's cute." My comment received a short, gruff sound. I knew he wasn't upset, but more affectionately annoyed.

"What about ingenious? Do you like that word better?" An affirmative sound, with the sensation of satisfaction, made me chuckle. "Who knew dragon egos were so prickly?" He didn't like that word any better than cute. "Hey!" I received a gentle slap on my ass from the flat end of his tail for my trouble.

A dragon's laughter sounds somewhat like a rain stick with boulders instead of pebbles. It rumbled through him, and that vibrated me. It was a stimulating sensation. Almost too stimulating.

"Unless you're part duck, you should flip over, so your feathers have time to dry." When he stopped laughing, I slid off his belly into the pool, then hoisted myself out. I walked over to the other half of the balcony and laid down on one of the lounge chairs to dry off. Xavior flipped over and shook out his wings. I didn't feel his footsteps, only a chill when the heat of the sun disappeared as Xavior came near my seat.

"You're quieter in your dragon form." I glanced at him, and he picked up one of his feet and wiggled it. "Ah, padding." Most predators had some kind of padding on their feet.

I closed my eyes and assumed Xavior would settle on the deck next to me. Instead, a slightly wet, forked tongue slid across my chest as I was about to doze off. I wrapped my hands around either side of the lounge chair to stay still. Xavior let out a soft growl.

Best guess, he'd try to see how far I'd let him go based on the curiosity and daring I sensed from him. Personally, I wondered how far he'd take it. Teasing was one thing, but I knew what he could do with his tongue. It danced across my skin but never seemed to drop below my navel, even though I was already half-hard from his attention.

The lounge chair moved, which caught me by surprise as he pulled it further out onto the deck, then straddled it. I could see from his shoulders to his abdomen. It didn't surprise me that he was excited. Before I could think about what to do next, his tail snaked its way between us and wrapped itself around his erection.

He stayed still as he used his tail to stimulate himself. A soft rumble escaped him as he slowly twisted and pulled. The feathered end brushed my body and made me shiver. *He's done this before.*

Xavior stretched out his wings and dropped them to the deck. It had the effect of giving us the illusion of privacy. When he ducked his head under and rested it near my shoulder, that's when I found out how long Xavior's tongue actually was, as it slid across my body and the tip touched my dick. I reached up and touched his cheek to give him my consent. He wasted no time as he wrapped his tongue around me. Xavior was no less talented in his dragon form.

"Fuck, Xavior." I watched the odd dance between his tail and tongue. While he used his tail to jerk off his dragon-sized dick, his tongue worked mine over and positioned his tail feathers to brush sensitive parts of my groin. It was, hands down, one of the wildest blowjobs I'd ever had. If you could call it a blowjob. Whatever the term was for it, he had me making a mess in no time. Then continued teasing with his tongue as he licked the cum from my chest.

I was so into what he was doing that I hadn't noticed the head of his leg-sized dragon dick in my lap. It was rubbing along my thigh and stomach, which was already messy.

"Are you close?"

Xavior gave a soft rumble in response. I pushed at his face, and he moved his tongue away from me as I slid my body down the chair until his cock rested on my chest. Then I used my hands to caress the parts that had been sensitive to my touch before. His tail movements became more erratic with each stroke.

His wings shook as a quiet rumble grew in his chest. I wondered about the wisdom of how close my face was when Xavior made a noise. The soft rumble changed to a combination of a whistle or snorting sound. It was the only warning I had before he covered me from head to waist in dragon jizz.

"Holy shit!" I laughed and tried to clean off his cum. I couldn't help but taste it, and the effect was like eating effervescent candy. Then a kind of buzz hit my system, like caffeine, but better. "Wait, did you just cover me with magical cum?"

Xavior folded his wings and took a few steps back from the chair. I watched as his eyes blinked slowly, then I looked down at myself. In the full sunlight, his dragon cum sparkled. Xavior seemed delighted by what he accomplished. His tongue darted out and licked at the mess he had made while I laid back and let him clean me off.

When he'd taken care of most of the mess, he shifted and climbed into the lounge chair with me and cuddled. We were quiet for a while until curiosity opened my mouth. "How did you learn to do that with your tail?"

"How did you learn to use your hand?" Xavior chuckled.

I couldn't help but laugh. "Sure beats using socks and hiding them in the dirty laundry basket."

My fascination with Xavior grew as magic worked through my system. I couldn't help myself. Touching him caused a euphoric response. When his scales appeared under my hands, it caused me to want more contact, more euphoria, more of him.

"Let's play a little game, shall we?" Xavior suggested.

The rules were simple enough. For each thing I did at Xavior's direction—order lunch, pick up clothes, grab us beers from the fridge—he let me touch him wherever for however long I wanted to as long as I asked first.

Each touch escalated into another task, which teased both of us until we ended up in bed. I had Xavior on his side, as I knelt holding his left thigh to my torso, and trapping his right leg between my thighs. Our position showed me his beautiful profile, and allowed me to fuck deeper into him, while I had access to his dick.

"Did you like what we did today?" Xavior said between my thrusts.

The connection between us was a live wire. Unlike the weird chocolate fiasco at his birthday party, I could feel that Xavior craved my attention. I leaned over and threaded my fingers through his hair as I built up a steady rhythm. "Yes. I liked it very much," I said as I pressed my lips to his cheek. He moaned as I adjusted slightly. "I love you, Xavior. Every single part."

I didn't move my hips much and continued to make small thrusts to stay inside him as much as possible. I didn't want it to end, and I couldn't fathom withdrawing from his body. My need was so great that Xavior could have asked me to do anything and I would have, if only he would let me stay like this with him. The part of my brain that would have thought it was irrational took a vacation.

"Kiss me, Gregor." He turned his head and caught my gaze as I leaned over him to reach his lips. Our lips and tongues met, and it was like completing a circuit. We came nearly simultaneously, panting and laughing softly from the high.

As we laid together, heedless of the mess, a bit of my rational brain tried to reassert itself. "If tomorrow you decide you need space, I wouldn't blame you." Even now, I couldn't stop myself from touching him. "I don't know how you aren't annoyed with me."

"I thought it was fun," he said with a smile. "I'd never come on anyone like that before, not as a dragon. The magical effects surprised me, too. Were you bothered by it?" Xavior caressed me, and I pressed my face into his hand.

"Maybe I should be, but I'm not. The game was a nice way of controlling it, so it didn't overwhelm me. The euphoria from even the smallest touch was really intense until I was used to it." I sighed as his hand slipped away. "I feel sated somewhat, but I still have an overwhelming desire to touch you."

Xavior grinned. "I wonder if it has something to do with the mating process."

"Oh? Why's that?"

"There are stories of dragons pushing themselves to the brink of death from mating. It's the reason families usually check in with newly mated pairs the first few weeks. And likely why they asked Freddie to spy on us." He reached up to trace his fingers along my forehead and then down to my temple. "No one ever mentioned the possibility of it affecting a non-dragon." Implying that it might influence a dragon, which added another item to the list of things to try once I had my potion.

I gave half a shrug. "Well, now we know, and I wouldn't mind us having fun with it every once in a while. Would you?" I trusted him to take care of me while I was high on his magic. I trusted him with all of me, and that was a heady realization all on its own.

Xavior grinned. "Fuck, I love you." I wrapped my arms around him as he kissed me. We pressed tiny kisses to whatever bit of flesh we could reach as we drifted to sleep.

LOCKDOWN

GREGOR

An alarm went off. I reached out to the nightstand to hit the snooze button on my phone. Nothing happened. The loud blaring noise continued.

"Ugh, shut it off," Xavior complained as he drooled on my chest.

"I'm trying." I reached out again and grabbed my phone this time. When I cracked an eyelid open and noticed it was 5:30 AM and my alarm wasn't set, I knew something was off. That's when I realized it was the room itself. "Lights ten percent." The lights came up, and because the system knew I was awake, it activated the holo projector above the sliding doors.

"Please remain in your room for your safety. Staff members will be with you shortly. This is a yellow caution alert." The message had no audio and repeated itself in several languages before it returned to English. The alarm stopped abruptly.

"Xav, what's a yellow caution alert?"

He lifted his head to look at me, then at the screen. He shook his head and dropped it back to my chest. "Means someone used magic, and it backfired."

"Shouldn't we be evacuating the building, then?" I sat up. Xavior's head dropped to the pillow next to me with a groan while I made a hand motion to the holo to see if I could obtain more information, but it showed the same message on every feed.

"The hotel has emergency shield spells that drop into place to keep guests safe. Once they have the rogue magic dealt with, they'll unlock the rooms. It's much safer to remain in a shielded spot than move."

"But we evacuate buildings for shit like this all the time." My training and instincts told me we should leave, not lounge in bed.

"That's because most buildings can't afford to shield every dwelling. Or worse, someone didn't request shielding to be added to their dwelling, even if they zoned for it. We'll be fine, Greg. Relax."

I eyed him and shook my head. It was still pretty early, so I followed his lead, turned off the holo, and went back to sleep.

A few hours later, I reached for Xavior and noticed he wasn't in bed, but I heard the shower. I smiled as I crawled out of our massive bed, snagged a condom and lube off the side table, and walked into the bathroom.

Xavior hummed as he used a bath brush to scrub his back. I set the supplies on a nearby shelf and watched. The humming slowly stopped as he turned to look at me.

"Morning," he said. I barely heard him over the shower.

I moved toward him and slowly took the brush from his hand. "Morning. Would you like some help?"

He laughed. "I think your idea of helping might be more fun, but our shower will take longer."

"You worried about wasting water?"

"No, of course not. They equipped this facility with state-of-the-art water reclamation. We could be in here for a week and . . ."

That's all I wanted to hear. I kissed Xavior, and he groaned as I used the brush to scrub his back. When I dipped it lower and washed his ass cheeks he laughed. I dropped the brush and smacked his ass with my hand. His laugh caught in his throat as his eyelids fluttered. He leaned his head on my chest as I caressed his ass with my hands. When I gave him another smack on the cheeks, he squirmed a little.

"Too rough?"

Xav shook his head. I knew he liked it already. I could sense that much, and his curiosity was mixed in with that.

I pressed my lips to his ear to ask, "What color are you?" It was our shorthand for anything that might wander into kink or power play.

"Green."

There was so much trust tied up in that one color. So much that Xavior was willing to let me explore. I took a deep breath and let it out.

"Shower off." The water stopped. "Steam, twenty percent." The vents opened, and hot steam flooded the enclosure. We kissed as his hands wandered to my waist. I could have let us go on like that forever, but I had other things in mind. "Turn around and lean against the wall." He did so, and he left me enough space to wrap my hand around his cock and smack his perfectly formed ass.

He made a gasping noise as I slowly worked him over. When he moved his hips to take advantage of my grasp, my other hand came down on his ass. "Did I say you could move?"

He chuckled. "Is that the game, then?"

"It is if you want it to be. Or you can move, and my hand brightens your ass cheeks a little more." He moved, and the swat I gave him was hard enough to leave my handprint for a few seconds.

I had never even imagined doing anything like this with someone, let alone someone I cared about. I was too well trained, too scared of hurting someone, and too scared that I really was all the things my mother told me I was before I left her house for good.

Xavior didn't move, and I rewarded him with a few more caresses to his cock before I stepped away from him. He stayed where he was. I sensed his excitement and curiosity as I walked over and grabbed the bottle of lube from the shelf.

As I approached him again, I opened the bottle. That's when Xavior tried to look over his shoulder. I brought my hand down on his ass, and he immediately faced forward again. "Curious dragon."

"Do you blame me?" I could hear the smile in his voice.

"No," I said softly in Xavior's ear. To be honest, I surprised myself a little. After everything we've been through, he still trusted me. Our connection had a lot to do with that, and I craved that trust between us. I think we both did.

I poured lube into both hands, then closed and dropped the bottle next to us. I wrapped my hand around his cock again as I caressed his crease. He made a pleasant moaning noise that lasted until I inserted my finger. Then he gasped as I watched his fingers spread wide and his toes flex. I alternated what my hands did with a push-pull method. To his credit, Xavior stayed still.

Water beaded on his skin as his scales danced across his body. I'll forever enjoy seeing that, knowing that I affected both him and his dragon nature. He grunted softly as I inserted another finger and tried not to move. His cock leaked all over my hand. I glanced down to see if it looked like it did when he was a dragon.

"Why doesn't your cum affect me when you're in your bipedal form?"

"Magic?" Xavior breathed out. "Maybe it's modified somehow? I don't know." His voice had a tremor in it that told me he was close.

"Huh. Interesting." I dragged out the phrase as if I had some devious idea in mind. I didn't, not beyond fucking Xavior senseless. He gasped as I stopped everything and I walked away to retrieve the condom I left on the shelf. Once I suited up, I returned to pick up the bottle of lube and applied a generous amount to myself and Xavior before I teased him further.

Xavior still had his hands on the wall. "When I press into you," I whispered. "You stay still until I say."

He nodded.

I angled myself and pressed into him slowly until his ass met my hips. It felt so good that I almost forgot what I was about. I wrapped my hand around his cock again, then leaned into him and whispered, "move."

Whatever I thought I was doing, it didn't matter. Xavior didn't hold back. He rocked on my dick and kept at it until I had to let go of his cock and hold on to his shoulders to keep myself inside him. "Fuck, Xav." I couldn't stop myself from meeting his thrusts. It wasn't long before I came. We were both panting. I reached around and helped him come with just a few strokes.

I kissed along his neck and shoulders as we breathed together, then I reached up for Xavior's hands and slowly brought each one down from the wall to cross his chest. I wrapped my arms around his and nuzzled his neck. We were content, and the only noise I heard from Xavior was a soft groan as I slipped out of him. Eventually, I let him go to take care of the condom.

When I came back, he kissed me softly. "Steam off," Xavior called out. "Shower on." The steam was quickly removed and replaced with hot water streaming around us. I leaned my head on his shoulder, and Xavior kissed my ear. "One sec."

He moved away to pick up a bottle of some fragrant smelling shampoo he liked as I patiently waited for him and held out my hand. But he didn't give me the bottle. Instead, he poured some of the liquid onto his hand and reached up to apply it to my hair. He moved behind me and continued to work his fingers along my scalp.

"What's this?" His finger traced a scar near the back of my head.

I chuckled. "Someone cracked a bottle over my head while I was doing a foot patrol. I spooked some folks that were breaking into a place."

"Is there a similar story about the little scar over your eye?" His fingers moved on as he massaged my head and neck.

I took a deep breath and sighed. "No. That was from training when I was a kid." Xavior's hands stopped and I stepped forward out of his grasp to rinse off.

He stepped in close and wrapped his arms around me, capturing mine. I leaned back into him as he kissed my shoulder. "I love you."

The sensations from that phrase were intense. Some of my own, and some Xavior's, threatened to have me in tears. He wanted me to be safe and was upset about how I ended up with the scar. It was a fierce love that encompassed his desire to protect, nurture, and see that I was happy. I understood because I felt the same. "I love you, too."

After that, we dried off and waited about an hour before requesting room service. An attendant brought it. It was our first opportunity to gain any outside information.

"Do you know when they plan to lift the shields around the rooms?" I asked.

The attendant shook her head. "Sorry, sir, not at this time. Only staff is permitted to move about the resort right now."

"Thanks for the information." She nodded, and I closed the door. "Maybe we should have stayed in our robes," I chuckled.

Xavior shrugged. "Usually, it doesn't take this long to clear an accident. So it must have been serious."

"Serious, like how?"

"Someone died more than likely. Which means they'll have to call in public safety and possibly cultural diplomats. If that's the case, we could be here the rest of the day."

"Well, that stinks. I hope the apothecary is open later. Mr. Uluke should be done with the potion."

"If not, we can have a courier bring it to us." Xavior walked over and sat at the table. "Might as well eat while we wait." I shrugged and joined him.

Xavior was right. As the hours went by, we lounged outside in the sun, then came inside and waited. The waiting turned into napping until a chime let us know someone was at the door.

"I'll get it." Xavior rubbed his eyes as he went to answer it. When it opened, a flood of people entered the room.

I bolted upright on the couch. "What's going on?"

"Xavior Brantley?" A person with dark brown skin, a goatee, and brown eyes, wearing dress pants, a button-up shirt, and a tie asked as he approached Xavior. If he wasn't from a local public safety department, I would be surprised.

Xavior held up his hand like he was in class. His worry came through our connection, and I took a step toward him. A person with skin the color of ash, dressed in a button-down and skirt, stepped in my way. "Sir, please stay where you are."

The goatee guy addressed Xavior. "We'd like you to come with us to answer some questions regarding your association with Bianca Cooper." He mirrored his partner and blocked Xavior from moving toward me.

"Why?" I asked. The way they kept us separated rang alarm bells in my head. Then I noticed an evidence imager and people picking up our things. "Did she file a complaint against him?"

"No, sir. She's dead."

REPERCUSSIONS

Xavior

Actions have consequences, and sitting alone in an interview room with two detectives I'd never met definitely had me thinking. If Bianca was dead, they likely found the footage somewhere of her talking with Greg and me in the hallway, which would give them a motive. Though I still hadn't processed that she was, in fact, dead.

They escorted Greg and I to a local public safety headquarters about thirty minutes from the resort. They brought us in together but quickly separated us for statements, which we both agreed to give. Based on the fact that both detectives were here with me, Greg was likely by himself in another room similar to this one.

"I'm Detective Benedict, and this is Detective Floyd. We'll conduct your interview until federal agents and the Envoy arrive. Are you alright with that?" Benedict was the attractive Black man in a button-up, slacks, and a tie. His partner, Floyd, was quiet. From their scent and gray skin tone, my best guess was half-fae.

I nodded. "Yes," I said, agreeing for the record that I was willing to give a statement. I could wait, but cooperating seemed the better answer at the moment. It might be the only way I would be allowed near Greg any time soon. My hands already itched from not being able to touch him.

"Could you state where you were at about five this morning?" Detective Floyd asked. Their sing song voice was mesmerizing but not distinctively fae. It made me wonder what else they were. But that was a mystery for another time.

"I was asleep with my partner."

"That would be Gregor Lyndon?"

"Yes." I rested my hands flat on the table in front of me. I wasn't restrained, which was standard procedure with people of interest unless you ran, tried to hurt yourself, or hurt someone else. It made the itch in my palms fade a little as I pressed them into the cool tabletop.

"How do you know Bianca Cooper?" Detective Benedict asked.

"We were engaged over three hundred years ago."

"Engaged? But not married?"

"That's correct."

"Did the relationship end amicably?"

"Well, if by amicably you mean she locked me out of her house, refused to talk to me, and told me it was over, then yes."

"Have you seen her before this week?"

"Yes."

"Could you elaborate, please?"

"Over the years, I've seen her from time to time." When the detectives looked like they wanted more, I gave it to them. "For companionship."

"Was that all?"

"Occasionally for work, but mostly for sex, yes." That response didn't have the reaction I was expecting from them. Which meant they had more information on me than I realized. If they knew about my relationship with Bianca, they also knew I was a dragon. There weren't diplomatic envoys for dragons. Though maybe there should be. Had her family supplied the information?

"Does Mr. Lyndon know about your previous relationship with Ms. Cooper?"

"Yes." Though I didn't elaborate on it more until recently, I'm glad Greg knew about it. To say it had been an emotional roller coaster these last two weeks was an understatement.

Detective Floyd was quiet. If they were half-fae, like I suspected, they could tell if I'm lying or not. Not that I lied. I didn't have to. Whatever Bianca got herself involved in didn't concern me. It pained me, though. I had cared about her once. Was I serious when I threatened her? Yes. Did I actually want her permanently dead? Not exactly.

"Were you here to meet Ms. Cooper for companionship?"

"No." I let the disgust with that idea resonate in my voice.

"It's not an unreasonable question, given what you told us. We've pulled your service record. It seems you and your partner were recently discharged from service for a separate incident involving a vampire coven in San Francisco."

"That's correct." I didn't like where this was going. I was entitled to counsel if they planned to charge me with something. Technically, I was allowed counsel before they started asking questions, but I was still trying to cooperate. I began to think that was not the best idea I'd ever had. The satisfaction I smelled from Detective Benedict made me think he was winding up to a point.

"Did you know that Ms. Cooper belonged to the coven that oversees the coven you had an altercation with?"

"No." That was definitely news. It explained why she'd been anywhere near San Francisco and the resort. The hypothesis that she was involved with the ambush was looking more likely.

Benedict nodded. He waved his hand over the table, and a holo screen materialized. "Tell me about this interaction?"

It was the night Greg and I went out dancing. Greg had danced with Bianca, and then she had come over to basically rub it in my face. I saw myself push Greg behind me and step close to Bianca. I winced inwardly. My body language was tense and threatening. There was no mistaking that, even though there wasn't any audio.

"She approached us, and I told her she was unwelcome." I'd actually threatened to kill her right there in the ballroom. The only thing that stopped me was the sense of Greg being upset and the distinct lack of provocation. You couldn't exactly kill someone for dancing with your partner.

"What about this interaction?"

Benedict waved his hand. The scene changed to the one in the hallway where Greg had been mesmerized by Bianca. He held me, and she stood nearby, touching both of us. He made another hand motion, and the audio was crystal clear. "Bianca, elements, so help me. If you hurt him, I'll kill you."

The footage ended once we walked into the restroom. Later, Bianca and Mark exited. There was a small time jump, then we watched as the fire crew and hotel staff broke down the door to rescue Greg and me. I stayed quiet.

"The hotel said you told them your magic had interacted with something your partner had taken. Is that true?"

I said nothing. I didn't know what to say. The detectives certainly had a motive now. When Benedict waved his hand again, I thought it would shut off the holo screen, but more footage came up.

The imager tracking me was a stationary one from the rooftop, mostly for observing weather and flying patterns. When you had any number of guests that could fly, it's not a bad idea to keep a watch on the sky. This time, it showed me flying from my balcony at about four in the morning. The time stamp was very helpful like that. Next, it showed me landing on another balcony shortly after. Then it showed me as I flew off and returned to my room.

"Is that you, Mr. Brantley?"

It looked terrible, but I knew I didn't kill her or Mark so I didn't answer the question.

A tablet came out. My service record replaced the surveillance footage as Detective Floyd projected it on the holo screen. DNA sample markers floated there in a long row. One marked as mine, and several others isolated to Mark and Bianca. Both names had a helpful tag next to them that said "deceased." There was a fourth line marked as "unknown."

Benedict waved his hand, and the unknown floated up to compare with mine. It was an eighty-nine percent match. The computer helpfully highlighted the sequences that matched and those that didn't. "Do you have any idea why we found your DNA all over the crime scene?" Benedict asked.

Somehow, Bianca, as her last act, figured out how to implicate me in her death, and Mark's too. "I exercise my right to legal counsel before I answer any more questions."

A Friend in Need

Gregor

I tapped my fingers on the desk in the interview room they had me locked in. It was standard procedure to separate individuals and corroborate their statements. The staff sergeant checked in occasionally and asked if I needed anything.

"Any news on whether the detectives are done interviewing my partner?" Sergeant Miller shook her head and quietly left.

No phone. No holo feeds. Just me and my thoughts. Sometimes Xavior's fear and nervousness would come through, and when it did, I tried to reassure him I was alright, somehow, by thinking pleasant thoughts. Though I didn't know how someone did that while waiting for information. When I thought I'd start climbing the walls from boredom, the door opened to the interview room. The very familiar face framed in the doorway was a welcome sight.

"Gina!"

"Greg."

I jumped up and wrapped my arms around her like a man given a lifeline. "It's so good to see you." Then I realized this was not Dallas. "Wait," I pulled back. "Why are you here?"

She gave me a sad smile. "Greg, why don't you sit down. We have a lot of catching up to do." I walked back to the interview table and took a seat.

Gina Kendrick was dressed in a white blouse and blue slacks that complimented her dark brown skin and natural dark brown hair, which was twisted up in a bun at the back of her head. Her shield was on her hip, along with an empty firearm holster. "Are you a federal agent now?"

Only federal agents carried weapons, but they were limited to when and where they could have them. Since we were at a public safety headquarters, they would have asked her to surrender her weapon upon entering the building.

Gina nodded. "When Sissy took the tech job in Dallas, I looked into that opportunity to work at the federal level."

"I remember that. The lead investigator from the FCIB tried to recruit you after we worked on that car theft case that crossed state lines."

"Well, I followed up and landed a post at the Dallas field office."

"That's amazing, Gina. I'm happy for you."

"Thanks." She relaxed slightly. Her movement drew my gaze to the tablet she'd put on the interview table. "As to why I'm here . . ." She tapped the tablet screen, then made a hand gesture to start the holo screen above the table. A three-dimensional analysis came up of a space that looked very similar to the resort room I shared with Xavior. "This is the analysis from the evidence imager used in Bianca Cooper's suite. The yellow markers you see are where we found pieces of Mark Denning, her co-occupant."

There were hundreds of yellow markers, or it seemed that way. So it was either a very targeted explosion, magic, or both, for someone to have blown up like that.

Gina changed the data. "The purple marker is where we found Bianca Cooper's ashes."

A large pile on the floor indicated Bianca was cremated where she stood. Sunlight couldn't have caused that. She was nowhere near the windows, and the resort had special

UV-blocking glass for its vampire guests. It was near the epi-center of where Mark exploded, for lack of a better term.

"Why are you showing me this, Gina?"

She gave me a sympathetic look. "How long have you known Xavior?"

"We worked together for a little over a year. I know that doesn't seem like a long time, but Xavior gets me in ways no one else ever has." I looked at my hands. When was the last time I touched him? The need to be near him felt like it was crawling up my skin and into my skull. Xavior had warned me, but this seemed extreme. Was it because we were under stress and I didn't know where he was?

"What happened with you and Keith?"

Gina's question brought me out of my distracted thinking. "Keith broke it off."

"Did Xavior have anything to do with that?" Her voice changed slightly, and that's when I realized she was looking for information.

"Gina, what are you asking exactly?" I leaned back. I trusted Gina with my life, but I wasn't sure if I could trust her with Xavior's yet.

She tapped a few more things, and the view changed slightly. "The green markers are where we found your partner's DNA."

It zoomed out and showed that Xavior's DNA was spread across the entire room, including the balcony.

"You think Xavior did this?" I stared at the screen in mild horror. He couldn't have. He had threatened Bianca, yes, but murder her? Why?

"We're only trying to figure it out, Greg. You know how this works. Did Xavior ever threaten or scare Keith?" Her voice had the same tone I used to reassure people so you could help them. I learned it from her.

I pressed my hand to my forehead. "No, not exactly."

"What happened?"

"They had an argument."

"What was the argument about?"

It was about me. It dawned on me that Gina was trying to establish a pattern of behavior. I dropped my hand and looked away. The carpet under my feet never seemed more interesting.

"Greg," Gina said gently, drawing my eyes to hers. "I know this is a lot to process, but you need to come to the realization that you might not know him as well as you think."

"No, I know him, Gina. Better than his own family." I believed it too. There's no way he could have been involved without me knowing it.

"What do you mean?"

"I'm connected to him. We're mated."

"Elaborate on that. What do you mean by connected?" She made a hand motion that shut down the display.

"We can sense each other. It's like an empathic ability but only shared between us. If Xavior had done what you said, I would know."

"Greg, have you thought about the fact that he's an older dragon? He could have ways of fooling your senses or possibly not convey emotions like you do."

"Come on, Gina. His service record alone would indicate that he's nothing like that."

"Maybe not his service record, but the information we received from his former employers, the Cooper family, indicates that he was completely capable of it. It seems he was a bodyguard and an enforcer for the Cooper family covens."

"That was three hundred years ago, Gina. He's not the same individual he was then."

She took a deep breath. "Maybe so."

"I know so." I lifted my head to look at her. "He's not a murderer, Gina."

"No, I don't think he did it out of rage or because he gets his kicks that way. He did it for you, Greg."

"No, no way." I couldn't even get him to report Bianca, so the idea that he'd murdered her to protect me seemed preposterous.

"Let me walk you through what we think happened. You and Xavior meet at work. Things are going well, but Xavior takes more and more interest in you. Possibly verging on obsession.

He engineers your breakup with Keith. Continues to work with you, while his focus on you escalates.

"You like him, and one day, he does something to make his obsession with you known. You move past coworkers to lovers, and things are fine until he dies and regenerates. Then, he comes back, and suddenly he sees all vampires as threats.

"His ex-fiancée turns up, and he feels threatened. He's worried about your safety. Cooper offers to talk, and he threatens her but doesn't do anything because you're there. He waits until you're sound asleep before he takes care of Bianca. In his head, he's keeping you safe."

It made sense. The kind of sense that, in a way, it was almost too perfect. Reason, motive, opportunity, all neatly tied up in a nice package, just waiting for someone to use it to destroy Xavior.

Gina didn't know that I was a Saint George Knight. I never told her. But if she knew about Xavior dying and the aftermath of that investigation, she had to know now.

"It's not possible, Gina."

"Greg, I'm sorry. I know you think you know him, but I don't think you do. Sociopaths can fool those closest to them. It wouldn't be the first time in history that an individual with deteriorating mental health issues did something reprehensible while everyone around them was none the wiser." She paused. "Maybe even to keep you from needing to use your ability."

I stood and turned away from the table, trying to keep my anger and fear from getting the better of me. It wasn't true. I concentrated on Xavior. He was scared, nervous, and longed for something. The moment he felt me, his emotions shifted. He was angry. I shook my head to clear my thoughts. He needed to know that I was okay. I tried to convey that I was sad, but safe. The anger faded, and the longing came back and threatened to overwhelm me.

"Greg?" Gina had come up behind me and touched my shoulder. "Can I call someone for you?"

I shook my head. "I don't want anyone else involved with this." I turned toward Gina. "Are charges being filed?"

Gina nodded. "He's asked for legal counsel. We're in the process of finding secure facilities for him. We're also waiting for the vampire covens Envoy to arrive. He'll want to interview Xavior as well."

I put my hand on my forehead. "I want to see Xavior. Please."

She patted my shoulder and nodded. "I'll see what I can do."

INSIDE A BUBBLE

XAVIOR

I spent a night in a holding cell before my legal counsel showed up. By then, I knew I was going through withdrawal. I felt like it too. I wondered if Greg was alright, but no one talked to me even though I asked.

"By the elements, kid, you look like shit." I lifted my head to see where the voice came from and saw a dragon dressed in a three-piece suit, with slicked black hair, yellow-gold eyes, and the stance of a lawyer.

"Hey Uncle Renard, it's nice to see you, too," I said with a slight stutter, which wasn't good. Mental facilities were shutting down. "Where's Vanessa?"

"Come on, Xavior. She may work for me, but you can't say you're surprised she brought your case to me instead of taking it on herself."

"No, you're right."

"She said she would help if we go to trial, so that's something."

"That's . . . comforting." I swallowed and tried again. "Where's . . . Greg?"

"Shit." Renard shook his head. "Hang on, okay. We're in the process of having you moved to a bubble. Greg will meet us there."

"Is he alright?" I tried to stand and nearly fell over.

"Sit your ass down, kid. He's mostly okay, only the shakes right now. But if we wait another day, you'll both be in the hospital."

I sighed and closed my eyes. The next thing I knew, I was in a quiet room without lights and a softer bed than the previous one, with a familiar smell pressed against my face. Greg's naked chest and chin came into view when I blinked my eyes. He was breathing gently, and I was afraid to wake him. I wanted to pretend we were home in my brownstone, enjoying a few quiet moments together before we woke up for work.

My relief at being near Greg again, the stress of being implicated in Bianca's death, and the odd grief that came with knowing part of my past was gone forever caught up with me. I squeezed my eyes against the tears and bit my lip to hold back the sobs that wanted to escape. Strong, gentle arms wrapped around me and held me tighter.

"Hey, it's okay. I'm here. It'll be alright."

Like I had pretended earlier, I did so now and tried to believe that Greg was right. Everything would be okay, if only because we were together. I sucked in a deep breath and crumbled. Greg held me tighter.

"I've got you, Xav. I've got you." Greg cradled my head and held me as I fell apart. It must have been torture for him. To some extent everything I felt he did too. He kissed my face and rubbed my back. I'm lucky in a lot of ways. Most beings that reach a certain age lack emotional empathy. It's not that they are bad people. They just don't have much that sparks emotional engagement anymore. My obsession forces me to do that. I have to seek new mysteries to fuel it. Through it, I find my emotional connection to individuals and my surroundings. I've always been grateful for that. My brother lost much of his empathy a long time ago. If I'm honest, he scared me sometimes.

When I finally calmed down, Greg brushed my face with his hand and kissed me. I nearly lost it again until he spoke. "Hey, you hungry? Your uncle helped me stock the kitchen. I know the holding cell sandwiches couldn't have been enough. Especially not right now."

Greg's face was wet too. I lifted a hand to his face to thumb away the tears and gave him a half-hearted smile until I saw the silver band wrapped around my wrist. "I don't remember how I got here."

"Your uncle said you passed out as they were about to move you. He negotiated a way for us to stay together since we're newly mated. They deemed it medically necessary." Greg lifted his arm to show me his own silver band.

The silver bands appeared as if they were flush with the skin. They weren't really silver. The coloring was caused by a nanite mesh that functioned in any number of ways. It took vitals, restricted magic, tracked movements, allowed someone into a location, or kept them contained to one.

My gaze drifted over the room we were in. It was modern, spacious but lacking in any kind of decoration. "It's a nice bubble."

"It was the closest place they could find that didn't have its own magic already set into the foundation. And the neighborhood is mostly vacation homes. This bungalow isn't going to be cheap." Greg ran his fingers through my hair as he smiled at me, but it didn't reach his eyes.

"That's if I'm convicted. Which is likely, since I have no way of proving I didn't kill Bianca and Mark."

"Come on, let's get some food. I'm not talking about a case on an empty stomach." Greg rolled out of bed, naked, and my brain wasn't thinking about food at that point. My hand reached out to grab his ass, and he moved before I could make contact. "No, that needs to wait. Food, talk, and then if we're not completely exhausted, we can revisit some grab-ass."

Greg tossed some clean clothes at me, and I pouted as I watched him put on a shirt and shorts.

"Fine. You win." In truth, food sounded good, but I sensed Greg was worried, too. If talking about this helped both of us, I was on board. Solving this mystery might save my life, but I worried that doing so might put Greg in danger. The covens were clearly behind the frame job, but why, and how?

As I pulled on clothes, I already smelled meat cooking and fries. When I found Greg, he was arranging toppings and bread buns in the kitchen.

"How many do you think you'll want?"

"Two, at least. All of it smells good. All the headquarters had was synthetic stuff, which was alright, but it left a taste in my mouth."

Greg smiled. "Well then hopefully my cooking is better than that."

I took a deep breath and sat on the other side of the kitchen island. There was no point in holding off the inevitable. "So, what are my current boundaries?"

"The bubble consists of the house and the backyard. They gave us a schedule of times you'll be allowed to shift. If you don't use it, you lose it. Flying isn't permitted, but they made sure the yard was large enough so you could spread your wings. I'm allowed to enter and stay here as long as my magic stays completely muted."

"Why?" I said, exasperated. "Your magic is very specific. There's no point . . ." Oh. It made me realize how much I thought of Greg's magic as dual-purposed. But he had stabbed me twice, albeit through no fault of his own. "They thought we might go out in a blaze of glory, huh?"

"The thought crossed several people's minds, which is why I had to agree to the monitoring band and magical control in order to see you." He turned to plate up a few burgers and put a few more on the tiny grill.

"Do they know about the healing aspect of it?"

"I mentioned it, but they decided that the overall risk outweighed my having access to it." He put the plate on the island, and I fixed up the burgers before they cooled off. I handed him one with cheese, lettuce, and mustard, while I fixed one up with all of that and onions, tomatoes, and mayo. Greg chuckled as I downed the burger in five bites.

"What? You were right. I'm more hungry than I thought."

"Good, because I made four more. And the fries should be done in another ten minutes."

We ate next to each other in companionable silence. By the time I'd finished my third burger and Greg had finished his first, he spoke up.

"Gina Kendrick, my old partner from Jefferson headquarters, is working with the FCIB out of Dallas. She was assigned to your case."

"That's good, isn't it?" It seemed like it was, but the doubt I sensed from Greg told me otherwise.

"They have a lot of evidence against you. Your DNA is all over the room and the balcony. Gina said that the working theory is that after your phoenix episode, you had a mental breakdown, decided all vampires were a threat, and took out Bianca and removed Mark because he was there."

My guts churned. I rested my elbows on the island counter and put my head in my hands. "It's perfect. I mean, if I was working the case, I'd think it was me too."

"Is it?"

Fuck. That question hit me like a blow to the face. I never wanted Greg to doubt me, or the trust we had in each other. It was clear someone had given him a reason to, maybe to protect him or have him testify. It's what I would have done.

I lifted my head and looked at him. "I did not kill Bianca or Mark."

He closed his eyes and took a visible breath. "Okay, okay. I believe you, but why the guilt? What's that about?" We'd only been connected a short time, yet he already understood me better than anyone.

I sighed. "Because I almost did."

"What?" He blinked. "Are you telling me that's reason your DNA was everywhere?"

"Kinda."

"There's no 'kinda' about it. What the hell happened, Xavior?"

Greg leaned away from me as I turned to face him. I knew then that our trust was fragile and had to tell him the truth. "You fell asleep, and I used my den to leave the room. They picked it up on the external imaging monitors. I flew to Bianca's balcony thinking if I confronted her myself, she'd leave us alone. Maybe singe the hair off her head. I don't know." I felt a knot in my throat and nausea. Everything I'd eaten threatened to reappear. But I needed to explain myself, especially to Greg.

"As I watched her feed off Mark, I snapped out of it. I realized my aging cycle was pushing me to protect you. I also knew that you wouldn't forgive me if I harmed someone else, regardless of what she did to us. Even if it meant that you'd be safe."

Greg stared at me but didn't say anything, so I continued. "So I flew back and got back in bed with you where I belonged. I didn't wake up again until the rogue magic alarm went off."

"That explains why your DNA is on the balcony. How did it get in the room?"

"I have no idea. Honestly. When I left Bianca and Mark, they were rather animated."

"Animated?"

"Fucking?"

Greg blushed. "Which is why they never saw you on the balcony."

I nodded. "Like I said, it's perfect. The detectives have all the footage from the dance floor, the hallway, and my flight to and from Bianca's balcony. With the information from the Cooper family, it makes me look exactly like your friend Gina suspects."

"The evidence imager picked up your DNA all over the room. It looked like a splatter painting. Mark's DNA did too. It appears as if you blew them up with your fire breath."

"They think it's my saliva all over the room?"

"That's what it looks like from the evidence."

"How did they explain the time difference between my flight and the rogue magic alarm?"

"Sometimes dragon abilities aren't registered with the internal sensors right away. If they did, the whole resort would have alarms going off all the time."

I got up and walked a few steps away. "Greg, we may have to face reality here. Maybe if I bargain with the feds, they'll keep me alive so you can at least have a decent life."

His face formed a scowl. He was annoyed, if not a little angry. "You're going to give up? Just like that?"

"It's not giving up. It's protecting you. You didn't sign up for this." The problem was that if the Cooper Coven was behind this, I wasn't sure what I could do to keep him safe from them.

"Maybe not this specifically, but I knew what I was getting myself into, Xavior, and don't act like I was thinking with my dick rather than my heart. I know you know better."

I turned back toward Greg. He stood and came to me. "I love that you're so stubbornly loyal once you've made up your mind, but in this instance, it can kill you, Greg. I don't know if I can deal with putting you in harm's way."

He reached out and touched my shoulders. "Listen to me. We're not giving up. Your uncle is looking at the case the federal prosecutors are putting together. The Envoy for the vampire covens is coming to mediate. And while Gina thinks you're a sociopath—"

"Seriously?" I shouldn't have been surprised. The evidence was telling the story so far, and if it had been me investigating, I might have come to the same conclusion.

"—I don't." He moved closer. "You did a bonehead thing. And you made me a promise. I expect you to keep it."

I smiled a little. Greg was right. It was a bonehead thing to stalk Bianca. We might have ended up here anyway, but that certainly hadn't helped. "I'm sorry I messed up our vacation."

Greg sighed as he moved his head from side to side. "You did, but you'll make it up to me once we figure out how to prove that you didn't kill Bianca and Mark." He pulled me into a hug, and it was worth everything.

I didn't know how we would prove anything, but if there was a chance at all that we could, I didn't want to give up. At least for Greg's sake.

Unexpected Arrivals

Xavior

We'd been in the bubble for a few days. There was an odd quiet that surrounded the place. The bubble worked well for many reasons, but it also disrupted interactions with the natural environment. No birds or squirrels. Even insects stayed away. There was a tree in the backyard that looked healthy, but it was known that bubbles maintained for an extended period caused plant life to eventually wither and die no matter how much you fed and watered it.

Bubble tech was based on the same shield tech that many public safety groups used to contain projectiles. Except, in this instance, I was the projectile. I could only leave if Renard, members of the local public safety office, or someone from the FCIB picked me up.

While Renard was my uncle, no one was worried about him helping me escape. For one thing, the wristbands were nearly impossible to remove, and the trackers it held disbursed through my body. It would take some pretty heavy spellwork to neutralize them all. On top of that, if he was caught helping me, he'd find himself in his own bubble, without his law practice and licenses. Besides, escape didn't sit right with me. Even if I couldn't be a detective any longer, I still had a hope that it would all work out. Maybe that was naïve, but me running wouldn't prove my innocence either.

It was nearly dawn, and the built-in alarm on my wrist reminded me I had a scheduled window when I could shift for an hour. So I left Greg in bed, went out to the living area, and opened the sliding glass door to walk into the garden. It was large enough for me to spread my wings and maybe even nest, but it wouldn't be my den. Nor would it be the balcony and pool we had back at the resort. It reminded me that all this was meant to be functional, not necessarily comfortable.

The metallic band beeped and started a timer. I took a deep breath and shifted. It wasn't as smooth as usual and felt like I was moving through honey. The tech was making sure it could handle me in dragon form while it still suppressed any magic I might use.

I opened my wings to give them an experimental flap as I settled into place. It was good to feel feathers and claws again and the moisture of the ground under my feet. I scratched a little at the dirt and grass to kick up the smell of it and let it wash over my senses. It was the only reason I didn't hear or feel Greg's approach.

The sun was coloring the sky when I finally noticed Greg in jeans and a T-shirt standing in the garden near the house. If I extended my wings, I could almost touch him. But, instead, I folded my wings, turned, and licked his face.

"Gah!" The laughter it induced was enough to make me rumble a little. It was nice to forget we weren't here by choice, even if it was only for a moment.

Greg caressed my snout and eye ridges, then my chin. It felt nice to have these small touches and his scent on me. "Make sure you take your full time, but I wanted you to know your uncle messaged me via the house system. He's coming for a visit."

I made an affirmative noise, and he chuckled. Maybe Renard could talk Greg into contacting his parents. Greg said he wasn't ready to. They would want to help if he did. It was likely my family was in touch with Renard. With most of them in Europe somewhere, it wasn't practical. They had responsibilities, and it was too early to tell what would happen. And I certainly wasn't prepared for Faith to give me an I-told-you-so speech.

It was better if I shifted before my timer went off. Being forced to shift was akin to putting honey back in a broken glass bottle. It hurt, and I wasn't that much of a masochist to endure it if I had a choice.

The house system signaled that Renard was here as I walked out of the bedroom dressed for the day. Greg had started coffee, and I could smell eggs cooking. "I'll get the door," I called out. There was a quick thanks in response as I approached the entryway. I found out Renard wasn't the only one waiting when I opened it.

"Morning, Philip. Jennifer." I glanced at Renard and tried not to be so awkward. "Um, Greg's cooking breakfast if you're hungry." I hadn't known what kind of reaction to expect, but Jennifer reaching for me and hugging me wasn't one of them.

I was on the verge of tears when she let go of me. "Gina, Greg's old partner, contacted us and explained what's going on. She gave us Renard's number, which I don't think she was supposed to do, but she used to eat dinner at our house."

"How much do you know?" I glanced at all of them.

Philip finally spoke. "Enough to know that it's serious. Especially since Greg didn't tell us anything the last time he messaged us. Renard filled in the rest."

"We don't know how much the covens are involved. Greg wanted to keep you both safe."

"That sounds like Greg," Jennifer said with a sigh.

"Well, come in. Please. Regardless of what Greg planned, you're here now. He'll be happy to see you." I led everyone to the living area. Greg had his back to us while he continued to make omelets. "Greg." He gave me a questioning hum in response. "We have a few more for breakfast."

He slowly turned around, and I watched as his gaze moved from me to Renard, to his parents. He tossed the omelet pan on the counter and came out of the galley kitchen toward us. Once he was wrapped in his parent's arms he started crying, which made me tear up.

"I didn't want you to worry or put you in danger. We don't know how safe it is right now." Greg dashed his tears away, and Philip touched his shoulder.

"Gina is worried about you. We're worried about you," Philip said, as he embraced his son again, then turned toward me. "We're worried about both of you. Gina," he shook his head, "has some interesting ideas about you, Xavior. We tried to persuade her otherwise." He glanced at Jennifer, then back at me.

"She's building a case. Interviewing family is part of it. I'm sure she's contacted my family, too." I thought the statement would reassure Greg, but instead he was more worried.

"Shit, please tell me she hasn't contacted Narissa." Greg glanced at his parents and then Renard. I was nearly staggered by the fear I felt from him. I saw Renard's nostrils flare, picking up the scent.

"Gina didn't ask us about Narissa. Does she know anything about The Order?" Philip asked.

"I didn't tell her, obviously, but she'd have access to what Lang might have put in our termination papers. Whether that's public knowledge, who knows at this point. Lang and the city council representatives found out somehow before I told Lang in our exit interview." Greg ran his hand through his hair.

"I can make a few calls. See if Narissa turned up on the discovery list. Try not to panic until we find out more." Renard turned and went for the house entrance. Phones didn't work inside the bubble. We could only use the comms system provided or Renard for external communication.

Greg looked at me, then his parents, and seemed to remember breakfast. "Um, let me finish cleaning up my mess, and we can all have coffee. I made a bunch of simple omelets if anyone's hungry." Greg walked past all of us as he wiped his hands on his jeans. Jennifer followed him and helped under Greg's direction.

"Why don't we sit down," I suggested to Philip, as the kitchen was busy enough with two people in it. He followed me to the living room area and sat in one armchair while I took a side of the couch.

Philip smelled upset but held it in. I could understand that, especially from him. He was in danger of losing his son for multiple reasons. As the silence grew, I reached for anything that would be a safe topic. I noticed the stamp on his hand. "How much time did they give you for a visit?"

"Forty-eight hours. Renard said there were multiple bedrooms here, so we thought we'd stay with you both for the night."

I nodded. "That's a good idea. Then my uncle can work on moving you to a safe location until this is all worked out."

"Will it work out, Xavior?"

I trusted Philip. He trusted me with Greg and with his concern about Narissa, his ex-wife and the leader of the North American Order of the Saint George Knights. So I told him the truth.

"I don't know. And I wish I could tell you something different."

He leaned over to grasp my hand. "I trust you. Alright? If you protected Greg, then to me, it's justified." He squeezed my hand. "Whatever comes next, we're here for you both." I gave his hand a squeeze in return. "Promise me, Xavior, that you'll do whatever you need to keep yourselves alive. I'm too young to bury my children."

I nodded because I couldn't think of anything to say. Not that I could have with the knot in my throat. I hadn't expected Philip to support me, but I also remembered when he told me to kill his ex and run if she came after us, so maybe we had more in common than I realized.

Soon enough, coffee was served and omelets were eaten in an odd silence. Renard joined us, and I took a deep breath before I asked him a few questions that were rattling around in my brain.

"Is there any plan to use a walk-back spell?"

Renard shook his head. "Initial tests of the space using your DNA came up inconclusive. The theory is that because dragon fire is magical, it destroyed the ether forensics would have used for the spell."

"Which further implicates me." If you practiced metaphysical magic, ether was the stuff that held our universe together.

A binding element that kept impressions of nearly everything that passed through it. A fancier name for it was luminiferous ether.

"I'm afraid so. Along with your CSI training." I groaned with frustration as Renard continued his explanation. "One of the FCIB's theories is that you killed Bianca and Mark with an initial burst and then tried to destroy more evidence with another burst."

The coffee and eggs weren't sitting well. I stood and went for the main bedroom then found myself in the bathroom vomiting up everything I'd eaten. A damp cloth was placed on my neck before I saw Greg as he crouched next to me.

"This isn't morning sickness, is it?"

The frank statement from him made me blink and then laugh. "Fuck, that would be our luck."

Greg sat down next to me as I put my head on his shoulder. His arm pulled me closer, and I covered my face while I cried into the damp cloth. He held me the whole time. When I finally calmed down, I answered him.

"It's just nerves. I'm pretty sure. Dragons rarely have morning sickness until really late in gestation, and it's usually because the egg is solid enough to take up space. It's a sign that we need to shift if we haven't already."

Greg nodded. "Good to know for future reference." He kissed my forehead. "Especially since my parents are expecting grandkids." I laughed. It was very much like Greg to be hopeful and solve problems. It's one of the many things I adored about him.

We sat like that for a long time until Jennifer found us. "Hi, guys." She bent down so she was at eye level with us. "Renard needed to leave, so he helped us bring in our luggage. He said he'd be back tomorrow to pick us up and move Philip and me to a safe location."

Greg nodded. "That makes me feel better."

Jennifer reached out and touched Greg's shoulder. "I thought it might." She patted his shoulder, then stood. "Come out when you're ready. You have all the ingredients for lemon-ginger shortbreads, so I'm going to take over the kitchen for a while."

"We do?" Greg hadn't mentioned it.

"I missed home," he said.

I understood, and so had Jennifer. She disappeared back into the main part of the house as I gave Greg a kiss on the cheek, and we held each other a little longer.

THE ENVOY

GREGOR

It was Monday, the second week of April, and so much had changed in such a short time. Two months after our work anniversary, we were ambushed by vampires, which caused Xavior's phoenix episode. Then, we had our first vacation, mated, and lost our jobs. His ex tried to murder us and died afterward, implicating Xavior in the process. It was an eventful second year together so far.

Today, Xavior and I were retrieved from the bubble location and brought back to the public safety headquarters to talk with the Envoy. This time they let us stay together, which surprised me.

Xavior's uncle entered the interview room. "Good morning. How are you both feeling?"

I looked at Xavior, and he nodded. "We're both doing fairly well, considering," said Xavior.

"Good. I will state that it looks better if you cooperate with the Envoy during their investigation, but you are not obligated to do so. Ms. Cooper was a valuable family member, and her family is most certainly seeking damages, but they could ask for more if they feel it's warranted."

"You mean they could ask for my head?"

"It's a possibility, Xavior. The Vampire Accords govern interactions between the living and vampires. It established their rights as the living undead, or an alternate unlife style, depending on how you view it." Renard shrugged. "A cross-species murder charge is usually handled at the federal level, but if the covens want to set an example, they could ask for the trial to be moved so that it's overseen by international courts. If they only seek a civil case versus a criminal one, they might leave it at the federal level, but it would be at the Envoy's discretion."

"Do either of you know the Envoy?" It seemed like a logical question since Xavior had some knowledge of the inner workings of the covens, and Renard was a lawyer.

Renard shook his head no, and Xavior nodded. "In times past, a dhampir usually held the position. An individual in the major coven families trusted to represent them and uphold the accords. Some appointees did better than others. It's said that the families take turns creating dhampirs specifically for the purpose." Xavior shrugged.

"What are dhampirs?" I hadn't heard the word before.

"They're a hybrid, like me, between vampires and humans, mostly. There was a rumor of a vampire-fae hybrid once, but whether they were an Envoy, I couldn't tell you."

The door mechanism moved and a lock was thrown. The three of us stood as a lone person dressed in a very nice suit, with fashionable, long, black hair and a decent tan walked into the room with an imager in hand. He tossed it into the air, and it activated with a blue glow around it. That glow meant it was scanning for magic signatures. Unless it was modified to do something else.

"Good morning. My name is Lennix Creighton. I'm the Envoy from the Coven Collective. I'm here to represent the Cooper family's interest as well as uphold the Vampire Accords. Please, be seated."

We sat, and the imager moved closer. The glow shifted from blue to yellow, indicating it was recording thermal temperatures. The silence grew longer as the imager cycled through all its functions, likely recording baseline feeds to be reviewed later after Creighton started his questions.

His mannerisms were matter of fact. I wondered if they trained him as an investigator. He reminded me of how federal agents sometimes approached interviews. "As I'm sure you've guessed, I'll be recording our interview. Shall we begin?"

We stated our names, date of birth, home addresses, species, and current occupation. It wouldn't have surprised me if Creighton asked about our sexual orientation at that point, too. Just for the record, of course.

"Mr. Brantley, could you describe the nature of your relationship with Bianca Cooper?" His voice was melodic and calming. Within moments, I blinked as if I was tired. Xavior squeezed my hand, and it woke me up.

"Early in my life, I was in a relationship with her, and I worked for her family," Xavior said.

"During your relationship with Ms. Cooper, did you ever enter into a financial agreement with her and her family?" the Envoy asked.

Xavior nodded. "I did. It was contingent upon marriage."

"For the record, what was the basis of the agreement?"

"All of my possessions and financial gains, except my den, would be the property of the Cooper family upon my death."

Xavior gave me a quick glance and another squeeze of my hand. I turned to look at Renard, and he nodded. I had a feeling he'd been involved or had seen the contract at some point.

Creighton continued. "Can you state the reason your engagement was called off?"

"Bianca threw me out of her house. I would say that calls off an engagement." Xavior let go of my hand and leaned forward. I sensed frustration from him.

"Was there ever a formal dissolution of the engagement?"

Renard spoke up. "As Mr. Brantley's legal counsel, I'd like you to explain why you are asking about a nearly three-hundred-year-old contract."

"As there was no formal dissolution of the engagement agreement, Ms. Cooper and Mr. Brantley were still engaged at the time of her death. Therefore, it's entirely possible that when Mr. Brantley realized Ms. Cooper was at the resort, he removed Ms. Cooper to eliminate her and her family's claim to Mr. Brantley's fortune." Creighton said.

"You can't be serious," Renard said. "If the contract was even still valid in the first place, then Xavior's phoenix episode would have nullified any claim regardless of whether the contract was dissolved properly since the two parties in question were not in fact married when either of them expired." It appeared Renard was only warming up. "And furthermore, since the Cooper Coven sponsors the Hargrove Coven, their involvement in Mr. Brantley's phoenix episode could be seen as exactly what you are alleging my client did to Ms. Cooper."

I was guessing because I didn't know the particulars of the contract, but if Xavior had died that night instead of resurrecting, the Cooper family could have made a claim to his estate based on the engagement. I'm sure his family would have fought it, especially since his sister Faith was so against Xavior's relationship with Bianca in the first place.

Xavior stayed quiet, and I followed his lead. If Renard wanted to argue with Creighton, then we'd let them.

"Envoy Creighton, unless you have any more questions relevant to the case, we're done with this interview."

Creighton glanced between Xavior and me. "I only have one. Did either of you murder Bianca Cooper?"

Xavior squeezed my hand. "No, I did not murder Bianca Cooper."

"Neither did I," I answered easily.

We told the truth. The evidence seemed to be otherwise, but at least we both knew that Xavior hadn't killed Bianca or Mark. Whatever happened, the Cooper Coven wouldn't end up with Xavior's estate. Not that they could have touched it if he was convicted, anyway.

They would have had to wait until after he served his sentence because if you could afford to support yourself, you were required to support your own rehabilitation and confinement. The only difference would be whether they considered you a violent offender. They placed those individuals in therapeutic stasis that worked as a virtual reality. You served your time without harming yourself or others while undergoing psychiatric care.

Creighton nodded. "As of now, I am advising both the FCIB and the Cooper family that the Vampire Accords were not violated in the deaths of Bianca Cooper and Mark Denning. While this does clear you of legal implications toward violating international law, this does not clear you of the charges the FCIB have filed."

The Envoy stood and gathered the imager. "For what it's worth, I hope justice will be served. Good day." Creighton turned on his heel, knocked on the door, and it opened and closed before any of us could respond to what he said.

As FCIB didn't need us for more questions, Renard escorted us back to the bubble. Once we were inside, I asked what I thought everyone was thinking, but no one wanted to say.

"What was the Envoy doing by dredging up an engagement contract?" We took a seat in the living room. Renard sat in a chair while Xavior and I occupied the couch.

Renard shrugged. "Might have been to establish an alternative motive, trick Xavior into saying he killed Bianca for another reason, or at the very least, try to gain some compensation for the Cooper family. Running a coven doesn't come cheap."

"But Creighton cleared me instead. Why?" Xavior clearly looked confused at being let off the hook so easily.

"Maybe he knew you were innocent all along. The covens go after what they want if they think they can get it. The imager Creighton had was likely feeding to an observer that reported to him. With the imager and his vocal power, he probably had enough information to make a determination." Renard folded his hands together.

"What vocal power?" I asked.

"You almost nodded off after he began talking. It's likely a vocal power that lets him put his subjects at ease or makes them speak truthfully," Renard said.

I looked at Xavior. "I don't remember falling asleep." I never knew I was so susceptible to vampire powers. Bianca did something similar, and it nearly got Xavior and me killed.

Xavior rubbed my shoulders in a gesture of reassurance, but I felt like a weak link at that moment. Especially if vampire covens were after us. Renard talked about next steps, but I only caught half of what he said.

"The FCIB would likely come up with a plea agreement, especially if Bianca's family pushed for it. We should hear from the team in a few days. Rest until then. I'll keep looking for more evidence." We assured Renard we'd do so and escorted him to the edge of the bubble, where he entered his vehicle and left.

Dinner was a quiet affair with fish and a salad. The domestic nature of it didn't escape either of us. This would be our life if we couldn't find any other evidence to exonerate Xavior. Here or in another bubble, I would be the only person able to leave.

Later in bed, with the room quiet and dark, I worked up the courage to talk about our future. "Who has the keystone for your den?"

"Renard does. As most dens become family property after a dragon passes, I made sure Renard requested it." Xavior looked up at me with curiosity in his eyes. "Why do you ask?"

I reached out and caressed his face. "I'm worried." After taking a deep breath, I continued. "Maybe we should ask Renard to draw up plans. I have a will that leaves everything to my parents. I don't have a lot at the moment, but what's left from the sale of the house they can use."

He rolled so he could prop himself on my chest. "You're not giving up, are you?" His voice was gentle, understanding even, but the hurt was there, too.

"No! No, I want to see this through. No matter what happens. We can endure this. I know we can. But we shouldn't assume things will go our way." I raised my gaze to the ceiling to keep from crying. The life we'd planned such a short time ago seemed to be slipping away.

He tapped my chest. I dropped my gaze to his emerald eyes. "First, I love you. Second, you've stayed by my side through all of this. I couldn't ask for a better partner." He moved and gave me a kiss. "Don't ever think I regret being with you or us. Whether we have five minutes or fifty years. You're my mate, Greg. That alone brings me so much happiness."

"Don't make me cry." I tapped his shoulder and chuckled to keep the tears away. It didn't quite work as Xavior reached up to brush his fingers across my face. "I don't want you to resent me. The whole reason you're in this mess is because of me."

"No," he gently corrected. "The whole reason I'm in this relationship is because of you. The legal trouble I put completely on Bianca and the covens. I suspect that our encounter with the pledges might have been their plan to get my estate. With Bianca gone, and the Envoy ruling in our favor, the covens can't go after it anymore."

We held each other for a time. I was nearly asleep when Xavior spoke. "We should have Renard take you to get my vehicle. If we're going to be here for a while, you'll need it."

"That makes sense. I'll call your uncle in the morning." Xavior went to sleep. While I tried to rest, my thoughts kept circling. Regardless of what we had wanted, this was our life now. The sooner we accepted it, the easier it would be to move forward and figure out how to live with it.

THE MISSING LINK

GREGOR

I didn't like leaving Xavior alone in the bubble, but he was right. His expensive vintage vehicle was at the resort, and would only take a few hours to pick up so we wouldn't have to rely on his uncle as much. My vehicle was back in San Francisco, which was an eight hour round trip. Until we could be separated for more than a day, it wasn't worth the risk. The pheromone addiction was definitely real, and we hadn't lasted more than a few hours before we both had problems.

"You're quiet. Is there anything you want to ask?" Renard's golden eyes turned toward me, and I gave him what I hoped was a thankful smile.

"I'm not sure where to start. How much do you know about me?" I looked down at the pair of shorts I'd worn for the fourth time in as many weeks. At some point, we'd need fresh clothes too. The ones we brought with us worked fine, but washing them every few days was a pain.

"Well, when you initially started working with Xavior, the family asked me to do a background check. There were a lot of concerns. Xavior seemed to think it was fine, but his parents were worried."

"Then you know about my family—my other family, I mean." He obviously knew before now, or he would have been more surprised when I mentioned Narissa being on the interview list. She was a problem we didn't need, given everything else that was going on.

Renard nodded. "I'm surprised it didn't come up in your service record. We only found it because of academic records and your father's first marriage certificate — which was very hard to find."

"I was disowned. It doesn't surprise me that my mother tried to erase as much as she could about my connection to the family." By the time I applied to the public safety academy, Jennifer was my mother in every way that mattered, and that's all that mattered to me.

"So we've gathered." Renard nodded. "Xavior's parents thought it would be more prudent for him to work with someone else, but he wouldn't have it." Renard smiled. "He said he found you fascinating."

I chuckled. "Don't tell Agent Kendrick that. She already thinks he's a sociopath."

"I'm well aware of Agent Kendrick's theories." Renard sighed. "I think she's concerned about her friend. If you were in her shoes, Greg, wouldn't you think the same thing?"

"Maybe." I thought about it a little more. "Probably. Especially now that we're mated. I would certainly think my judgment was affected."

"Exactly." He tapped a few buttons on the console and turned toward me. "Greg, I want you to think about your future. They could levy a severe sentence on Xavior based on the evidence."

I realized that, but I had already made up my mind. "I appreciate your concern, Renard. But I didn't go into this with my eyes closed. I love him. Whatever comes next, we'll figure it out together."

He shook his head. "I had a feeling you'd say that, but I had to try." He turned back toward the console and checked the monitors. "We should be at the resort in ten minutes. If you have any problem with the staff, let me know. I called them earlier, and they know you will be picking up Xavior's vehicle."

"Thank you for everything. I know Xavior appreciates your help as well."

"Don't thank me yet." He adjusted our course as I watched. "Xavior's facing two counts of premeditated murder. I'm trying to have it reduced, but federal prosecutors won't budge. The evidence supports a crime of passion, at best."

"But the Envoy from the covens cleared him. Doesn't that count for something?"

"It only means that the coven won't be able to touch Xavior's estate, no matter the outcome." Renard shrugged. "Though that will be little comfort if he's in a bubble for the next hundred years or has his head cut off."

"Is that a possibility?" I knew it was, but I didn't want to think about it. Life without Xavior would be a cruel joke.

"Based on the evidence, yes." Renard was matter of fact about it, but his tense shoulders and the way he drove the vehicle betrayed worry. "Which means, if I can't turn up any other evidence, your other family will become involved. For your sake, I'm hoping to keep them out of it."

I nodded. My stomach churned, and bile collected at the back of my throat. Thinking about my mother or any of my relatives laying a hand on Xavior made me sick. If that happened, I'd be powerless to do anything about it.

Executions were very rare, but when they happened, they were swift. The last one I could remember was a troll that had incurable cancer, and she was in so much pain that she had a berserker fit that wouldn't stop. They finally stopped her with a combination of spells and drugs only after she smashed up half of Kansas City, including a major bridge that caused several injuries and deaths. They reported that when the troll died, she thanked the people in the room. I doubt Xavior would do the same. The last official dragon execution was over three hundred years ago.

Xavior was innocent, but he felt guilty enough about Bianca and Mark that he was prepared to be sentenced. He hadn't exactly given up, but he was more worried about me than concerned about himself.

Renard pulled into the resort driveway, and the vehicle attendant opened my door. "Greg, it's not hopeless yet. We have time. There are more interviews to do, and the Envoy clearing you both gave the prosecutors some cause for concern. Personally, I wouldn't want to be Creighton when he tells the Cooper family he ruled in Xavior's favor. They aren't likely to take it well."

"That surprised both of us. Xavior still doesn't know what to make of it."

"Neither do I, but I'm working on things here. Promise me you'll take care of my nephew while I try to figure this out."

That was an easy enough promise to keep. "I will, Renard. Thank you for the ride."

He nodded and drove off while I approached the vehicle stand. "Hi, I'm Greg Lyndon. I'm here to pick up Xavior Brantley's vehicle."

"Certainly. It might be a few minutes. We moved it to a long-term storage location for safekeeping."

"Okay." I stood there for a moment, then remembered the potion. "Actually, could you give me thirty minutes? I have something I need to pick up." The attendant nodded and wrote a note. I went inside and wove my way through the resort until I found the shop I needed.

"Mr. Uluke?"

The shop was quiet. If I could pick up the potion, at least that might give Xavior something to look forward to. Something we could do together that would lift his spirits. The more I thought about it, the more I hoped Mr. Uluke had it ready.

"Hello, Mr. Uluke? It's Greg Lyndon. Are you here?" I walked further into the shop and approached the desk. There was still no answer. I waited for a little while and was about to give up when I heard a clatter from the back room and a loud squeak. I threaded my way through a hall that could be better described as a rat's nest than a passage with things stacked up on either side of it. There was barely enough space to walk through sideways. When I reached a workshop area, I found Mr. Uluke covered in a green substance. "Are you alright?"

"I'm fine. Just fine. Why are you back here? What do you want?"

His reply was in stark contrast to the helpful shopkeeper I'd met before. "I'm Greg Lyndon. You were making a transfiguration potion for me."

"No, I don't think so. You are mistaken." He fidgeted and didn't meet my eyes. It surprised me that he lied.

"No, I'm not. I have the charge on our room bill to prove it. You said it should be done by now. I'd like to have it, please."

"I'm sorry. No."

"No, it's not done, or no, I can't have it?"

"It doesn't matter. Just leave, please."

"It does matter." I was frustrated with this circling conversation. I had spent a lot of Xavior's money, so it mattered. I couldn't go back empty-handed. "Look, if you won't talk with me. I'll have the hotel manager come here. You can speak with them about why the potion I paid for isn't completed well past the time you said it would be."

Uluke scurried over to me and grabbed my phone as I took it out of my pocket. "Please, don't call. I don't want any trouble. The man who came here said if there was trouble, he'd hurt me more and mess up my shop."

"What man?" Someone had scared him badly. He shook like a leaf while I asked questions.

"The man that asked for your potion. He punched me and broke my tail." Uluke pointed to the stump that was left of his tail.

"Did you give him the potion?"

"Yes, yes! It hurt too much. I kept a small amount to replicate it, but you came back too soon. I promise I'll have it done next week."

"Never mind that now. Do you have security cameras in here?" Mr. Uluke nodded.

"Good. Can you show me the footage from the day the man showed up?" Another affirmative from Mr. Uluke, and five minutes later, I was staring at the man who walked out of the shop with my transfiguration potion.

"Did he give you a name?"

"No, not one that I remember," Uluke said.

I took a picture of the frozen frame image from the holo showing the man who accosted Uluke with my phone, then called Gina. Thankfully, she didn't send me to voicemail.

"Greg, you shouldn't be calling me right now. You need to go through your lawyer." It was good to hear her voice, even if she was annoyed with me.

"I know. And I know this isn't standard protocol, but I have something here I think you should see."

"And what is that?"

"I don't know what it is other than a theft, but I have a hunch that it's something more and involved with Xavior's case, and I suspect you're the only person who might be able to track it down."

I heard Gina sigh over the phone. "Alright, tell me where you are. I'll meet you."

I gave her directions and tried not to get my hopes up.

EXONERATED

XAVIOR

It was the first time that the nanites under my skin seemed to itch like they were burrowing deeper. I knew it was psychological, but I couldn't help it. I was worried. Greg had called to let me know he was at the public safety headquarters. I couldn't tell over the phone if his abruptness was from stress or excitement. Whatever it was, I sincerely hoped something else hadn't turned up that placed Greg in as much hot water as me.

Renard returned to pick me up at Agent Kendrick's request. Neither of us had more to go on other than where Greg was at the moment. "I guess we'll see what they have when we arrive. Is there anything else I need to know?"

"Not that I know of." My uncle gave me a look. "I'm being honest! Can't you trust your nose?"

"I'm your lawyer, Xavior. You pay me to scrutinize things, not trust my nose." The ride in his vehicle to headquarters was a quiet one after that rebuke.

Once we arrived, the desk sergeant escorted us to an interview room, where we waited. Renard messaged Greg but received nothing. "This wouldn't be about a plea deal, would it?" I was worried that they were talking to Greg about it before me, maybe preparing him for the worst or trying to convince him to be a witness.

My uncle shook his head. "It could be, but last time I talked with them, they didn't want to do a deal. I still have at least two more weeks for discovery. There's a lot of footage to go through and a timeline to confirm. We don't even have a date for an initial hearing."

I stayed seated, but I wanted to pace the room. Greg had been gone most of the day. My vehicle was in the parking structure next to the headquarters, but I had no way of knowing if Greg brought it here or if it was on its way to being impounded.

"Let me see if I can find someone to give us some details." Renard got up and headed for the door just as Greg opened it.

I rocketed to my feet. "Are you alright? What's going on?" My feelings were in my throat I was so happy to see him.

He smiled, and there was a light in his eyes I recognized from when we solved cases. He crossed the room and wrapped me in a hug, and I hugged him back. The sheer joy I sensed from him nearly made me cry.

We finally separated when someone cleared their throat from behind Greg. He chuckled. "Xavior, let me introduce you to my former partner and the agent working your case, Gina Kendrick." I offered to shake her hand. No reason I couldn't be polite.

"I'm sorry we didn't meet under better circumstances." I meant that. Greg thought a lot of Gina. It bothered him that two people he cared about were at odds.

She shook my hand and gave me a cryptic kind of smile. "Likewise, but I think Greg might have found something that I think you should see." Agent Kendrick walked into the room and activated the holo screen. She brought up the evidence board with the DNA markers.

"So we know they found your DNA at the scene." Greg reached up and traced a finger that created a highlighted circle around concentrated dots representing where my DNA was found. "But there was a discrepancy."

He pointed. "This collection matches you nearly perfectly, and it's all located on the balcony." He pointed to the interior dots of evidence in the hotel room. "However, this collection is only a seventy-nine percent match instead of ninety-nine."

"So the eighty-nine percent they originally had was an average to account for anomalies like fire causing DNA degradation," I offered, which was ironic since I was the primary suspect. Uncle Renard made a noise to remind me to shut up.

Greg nodded. "Exactly, until I found out that our transfiguration potion was stolen." The smile on his face was everything. It was the sun coming out after a long thunderstorm, and I couldn't look away.

"Stolen? By whom?" Renard asked.

"This individual." Kendrick brought up two pictures, and it revealed Mark Denning bumping into Greg, and another of Mark walking out with the potion. They had two different timestamps, several days apart. It was clear that he had something in his hands in the second one.

"Mr. Uluke is giving his statement. They forced him to hand over the potion, though he warned them it was volatile. When I went to pick up your vehicle, I remembered the potion. That's when I discovered the theft. He took a sample of the potion intent on making another to cover the loss, but I talked him into giving us the remainder of what he had instead." Greg was smiling, but he wasn't done yet.

"Xavior, it's a match for your DNA in the room. Not only that, but it's a partial match for me too. Not enough for my DNA to come up in the system, but when we matched it to the potion, which combines our DNA, our combined sequences matched."

We stood in silence for a moment. I looked at my uncle, and he looked—impressed. It was hard to impress my uncle. Personally, I was proud. Greg was my mate, after all. It slowly sunk in that Mark and Bianca had used the potion. "So, you're saying that Mark used a tailored potion on himself, and he blew up and took Bianca out with him?"

Greg nodded. "It lines up better with the timeline, too. You were out on their balcony around four, and they had to have taken the potion before Bianca planned to sleep for the day.

Mark had a violent reaction that killed them both and triggered the magical wards around the time we heard the resort alarms."

"Is that true?" I looked at Agent Kendrick.

"It appears so, Mr. Brantley. I have a CSI team reviewing the evidence based on this new information. Once we have everything independently verified, I'll make a recommendation to the federal prosecutors."

"How long will that take?" Renard asked the vital question while I smiled across the displayed evidence at Greg, who couldn't stop smiling either.

Kendrick looked at Renard. "We have teams working on it now. We'll know for sure in two days." Kendrick shrugged. "If you could escort these two back to the bubble, we'll be in touch as soon as we've double-checked everything."

Renard nodded, then pointed at the door. "Shall we?"

Greg reached for my hand, and I took it as we walked out of the interview room together. Greg gave a nod to Agent Kendrick as we left.

We still had to follow procedures until the investigation cleared me. My uncle drove me back to my bubble, and Greg followed in my vehicle. Once we were back, Greg and I ate dinner, cleaned up a bit, and flopped into bed. We gravitated toward each other like magnets.

"You're brilliant." I took Greg's hand, brought it to my mouth, and kissed his knuckles.

"You've said that already."

"I mean it every time."

"I got lucky, Xav. If Uluke had replaced the potion, I never would have figured it out." He gave my hand a squeeze, then let it go to brush his fingers along my face. "I can only assume that he hadn't expected me to return. Why waste expensive components on a client that wouldn't ever show up again?"

"Maybe something would have come up in the security footage."

"They were focusing on interactions between you and Bianca. They thought they had the case wrapped up."

"Hey." I touched his face. "Stop thinking like that. How many times are you going to replay what you could have done sooner in your head when you had no control over it?"

Greg sighed. "You're right." His hands moved to my shoulders and I moved into his arms. He held me tight, and I sighed in comfort, though I sensed Greg trying to settle his worries. I could only reassure him with my own feelings. He slowly relaxed, and then a tiny disappointment crept between us. I didn't think he was disappointed in me exactly, but I made a guess.

"We'll figure out another way for you to fly with me, I promise."

He kissed the top of my head. I felt him smile into my hair. "Okay."

In his heart, maybe ever since Greg learned about dragons, all he'd wanted was to be near one. To protect them. What he got was a brash, loud-mouthed punk that enjoyed looking for danger rather than playing it safe.

You'd think I'd be more of an adult after all this time, but I tried that. With Bianca, I thought I was a grown-up. I thought I knew what I wanted when everyone around me hated my choices. Now, they might hate my choices, but I know I did one thing right. Greg wasn't a second chance at an average dragon life.

I was more determined than ever to take every moment we were given and make it count. Jordan understood more than I realized when he gave me his awkward blessing. Genuine friends often do. It made me wonder what his partner had been like. I wish I had met her. She must have been a fantastic person to have made such a lasting impression on him.

"I can hear you thinking." Greg's hands moved along my back. I felt my scales respond. It was as comforting as being held by him.

"I think we might need a vacation from our vacation."

Greg laughed. "That's possible. You wanna know what I'm thinking?"

"Always."

He rolled me onto my back, and I looked up at his large brown eyes. "Maybe we should move in together."

I don't know if he saw the shock on my face or felt it, but he laughed, and I was ecstatic. "Yes! Please! Absolutely!" I buried my face in his chest and kissed him wherever I could. Then I halted. "Wait, is this because of our reaction to the pheromones? Because we can figure that out. Stressful situations make it harder, but once we're home . . ." He kissed me to shut me up. Once we stopped, I knew he was sincere, not just concerned for my safety.

"Xavior. We've talked about building a life together and children. The one thing we didn't talk about is where we want to live."

"Well, we have a lot of options. I have the brownstone and my estate in San Francisco. A flat in London. A villa in Spain, close to my parent's estate. Jordan and I have a luxury high rise we own in Hong Kong. He stays there a for business, but I'm sure we could rent something there if you wanted. Oh, I have a small house in New Zealand. I haven't been there in a while, but you might like that too. And if there is some other place you'd rather live, we can find something. Wherever you want to go, I'll make it happen."

Greg was quiet for a long moment. "I've lived in three or four places, and most of those were along the west coast. I've never been overseas."

"Well, that's what we do then. We'd planned to visit my parents in Spain, anyway. Then we can visit my sister and her brood in England. After that, we can go wherever you want."

"That sounds good." He eased himself down to rest his head on my chest, and I wrapped my arms around his shoulders. I sensed some confusion and excitement, but I let that be. We'd talk more about it once we were out of the bubble and the life we spoke of became more of a reality than a what if.

As Greg fell asleep with his head near my heart, I thought about everything we found out today. Why would Bianca and Mark have taken such a risk? Bianca wasn't unaware of magic. Maybe they didn't know how volatile the potion was? She could have ordered Mark to take it, but if that was the case, why? She mentioned another plan when she locked Greg and I in the resort restroom. Was the potion part of it? Her DNA was in the ashes they found, but if there was a discrepancy in what they collected from the ashes like there had been with mine, were they actually her ashes? And if they weren't hers, whose were they?

I took a deep breath, and Greg moaned softly. For our sake, I needed to let this one go. Greg cared about Gina and her family. If the pile of ash wasn't Bianca, then we'd be sending her after the covens. I refused to send her into a tangled web I'd barely escaped several times over.

Another thought occurred to me before sleep claimed me for the night. The Envoy, Creighton, never asked us about the details or the evidence already collected in the case. He only asked if we had murdered Bianca, and he hadn't asked about Mark at all. It pointed to Creighton knowing more than he let on, though with his ruling on record, it meant the covens couldn't come after me or my estate, especially with Bianca out of the picture. Given what I knew of the covens, Creighton might have set himself in opposition to those he represented. I hoped for his sake that it was worth it.

"Xav," Greg mumbled.

I kissed his forehead. "Shhh, I'm right here." He relaxed as his breathing slowed until he was asleep. I let the calm and tired feelings we shared lull me out of my thoughts and into a more peaceful slumber. Greg was enough mystery for me. He would always be enough.

FAMILY GATHERING

GREGOR

Gina came out to the bubble personally to remove our nanite bands. I'd never been so relieved in all my life. We even had an escort to the local airfield. Xavior's uncle arranged a private flight to Spain for us, along with new clothes for the trip.

"I'm glad everything worked out, Greg." Gina hugged me as we stood on the tarmac while they prepped the plane.

I hugged her back. "Me too." I gave her another hug and let her go. "Tell your partner I said hi and give the kids hugs for me."

"You stop by when you get back, you hear me? Don't let this one get you into any more trouble." She pointed at Xavior.

Xavior made a "who, me?" face, and I laughed. "I'm pretty sure we'll manage."

"Thank you for everything, Agent Kendrick." Xavior held out his hand. Gina took it and then offered him a hug, which he accepted.

"Take care of my friend, Brantley." He released her and nodded. "Now, will you two get out of here already? I have a ton of paperwork and a spouse that I'd like to see before you all give me more gray hair."

"Yes, ma'am," Xavior said and moved toward the plane. I took his offered hand and we headed up the stairs. I gave Gina a last wave as they closed the door.

Xavior's uncle was in the first passenger seat. We sat across from him for take-off. We made small talk while we ate dinner. After the dishes were cleared, Renard reclined his seat.

"Why don't you two take the guest suite. Just . . . be quiet."

Xavior was up and moving before I could say anything. I followed him and grabbed our bags. We washed up separately because the bathroom was tiny. Once we were ready for bed, we found it was just long and wide enough for both of us.

I held up my wrist to look at the slightly pink flesh left behind by the nanite mesh. Xavior did the same, then laced his fingers with mine. "Are you ready to meet my family tomorrow?"

"As ready as I'll ever be, considering everything that happened."

"Well, like my father said, I've never been one to pick the safe option." We chuckled and kissed as hands wandered. But mostly, we held each other and slept.

We woke about an hour before we landed to eat breakfast and dress. As the plane touched down, the mag slides gently locked and floated the gulf stream toward the hangar. Xavior's uncle left the plane first. We lingered for a moment, making sure we both looked decent.

"Don't be nervous, okay?" Xavior smoothed his hands over the button-down shirt and tie I wore, with gray slacks and matching dress shoes.

He picked a bit of lint off the new shirt and I chuckled. "I'm not the one that's nervous," I said.

"Sense that did you?"

I shook my head and caught his hands as he smoothed my shirt again. "Whatever happens, we're together. That's all that matters. Whatever your family decides about me, I'll never keep you from them."

Xavior visibly swallowed and then nodded. "How do I look?"

"You look great." He wore a plain T-shirt with an open button-down over it, jeans, and his preferred pair of high-top sneakers. He was dressed almost exactly how he had been when

I met him that first day at headquarters. I kissed the knuckles of the closest hand before they slipped from my grasp.

He handed me a pair of sunglasses and put a pair on himself. "Shall we?" Xavior led the way through the plane, and we exited down the short set of stairs to the hangar floor. Once the sunglasses adjusted to the dark hanger, I saw his whole family, or as many people as could be here for Xavior's return. He walked forward to greet his mother first who hugged him, then his father and sister. The only family that seemed to be missing was his brother Denis. Trevor stood next to Faith with their daughter Lena. And there were several other dragons, likely children of the aforementioned couple, standing behind them with their mates, who all reached out to welcome Xavior.

I stayed back near the plane with our bags as his family greeted him and loosened my tie and collar as the heat rose in the hanger.

"Xavior, mi hijo, are you forgetting something?" Corley asked. She stood out from the dragons. A faint light circled her as if a hand was in front of a candle flame on a dark night. Her bright amber eyes looked at me, and I lifted my sunglasses. The light she radiated became brighter. She was as tall as Xavior's father, with bright red hair and reddish skin with pink and orange undertones and masses of freckles. Xavior caught his mother's look and turned back toward me, came over to take my hand, and brought me into arm's reach of the group.

"Faith, Mother, Father. This is Gregor Lyndon, my mate." They stared at me for a moment. I wasn't exactly sure what to do next with fifteen dragons and a phoenix. It occurred to me I should have asked Xavior about protocol. As I watched, all of them, except Xav's mother, took a very discreet sniff. I'd seen Xavior do it often enough when he met someone. I stayed where I was and waited.

Faith separated from the group first and came toward me. Her long black hair was braided, and her emerald eyes, both traits similar to her father's, caught my gaze. She was definitely her father's daughter, as they had the same light brown skin tone, while Xavior and Denis looked more like their mother. Faith was my height too, so it was effortless to look her in the eyes as she stood centimeters from me and laid her hands on my shoulders.

"Gregor." She leaned toward me, and her forehead touched mine as she gave me a pleased smile. "Welcome to the family." She let go of my shoulders and opened her arms. I took that as the gesture it was meant to be and gave her a hug. Her arms wrapped around me as she laughed softly and patted my back. The relief I felt was momentary as Faith let go of me and her mother took her place.

"Welcome, Gregor." She hugged me, and I hugged her back. Then she whispered. "We protect our own, including you. I expect you'll do the same."

"With my life," I whispered. She released me and gave me a nod. The rest of the family circled us and I was introduced to more family members via names, hugs, and handshakes.

Ransford approached me last. He gave me a nod and shook my hand, then patted my shoulder. "Be welcome. Come." He let go of my hand and reached for Xavior. We were on either side of him as he walked us away from the family toward a vehicle. I watched as a couple of family members ran ahead with our bags and put them in the storage compartment, then left to return to the larger group. "I've arranged for transportation to your villa and had it opened for you, mi hijo."

"Thank you, I appreciate that, Papa," Xavior said as Ransford released us and stepped forward to open the door of the vehicle.

"I'll expect you at dinner tonight. Tu madre has planned a feast. No excuses, mi hijo, am I understood?" Xavior nodded, and Ransford reached for him. To my surprise, he hugged him. I hadn't expected that, considering how formal Ransford had been with us in front of everyone else. Maybe the illusion of privacy and the fact that we were downwind now was enough for Ransford to relax. He grasped Xavior by the neck and smiled at him. "I'm glad you're home."

He turned from Xavior to me and came over to squeeze my shoulders. It was just short of painful. A warning not to hurt his son, perhaps. "Gregor, be welcome." We nodded at each other, and Ransford left us where we stood as he walked back to his mate.

"He likes you." Xavior sounded surprised.

I was definitely relieved. "You pick that up from his scent?"

Xavior nodded. "Hard to hate a man that single-handedly kept his son sane and out of long-term confinement, or worse."

"I'll try to stay in his good graces." We climbed into the vehicle. Once we closed the door, the automated driver started and drove us toward the place Xavior and I would call home while we were in Spain.

THE VILLA

XAVIOR

"When was the last time you stayed here?"

I had to think about it. The west coast of the United States had been my home for some time now. Even when I visited my parents, I stayed at the manor. "A few years at least." Greg's eyebrows raised. "It hasn't been empty that whole time. I rent it out, and my family uses it." Greg nodded as he put our bags down.

The entrance was a double-door foyer that led into a small greeting area. Beyond were a pair of French doors that went into a courtyard with a fountain surrounded by a pond in the middle.

"Let me walk you around." I picked up our bags, and Greg followed. "It has three rooms, two guest rooms, and one main suite." I nodded to a room as we passed it. "Extra bathroom here off the main living area. There's another between the kitchen area and the other guest room." The living room was an open space with a bank of windows that looked down the mountain.

"Bean bag chairs, pillows, blankets, and books? It looks like your den." He wasn't wrong. The walls were floor-to-ceiling shelves stuffed with books.

"There's an entertainment holo that projects from the ceiling. Old tech, but it still works." Greg nodded. "Come on, the main suite is this way." We passed another set of French doors to the courtyard, then a little further, we turned right and stopped in front of a large Spanish-style interior door.

"What's the door behind us?" Greg asked.

"Storage mostly. Linens, towels, extra clothes, and toiletries." I turned back to the door and opened it. It was similar to the living room in that it had a large bank of windows facing out with another pair of French doors in the middle that led outside, and across from that set was another set that led to the courtyard.

Greg gasped a little as he walked in behind me. I smiled at his reaction. "Like it?" He looked at the extra-large four-poster bed that stood along the left wall. Across from the bed was a fireplace with a small coffee table and chairs set in front, and next to it was the entrance to the bathroom and closet. "Let me show you where you can put your things."

"If I thought the bedroom was impressive, your bathroom is massive," Greg noted as he walked in. It contained a large Spanish tiled tub with the commode and bidet to our left. The walk-in closet was to the right and spacious enough for two people. There was a small pedestal sink next to the entrance with a small table for hand towels and other products.

"I'm glad you like it." I took our bags and walked toward the closet, intent on putting things away while Greg explored more. As I finished unpacking, I heard a cork pop. I shut the drawer and walked out into the bedroom to see Greg pouring two glasses of champagne.

"From your Uncle Renard," he said as he handed me one.

"Where did you find it?"

"Next to the bed on the nightstand." Greg chuckled. "He might know us too well."

I laughed. "It makes sense. Most newly mated couples disappear for weeks. Other mated family members will take turns making sure they have food and water or hire someone to do it if they aren't nearby."

"How does that work with the competitive nature between family members?"

"There's friendly competition at larger gatherings, but no one wants the couple to expire if they can prevent it."

"That's happened?" He looked at his champagne flute as if he'd rethought the wisdom of pouring a glass and relaxing.

I nodded at first and made a face as solemn as I could manage. When Greg looked like he might faint, I shook my head, drawing a soft chuckle from him. "Not in a long time. Medical intervention and all that."

"Well, here's to not expiring under any circumstances, and your family liking me enough not to fry me on the spot." I clinked my glass with Greg's, then took a drink. The bubbles woke me up a bit and gave me other ideas as I watched Greg take a few swallows and noticed a very distinct mark on his neck. It was likely my whole family had seen it, but I knew I'd tucked his shirt up around it before we left the plane.

"Greg."

"Yes, love?" he said as he set down his nearly empty glass and went to pour another.

I walked toward him and set my glass next to his. When I reached for his tie, he was a bit surprised, but as Greg usually does, he went with it for the moment as he straightened and turned toward me. I undid the tie and removed it. He watched with an interested gaze. "Tell me, love, did you plan on showing off, or was that an accident?"

"Showing off?" Greg's confusion was amusing until I reached up and caressed the slight bruise. His eyes widened, then narrowed as a smirk appeared on his face. "Well, if they need-ed secondary confirmation, we belong together, besides scent, they have it," he said with a soft laugh. "If you were that worried, you should have been more careful about where you put your mouth." Greg's fingers brushed a similar spot on my chest, and the slight pain made me take a sharp breath. I was surprised it still smarted, but that could be a testament to the effort Greg had put in to mark me in the first place. Dragons don't bruise easily.

My hands moved to his slacks. "Let me correct my mistake," I offered as we looked into each other's eyes. Greg's hands moved, not to stop me, but to unbutton his shirt.

"If you feel it's necessary," he said as he took his shirt off, then reached for my jeans while he toed out of his dress shoes.

Once we had each other naked, lips and teeth took over as we maneuvered onto the bed. I still had Greg's tie in my hand. Once I had him under me, I asked a simple yet important question.

I showed him the tie. "What's your color?"

Greg grinned. "Green."

"Good. You can pick. Wrists tied or blindfolded." We hadn't done anything like this before, but we talked about it. Though with most of our discussions, it was me being tied up. I could see Greg calculating what might come next, depending on what he picked.

"Blindfold."

"Good choice. Lift your head." Greg lifted to his elbows even though I was straddling his abs. I could feel his stomach flex under my ass as I wrapped the tie around his head. I made sure I tied it to the side instead of the back so we could undo it quickly. Once I had it in place, I touched his shoulder so he'd ease himself back down. "Comfy?"

"Yeah, so far." Greg's hands drifted to my thighs and began caressing closer to my groin. I let this continue for a few moments until I pushed away from him. He made a slight noise of protest, and I chuckled in response.

"Relax, I'm just grabbing a few things."

"Like?"

"So impatient. You'll find out soon." I summoned the items and brought them to the bed. I began with massage oil and poured the cool liquid across Greg's chest. He slowly relaxed as I avoided his groin. Then I had him roll onto his back and massaged everything but the crease of his ass. It took me some time, but I massaged Greg into a pile of mush.

"Greg," I called to him softly. In return, I received a sleepy response. "Do you remember the massage we had at the resort?"

He nodded as I coaxed him to roll onto his back, blindfold still in place. "Sure," he chuckled. "I also remember our conversation later that night." About ogre hands, and how large they were and all that implied.

"Good, good." I was a little excited to see what he would do next. I picked up a toy from the nightstand as I straddled his abdomen. "Hold out your hands." I put the rather excellent replica dildo in Greg's hands, and his mouth fell open. "Turns out, the resort sells replicas, and some of them have magical properties. This is Chuck's."

"Holy shit," he said as he laughed. As large as his hands were, they could barely fit around it. "Are those piercings I feel?"

"Yes, several of them." I guided his fingers along the toy to the piercings, then brought it to the base where Chuck had other enhancements.

"Is that what I think it is?" His finger toyed with the replica's anal opening. I watched as Greg swallowed. "Are you going to fuck me with this?" He wasn't sure what to do with it, so I took the toy out of his hands and set it on the nightstand.

"No, unless you want me to. Do you want me to?"

"No!" We both laughed at his outburst.

"Okay then." I chuckled, and leaned over to kiss him. "It's nice to hear you laugh."

"It's nice to laugh." Greg's hands moved to my hips. I reached for them and brought them to my face. When I sucked his thumb into my mouth, he gasped softly. I watched his chest rise and fall, his throat move with each gasp and swallow as I teased.

Greg's free hand drifted down my chest and grasped my dick. I thought about denying him, but decided against it. I moved on from his thumb to his right two fingers, wetting them to the point drool ran from my mouth. Greg valiantly kept up with his hand job, though my tongue wrecked his rhythm a couple of times. At the same time, his very solid cock gently brushed against my ass.

With my free hand, I magicked the bottle of lube from the nightstand into my palm. The familiar sound of the cap opening made Greg pause as he concentrated on what I was doing.

When I took his fingers from my mouth and poured lube onto them, he smiled.

"Get me ready," I said, though the words sounded rough to my ears. I lifted off Greg's chest and moved forward to easily guide his hand between my legs and his fingers to the right spot. Never one to misunderstand directions, Greg worked the lube on his hand into my ass and then slowly penetrated my hole with one finger, then another as he continued to jerk me off.

"Fuck, that feels good." I squirmed on his fingers and bit my lip as he eased me open. The smile on Greg's face went from gentle to almost sinister as he concentrated on pressing and pulling all the right buttons to get me off.

His brown eyes were still shielded by his tie, but when I poured more lube in my hand and reached behind my back to grasp him, he bucked to chase the sensation. The movement rammed his fingers into my ass, and we both gasped.

A switch was thrown as Greg went from passive to determined. "Condom?"

I shook my head, then realized he couldn't see me. "No, not this time. No more barriers between you and me."

"You sure?" Greg sat up as I slipped onto his lap, his hard-on pressed into the crease of my ass. Not seeing his dark brown eyes bothered me. One, because I know if Greg saw my face, he probably wouldn't have asked that question, and two, I know Greg asked because he probably sensed that I felt some mixture of fear and excitement. I removed the blindfold.

"Yes. I'm sure. We're safe, near my family, and I absolutely am not taking our relationship for granted any longer."

Greg pulled me to him and held me tight. The combination of joy and lust was odd, but comforting. "Are you in heat, then?"

"No, not yet." He only looked slightly disappointed. "But I suspect the longer we use condoms, the longer it will be before it happens."

"So, practice?"

I chuckled. "Isn't that what we've been doing?"

He laughed, then his voice took on a heated edge. "Maybe." His two fingers ventured back into their previous location with ease, which I rode until I was panting with each thrust. A soft whimper fell from my lips as he pulled his fingers out and replaced them with the head of his cock.

"Xavior, look at me." I hadn't realized I closed my eyes. When our eyes met, he thrust his hips up as I slowly worked myself down onto him. "Fuck, your face is everything. I love the way you look at me, the way I can sense how you feel. I love how well we fit together."

A shiver shot through me as he filled me to the hilt. We held each other for a moment before he moved. While he stayed inside me, he picked me up and maneuvered so that he sat on his heels with me in his lap. I wrapped my legs around him as his strong limbs and hips made coordinated efforts to drive himself into me while I came apart in his arms.

Greg grunted into my chest as I held onto him. Each thrust was an exclamation point to his words, which made me gasp with each pass until he adjusted and the head of his dick grazed my prostate. Another pass brought me as I lost myself, splashing cum across his chest. That triggered another signal for him as his hand came up to my neck and held me still as he practically rammed himself into me while we gazed at each other. He watched me until the last moment when his orgasm stole his gaze from my eyes and a breath from his lungs as he filled me with warmth.

We laid down with me still on top of him, him still inside me. His hand caressed my face. "Whatever happens, I'm here, alright?"

I nodded. "Even if my parents press us for a date?"

"A date for what?" Greg looked confused for five seconds until he put it together and laughed. "I don't care. Do you want a date? I'll give you one."

"Seriously?" Why was I even surprised that Greg had thought about this already?

"We're already mated, and your niece called me uncle. Being legally tied to you is a formality, isn't it?"

I grinned at him and sighed as I relaxed. "Yeah, mostly." I tapped his chest with my fingers. "But don't give in quickly, or we'll be planning a ceremony next week instead of enjoying our vacation."

"Ah, so honeymoon first, then marriage?"
"Something like that." I chuckled again. "Do you blame me?"
Greg shook his head and held me tight.

A FAE'S TRUCE

GREGOR

After we had stayed at Xavior's villa for about a month, we still didn't give in to his parents about setting a date. More specifically, I didn't. His family knew Xavior wouldn't budge. I wondered if his engagement with Bianca was so long-lived because Xavior liked the idea of marriage, but didn't want to actually be married. Or maybe he knew all along that his connection with her wasn't what it should have been. His family didn't care that we hadn't proposed to each other or said we were formally engaged. They assumed the mating connection was reason enough.

While we had distance from our previous lives, it would take time before we were completely comfortable moving on from dating. Though I can't imagine how dire something would have to be for us to break up. If murder charges didn't do it, I doubt anything would.

We planned a long dating period, then maybe an engagement, but who would propose first was up for grabs. Xavior and I had taken to teasing each other about it. Perhaps the whole thing with Keith had put me off the idea of marriage altogether, too. The ring I'd tried to talk Keith into taking, I sold around the same time as the house. We hadn't spoken to each other since.

If he knew about how Xavior and I were dismissed, he never reached out. I was strangely conflicted by his silence. I didn't want to hear from him, but I wanted to know if he even cared what happened to me. It was another thing to speak with my therapist about.

With the charges dropped and the civil investigation by the coven cleared, publicly, the covens had to leave us alone. My parents could go back to their house, but Renard assured us he had extra security added to their place for good measure. The last time we spoke, they seemed well, and we had plans for them to come to Spain for Christmas and meet Xavior's family.

While I missed my parent's cooking and our weekend get-togethers, Xavior's family more than made up for it. Every Wednesday, Xavior and I would dress up and head over to the manor. Most of his family was there. Faith and Trevor attended with any of their brood who were visiting. Xavior's parents were overindulgent and always had everyone's favorites.

One night, Denis came up in conversation.

"Has anyone heard from Denis?" Corley, Xavior's mother, asked. "Xavior, has he called you?"

Before he could answer, Faith spoke. "Apparently, Denis is working on some project for the USEA to see if magic works on the moon." She took a sip of wine, and Xavior's mood shifted to a note of worry. "From what I understand, he and Emory are working on it together." Emory was Denis' mate.

"Well, that's lovely news, though I do wish he would contact us more often." There was a pause as everyone continued to eat. "Xavior, what are your plans? Should we be expecting whelps?"

I offered my hand, and he took it. It was better to head parents off with something else rather than have them create their own expectations, so Xavior had told me. So I spoke first. "Xavior and I are working on a plan to start a security consulting business. Xavior has quite a few connections, and we think we'll be able to take clients on full-time in six months."

Ransford, Xavior's father, seemed to have his doubts. "Is that really what you'd like to do? Both of you? Xavior always had a knack for art acquisition and history. Maybe something along those lines would be much more lucrative."

"Probably so. But Greg and I wanted something we'd both be interested in, and this fit our skills."

"Ah. Well. Far be it for me to criticize, but I rather thought the two of you would want something a little less dangerous, considering all that has happened in a short amount of time."

Corley, Xavior's mother, gave Ransford a very pointed look that said to leave well enough alone. Xavior, however, pushed things.

"We've made connections with the European Saint George society. Greg had an initial interview, and they plan to take him on and certify him. He'll be recognized for his unique skills and abilities, which will be fairly lucrative all on its own."

The whole family stopped eating. Sometimes I think Xavior honestly enjoyed lighting matches and tossing them into the middle of a powder keg of dragons to see what would happen. Corley only shook her head and sighed. Most of the time, they forgot I could hurt them.

Xavior's nephew, Gavin, interjected. "I've been poking into the histories, and it's possible there were other relationships between the Knights and different dragon families. I have nothing concrete yet. But if you learn anything while you're training, Greg, any history that might be useful, I'd be interested in hearing about it."

"Sure, I'd be happy to help if I can." Gavin loved dragon history. From the few interactions I'd had with him, he would tell me small tidbits from time to time. He also enjoyed playing peacemaker. He redirected many family arguments or issues during dinners. I owed him already for the number of times he had helped me navigate sticky family discussions. Especially ones that involved Xavior. It wasn't hard to see where Freddie learned her skills.

When we returned to Xavior's villa, he removed his suit jacket, loosened his tie, and went to the wet bar in the living room. "Scotch?"

I nodded. "It went better than we thought it would."

"They hate it." Xavior sighed. "They've always hated everything I've done."

"Everything?" I asked in a tone that said Xavior was exaggerating, and he knew it. He brought me a glass and sat next to me on a bean bag large enough to be a bed all on its own. "They're worried about you. You've been through a lot, Xavior. They've almost lost you several times in one year alone. They're right to think that we're tempting fate."

"Do you think that?" The question made my heart hurt.

I sighed and wrapped my arm around him. "We both did. Remember? It's why it took us three months before we did anything that would make it permanent." I kissed his temple. "The ring gives us some measure of safety. With or without it, I would have come to the same conclusion. I love you. That won't ever change."

"Even with family dinners?"

"Even with family dinners." I caught his gaze and gave him my best smirk. "You warned me."

He grinned. "I did."

The next day, when a package was delivered by a courier, I thought it might be a peace offering from his family. It had happened before. Small presents with notes which offered an apology—everything from wine to books to cuff links. Xavior did the same. The whole family worked to keep the peace, knowing being in proximity to give a verbal apology wouldn't help the situation. Territory and tempers went hand-in-hand at times, and they were all old enough to know that it was irrational behavior, but they couldn't help it. Hence the presents. However, this one was different. A fae stood at the door with an elegant wood box. They didn't mask themselves with glamour. Their skin was dark purple. I wish I knew what that meant.

"May I help you?" I asked.

"Is Gregor Lyndon available?"

"May I ask why you're inquiring after him?" My instincts perked up. The only people that knew I was here were Xavior's family and my parents.

"I was instructed to deliver this to him directly."

"Who is it from?"

"Jordan Gohansberg."

I knew enough to ask questions before accepting the package. "Is there a note?"

It was the first thing I could think of that wasn't flat-out asking if Jordan meant to harm me somehow. Can't insult a fae, make them promises, or accept gifts without knowing the fae offering them extremely well. Also, saying thank you was a risky thing, as many fae often saw that as acknowledging that a favor was owed. While Xavior might not have given it a second thought, I'd never directly met Jordan, so I decided the caution was prudent.

The fae produced a note with a slight smile and held it out to me. I took it and was surprised at the contents.

Hello Gregor,

If you read this before you touched the gift, you are indeed a wise man and worthy of Xavior. Within a moment or so, you'll also realize that Xavior hasn't ventured near the door. It's a small stasis spell that will break once you accept or reject the gift.

Xavior is precious to me. He always will be. When he asked me for this favor, I considered denying him, but alas, I am a fool in love with someone that loves another. If he asked for the moon, I'd grant it if it was in my power to do so.

Please love him as fiercely as he deserves. Keep him safe as much as anyone can keep a curious dragon safe. And live with no regrets.

I hope someday soon we can be friends. I would not want to live with animosity between us, for Xavior's sake.

If you take this gift, I will see it as a sign of goodwill. Accepting it will not harm you, nor will the contents until such time as they are activated. What happens afterward is entirely up to fate and magic.

With Warm Regard,

J.

P.S. Happy Birthday

The fae looked at me, and I looked at them. I took a deep breath. Making friends with Jordan gave me mixed feelings. He was one of Xav's oldest friends and lovers. I couldn't erase that. They had a history longer than I'd been alive. Jordan knew that too and had decided, in his own way, to make peace with it. If he could, for Xavior's sake, then I would too.

"I accept the gift. Please relay my gratitude and warm regards." The fae handed over the box. Once it was in my hands, I felt a slight pop in my ears. The stasis spell, more than likely. When Xavior reached the door, he looked surprised.

"Who sent it?"

"Jordan."

His eyes widened. I could almost read the thoughts there and the instant concern he had at the object I held in my hands. "It's alright. We have an understanding. At least I think we do." I handed Xavior the note for him to read.

His face brightened with embarrassment. "Oh, wow."

"Did you know how he felt?" It wasn't like Xavior to completely disregard someone's feelings. The favor he'd asked for had to be something he didn't think he could trust with anyone else. If it had been for him, it made sense for him to ask Jordan. He apparently crossed a line he didn't know about when asking for whatever was in the box.

"Yes. I knew, but I thought... I don't know what I thought, but it's very apparent that I had not considered how much he cared about me when I asked for the favor. He's very good with these kinds of things, and I trust him. I'll have to make it up to him somehow."

Xavior knew I didn't like to make a big deal out of my birthday. We had spent the night at home enjoying time together. While the small surprise he put together for me last year turned out alright, I wasn't sure about this favor Xavior had arranged. Fae had a way of using the most mundane information to their advantage. "Jordan knows my birthday?"

"No, not exactly. I was hoping it would be here in time for it. It's only a week late."

And what's a week to a fae? It was a favor, after all. "What am I going to find in the box?"

"A dream." Xavior smiled. "Happy belated birthday, Greg."

A Dragon's Color

Gregor

I looked at him and shook my head slightly as he walked with me to the kitchen. I put the box on the counter. "What do you mean?"

"Well, seeing as your transfiguration potion was misused, I thought I'd seek a more secure avenue to obtain another one."

I opened the lid, and inside was an opaque light purple liquid with another note. "Color will change to a dark purple when ready. It must be taken within twenty-four hours of activation. To remove the magic—submerge yourself in a body of water."

"Hey, Xav?"

"Hmm?" he hummed as he looked over the potion.

"What does it mean when a fae shows a deep purple color?"

"Mostly that they are excited and or curious for some reason. Something important is about to happen, but they might not know what exactly."

"Oh." That seemed way too accurate for the moment. "I thought you said it wasn't a good idea to take a potion like this around your family."

"It's not, but we're here, and my family is out of the area for the weekend. With that in mind, I asked Jordan to help me find someone we could trust to make the potion."

"Am I going to explode if I drink it?" I definitely didn't want to end up like Mark.

"I don't think so. The potion Mark took already had your blood in it. Mr. Uluke used a stasis spell on the potion instead of waiting for you to activate it, and that probably made it less stable in some ways. Some prefer that method, so they don't need the trouble of instructions."

"What do you owe Jordan for helping you with this?" Favors from fae were not cheap. I knew Xavior offered him something in exchange. It was one thing to spend money, it was quite another to owe a fae.

"I had a collection of first editions Jordan wanted for a while. So no, I don't owe him anything, if that's what you were worried about."

I took a breath. "Good. Okay. That makes me feel better. Though I feel like I've cost you a lot lately."

Xavior grinned. "You're worth it. Besides, I got a refund from the resort on the potion. I had them put it toward a membership for you. That way, if you wanted to invite your parents to stay with us next time, you can."

The grin on my face was pretty big. I could imagine what my parents would think of a place like the resort and Dragon's Grove. It was nice to think of spending time with them there in the future, though maybe not in the clothing-optional areas.

"Thank you, Xav. That's very sweet of you." I leaned toward him and gave him a kiss.

He smiled. "I'm glad you like the idea, too. Your parents seem the type to be laid-back enough to handle it."

"They would definitely get a kick out of it. They travel a lot now that they're retired. Maybe we can figure out something for their anniversary."

"We can definitely set that up."

There was a long pause where we looked between each other and the potion, sitting there waiting for me to use. If Xavior's family were out of the area for the weekend, then we needed to take advantage of that.

"Guess there's no time like the present." I snatched the bottle out of the box and wandered to the main suite to exit the villa to the large backyard and forest that partially surrounded us. Xavior followed.

"Do you think it will be instantaneous?" I was excited and a little scared. If I blew up, at least Xavior wouldn't have to clean me off the walls of his villa.

"I'm not sure. It might be. You should remove your clothes to be safe."

Xavior took the bottle from me, and I stripped down to my socks, willing to sacrifice them to keep my feet warm. He handed the bottle back to me, and I cracked the seal. Something jabbed my finger. As I watched, several drops of my blood dripped into the flask. It swirled, then settled on a purple that was nearly black in the shade of the trees.

"Moment of truth?" Before I could open the bottle completely, Xavior kissed me. "What was that for?"

"Luck." He smiled and stepped back.

I moved toward the center of the clearing in nothing but my socks, opened the bottle, and downed the whole nasty, snotty concoction. I didn't seem any different at first. For a long moment, I thought it hadn't worked. But then my vision shifted. The light outside was bright, and I shielded my eyes from the spectrum of colors that flooded in. Xavior rushed to my side as I became dizzy and caught the flask before I dropped it.

"It's alright. Greg, can you look at me?" I blinked a few more times and tried to look at him even though the sun was now blinding. Xavior smiled. "It's working, I think. Your eyes are ruby red, and your inner eyelid just blinked."

"There are a lot of colors."

"You'll grow accustomed to it. Breathe, though, or you'll pass out."

"Breathe?" The air burned my lungs as I gasped. Scales burst across my skin, and I dropped to the ground as the transformation took over.

"Greg. Gregor . . . wake up, love."

I didn't want the gentle hand to stop caressing my jaw. The pleasant sensation sang through my senses. When that same hand grazed my snout, I opened my eyes. I could see Xavior, barely in my field of vision for the length of my nose.

"There you are. Can you stand?" He had concern on his face, but there was a deep sense of pride as well. His smell told my brain that he was home, safe, and my mate.

A clawed foot and then another moved at my request, though I didn't recognize them. When I stood, it was on all fours. The view jarred me. I was really tall. Much taller than Xavior. He grinned at me. I lowered my head and gave him a soft sniff. He laughed and rubbed my snout, sending one sensation after another down my whole spine and back.

"I'm going to take pictures. You should see this later. You look like opals or pearls, with streaks of green scales, no horns but several skull protrusions, like a crown on your head." He took out his phone and pointed it at me. I stood still so he could take pictures. "You're bigger than me, that's for sure."

I chuffed out a laugh.

"Okay, asshole, no need to be a dick about it." Even as he said it, he was grinning.

Xavior's smell was intoxicating. Was this what pheromones smelled like to him all the time? Mixed with my senses, I picked up happiness, surprise, curiosity, and lust. Once he'd taken his pictures, passion and desire were the most predominant. I bent my head down and gave him a soft, teasing lick.

He pushed me away for a moment. "Why I expected that you'd want to do anything else shouldn't surprise me. Don't you want to try flying first? Or wander around sniffing things?"

The grunt that came out of me made him laugh. I wanted him and wanted him to have this experience as much as I did.

"Alright, but I want to try something first. Give me a few minutes?" I hummed my approval.

He dashed back into the house and came out with an imager, and tossed it into the air. "It'll take pictures of us together as dragons."

It shot up and took a picture of me and made me blink, though I knew the light it emitted wasn't on the human spectrum. Xavior stripped and put his clothes next to mine. Moments later, he shifted and stood with me in the clearing.

My eyes picked up so much more about him in this form. The brilliance of his scales and feathers. The play of colors along his body. While he was smaller, it wasn't by much. The first thing I did was bend down and rub my face along his head and neck. My eyes told me I'd left my scent markers behind. He did the same, and we continued like that, circling each other until we relaxed together.

I moved slowly, working on instinct and smell. I had to be careful with my precious mate. Xavior was not fragile, but I would not risk hurting him with my claws or teeth. Even in this form, I was aware of my ability. And the ring. It had shifted with me. I felt it on my finger, or rather clawed toe. That reassured me.

I kept my head in contact with his body as I moved. He stayed still as I put one leg between his hip and his hind leg and then slowly brought the other around to keep his hips in position. He dropped his head and front half as he raised his hindquarters higher and moved his tail so that it looped around my waist. That exposed his scent more than anything, and I thrust myself forward on instinct.

There was a soft squawk as I found myself pressed into Xavior's seminal canal. The stimulation was intense, as if his body had taken over. I didn't have to move much. My entire length was aroused, making me desperate for release. My follicles were caressed with every contraction of muscle Xavior made. There were the occasional stray thoughts about whether it was safe for us, especially Xavior. But instincts drove me to mark him. He'd never been with another dragon, and now he never would be.

As I neared my dragon body's ultimate goal, a tremble along Xavior's body came back to me as he made a very satisfied moan. Those vibrations did me in as I lost myself in him. He hummed with pleasure as we swayed there for a few moments.

When I released his hips, I felt wetness on the ground and noticed the dew-like sparkle of his own release. I backed away first to let him right himself. Instead of getting up, he flopped down and curled himself into a sleepy ball. As I watched him, feeling lulled into a similar stupor. As best I could, I wrapped myself around his warmth. It occurred to me then that I wasn't a fire dragon. I was cold, but not unbearably so. His warmth made me nuzzle my head into his side as much as I could without catching his horns or my bone crest.

Before I faded into a dreamless sleep, I noticed the soft buzz from the imager floating above us like a silent sentry as it captured everything.

A MATE'S DESIRE

XAVIOR

The weekend proved not to be enough for either of us. Instincts ruled us as we woke, fucked, then slept. The imager continued until it ran out of power and dropped to the ground near the house because it couldn't return to its charge point.

When I shifted back, my body ached in places I'd never felt before. Greg turned back into his bipedal form while he slept either by luck or instinct. Even as I picked him up and carried him into our room, he didn't wake.

I fed myself first, half-starved from all our activity. The backyard looked like some mad gardener had prepped it for an odd design with all the furrows our claws had made in the dirt. When I'd eaten my fill, I made a plate of food piled high with protein and carbs, grabbed a jug of water, then returned to Greg's side.

He continued to sleep even while I cleaned him up. Then I took a shower. What finally roused him was a thick slice of blue cheese I nearly pressed into his nose. A curious look appeared on his face before he opened his eyes. The odd smile that went with it charmed me, as usual. I moved the cheese and pressed a kiss to his lips.

When he opened his eyes, I held out the cheese. "There's my sleeping beauty. Hungry?"

He made a curious look and reached for his ears, moved his jaw, and stared at me again. "Is everything alright?" I asked.

Greg rubbed his ears again and tried to yawn, then tilted his head to one side, then the other as he sat up.

I touched his shoulder. "Greg, are you okay?" The more he moved his head, the more distress I sensed.

He shouted. "I don't know what you are saying!" His words were a little slurred. "Xavior! I can't hear you!" He pointed to his nose. "I smell concern and worry. Did the magic wear off? I don't understand."

I shook my head. "It's still part of your scent." I tapped my nose and pointed at him. He nodded. I got up, and he grabbed my arm. I held up a hand, took the plate, and shoved it at him. "Eat."

Some part of him must have realized how hungry he was because he shoveled food into his mouth like he had a dragon-sized appetite. I chuckled as I kept tabs on him while looking for something to help us communicate.

"It's been four days since you took the potion," I said into my phone. It converted my voice into text. After a couple of tries, Greg spoke at a mostly average volume.

"Four days? I remember being able to hear you after I shifted."

"So I didn't fuck you deaf then." Greg nearly choked on a piece of cheese when he read the text.

"Any side effects? You don't smell like you're in heat." Even with his odd reaction to the potion, he was still worried about me. His concern made my heart beat faster as I thought about how lucky I was to be with Greg.

I smiled. "I feel fine." He nodded as he read my words and continued to pick at the nearly empty plate.

"I put the imager on the charger and set it to download. We'll have our own sex vids to watch later." That earned me a gentle slap on my thigh. I laughed but noticed Greg only smiled. He indeed hadn't heard me, or he might have laughed too.

"Do you think it's permanent?" His smell was tinted with a faint bit of worry. Though it wasn't enough to drown out his excitement.

I shrugged. "We can test that theory. I could put you in the tub."

"No!!!! Not until I get to fly!!!" I winced at the volume, and he cringed a little and said in a softer voice, "sorry."

"Okay. It's okay." I grinned at him and caressed his face and head. "More food?" He nodded.

If anything, Greg was determined not to let the magic go to waste. He wanted to fly, and I didn't blame him. If we washed it off without flying, and he was still deaf, then he'd feel like he missed his chance. Even he knew that some magic tricks couldn't be repeated.

When we finished eating, we ventured back outside. I brought my phone with me. "You should be able to shift. Think about being your dragon and how it felt to be in that form." Greg nodded and moved away from me. He shifted reasonably quickly, as if he was born to it.

A roar rumbled out of his throat, and I looked up at him. "Fuck, that was loud." His head swiveled down to look me in the eye. "Did you hear that?" He gave me a gentle nod.

"So, you're deaf in your bipedal form, but you can hear just fine as a dragon?"

He nodded again.

"Weird." I shrugged. "Okay, here's what we'll do. There's a slope I use for a runway. It's a short walk into the forest. I'll shift and lead us there, then show you how you can use it to take off and land, okay?" Greg nodded his opal head. "Good. Let's fly then!" I shifted and led us into the woods.

FLIGHTS OF FANCY

GREGOR

Xavior trundled along through the woods he called home. I followed behind, but not so close. I wanted to fly, not fuck him. Well, not this minute, but pheromones were doing a number on my libido. How Xavior kept his hands off me for so long, I'll never know. I wouldn't have had willpower enough with a dragon nose and my natural instincts urging me on.

We broke through into a clearing, and I recognized it as the place Xavior had indicated by the gentle slope. It seemed short, but I knew nothing about flying. He kept walking, and I followed him to the end of the slope, where there was a drop-off. It was about two stories down. For a human, a drop like that would kill or severely injure them. A dragon might take a few injuries, or at most a broken wing.

I looked at Xavior, and he motioned with his head that we needed to go back up toward the top of the slope. So I followed him up the hill and felt the wind as it slid through the passage and rustled the trees.

Once we reached the top, Xavior turned, galloped down the slope, opened his wings, then leaped into the air. A few wing flaps, and he was cruising the wind currents that I could see form and glide under his wings as he banked and turned. I made a chuffing noise and hoped that conveyed my delight. I'd be surprised if anything from my dragon throat made sense.

He banked again, angled his wings, and swooped down into the path, then turned them again, gracefully landing with a few rapid flaps. If I'd had hands at that moment, I would have clapped.

As he approached, I got a nod for me to try. My excitement turned to trepidation. What if something happened? I glanced down the slope and shook myself, extended my wings, and folded them back in. Xavior sensed my anxiety, if not smelled it. He caressed my side with his snout and made a soft rumbling noise of reassurance.

I looked back at him and blinked. He blinked back, and I went for it.

Down the slope, right near the same spot where Xavior opened his wings, I did the same, and it was as if the very wind itself boosted me higher. It hugged me as if I was an old friend that had come home. I roared in my excitement and banked where I saw the air currents shift and move.

Moments later, Xavior joined me. Whatever people thought of two dragons above the mountainside, I didn't care. We flew side by side and played with each other as we darted around. I easily passed him a few times as I gained speed. It belied my size that I had more speed than Xavior. We had to have spent several hours aloft before Xavior became tired and directed us back to the slope.

I noticed lines marking the slope in the dark. They weren't even and looked like a chemical marking according to my dragon eyes. As if someone had put down long, wobbly streaks of fluorescents.

Xavior landed first, moved to the slope's top, and waited for me. I focused on gliding into the path of the hill and only adjusting my wings when it seemed I was off. When I put my feet down, it was as if the wind set me down itself. I folded my wings, and Xavior made a surprised noise. Was he jealous? No, pride. It was pride and envy. He rubbed his snout along mine and down my neck. The satisfying feeling I had from him bolstered my own. I flew with my mate and landed as if I was born to it. As if I was meant to be the dragon I was now. How could I ever give this up?

We walked back toward the house, and I watched as Xavior stopped to piss. Moments later, as his urine reacted with the air, it turned into a yellow-green marker. I could smell it too. So what I'd seen on the slope wasn't artificial. Xavior had marked the path at some point these last few weeks while we stayed in his villa, so we could easily see it at night.

I looked ahead of him and noticed the path had faint markings that led back to the house. It was then that I realized we were walking in near darkness because trees blocked most of the light. As a human, I never would have found my way back through. The markings Xavior made were extra. We could still see, but why struggle if you didn't have to?

Once we arrived at the house, Xavior didn't shift and neither did I. I thought he might want to indulge in our dragon forms a few more times before we turned in. I made a suggestive vocal noise and rubbed against him, but he gently brushed me off, then approached the house.

The disappointment at being denied faded quickly as Xavior walked into the house—as a dragon. The sliding glass rippled around him, and then he disappeared completely. I wasn't sure what to do until he stuck his head out and prompted me to follow.

His den! I walked toward the house and pushed a foot in first, and realized that the portal even accepted me in this form. Once I knew that, I went inside. The den had expanded upon Xavior's entry, and once I entered, it adjusted again. I moved along the hallway of journals and books until I reached his nest.

The nest was much larger now, with more pillows and blankets. Xavior came toward me and nudged me toward the nest. I went to it and rearranged it until it supported me in pure comfort, indicated by my contented sigh as I situated myself.

Xavior approached me from behind and used his feet to rub at my hindquarters. I instinctively moved my tail so it would wrap around his midsection as he mounted me. The sensations were intense. In the back of my head, I knew we had spent most of the weekend doing this to each other, but in the heated frenzy of need, pain, and carnal lust, I hadn't really focused on what it felt like.

This coupling was different. I held still, and Xavior barely moved. We weren't as driven as before, but we shared a deep desire to be joined. My muscles contracted and moved around his length while he adjusted every so often so that he stayed deeply seated inside me. The easiest thing to equate the sensations to was a massive vibrator with different settings all along its length, with thousands of slight movements that stimulated the follicles along his penis and the muscles in my seminal canal.

I knew he was close because he clenched his front feet on my hindquarters and made small hip thrusts, then a final one that pushed him as deep as he could go. I felt him release, which caused me to shiver with pleasure. For dragons, especially on the receiving end, it wasn't necessarily the physical aspect, not that it felt terrible; on the contrary, the stimulation was pleasurable. But it was the warm-up, as if nature had designed dragons in such a way to give them the best chance for survival. It was Xavior's spend that triggered even more pleasure. As the magic-infused cum coated my insides, it was as if someone had injected me with sexual euphoria. I couldn't move. I didn't want to.

When Xavior removed himself, I barely noticed. I couldn't lift my head, and my brain was overstimulated. There was a brief thought of food which I pushed away in favor of sleep and the possibility that I might regain enough strength to return the favor when I woke up. Xavior padded around me, then adjusted the nest slightly until he laid down next to me. His head rested on my midsection. I moved my head to mirror him as we made slight movements to press closer to each other. We drifted off, listening to how our hearts synchronized beat for beat.

WINDS OF FATE

XAVIOR

We lost another day or so in my den. I honestly don't know how dragons survived past their initial matings with other dragons. It was a kind of brutal joy. Likely also had to do with the sheer amount of magic dragons fucked into each other. Or that was my best guess.

Greg was still asleep, and he hadn't shifted either. I left the den as my hunger for food overrode my need for sex. One shower and a fresh pair of clothes later, I checked on Greg. He continued to sleep, and I grew worried.

The last time this happened, he shifted back while he slept. His heart rate was steady and his breathing was even, so I hoped he would sleep it off. But the next day, he groaned in his sleep. I sensed discomfort and exhaustion but didn't become concerned until I felt moisture on his scales. Dragons, regardless of subspecies, didn't sweat as far as I knew. Something was wrong.

The Alexanders had been our family physicians for as long as I could remember and were an exceptional group of mages. At some point in their family tree were fae ancestors. Often mages were drawn to others with magic. It's what continued to give them magic in their bloodlines. The Alexanders hadn't married into our family yet, but it would surprise no one if someone in their family did at some point.

Catherine Alexander, head of the Alexander family, standing on my doorstep was a welcome sight. I'd known her since she was a babe in her father's arms. Now she was nearly three-quarters of a century old but barely had a wrinkle or gray hair. "Thank you for coming, Catherine."

She moved inside and waited for me to shut the door. "I hadn't realized you'd returned to Spain," she said in Spanish. I answered her in kind, afraid that I would alarm Greg if he overheard us speaking English.

"Only recently. My mate and I came to relax and meet family."

"But that's not all, or I wouldn't be here."

I nodded. "Please, follow me." I led her back to the portal in the main bedroom. She'd been through dragon dens often enough to know the routine. I offered my hand and she accepted it without any hesitation as we passed through the entrance.

When we reached the nest, Catherine made an admiring sound. "They're beautiful, Xavior. I've never seen one with this coloring. Where did you meet them?"

"Well, that's a long story. But the short version is: Greg isn't really a dragon."

"Oh? How do you mean?" Catherine swept her dark brown hair up into a quick bun at the back of her head as she walked toward Greg. Her brown eyes critically examined his form. Her tawny hand was a stark contrast to Greg's pearl-like scales as she touched his side and found moisture where it shouldn't be, and frowned.

I gave her the quickest explanation I could. She clicked her tongue at me. "Transformational magic is always risky. When he went deaf, you should have broken the magic then. But we're here now. Let me see what I can do for him."

"If there's a way to make him shift, I could put him in the bath and wash the magic off." Catherine nodded as she continued to look Greg over. "I apologize for the state of the nest. I didn't want to move him, so I cleaned up what I could."

She chuckled. "You think I haven't seen a mating nest before?" I gave her a silent shrug. "I'm probably one of the few people in the world that has seen these things and not be mated to a dragon.

"He's not like you and your family. You all run hot. He's cold to the touch. Do you know what kind of dragon he's mimicking?" I shook my head. "Hmm, well, easy enough to take a sample." She did so, and Greg groaned as she removed a loose scale. It shriveled in her hand and then crumbled into white flakes.

"What does that mean?" I'd never seen a scale do that before. I shed plenty, and they never disintegrated like that.

"It's likely that whatever is going on, his body is keeping him in his dragon form to protect him. If he shifted, he'd likely be in a worse state. This form is costing him but protecting him, too. When was the last time he ate?"

"Two days ago, maybe?"

Catherine eyed me. "You're looking a little worn out yourself, Xavior." She picked up her bag and moved toward the entrance to the den. "Let's make some broth and see if we can get him to drink it. Magic takes fuel, and if he's overexerted himself," she gave me a pointed look, "his body will work overtime to protect him from something detrimental."

"Okay. What do you need?"

We worked together as I made containers large enough to feed a dragon. I remembered a large clay jug that had a spout that would make it easy to pour. Once I had three of them made, Catherine weaved a spell to fill them with broth. Not only was she a skilled healer, but she also knew survival magic. Once the jugs were filled, I moved them next to Greg. His breathing was shallow, and his groaning became more audible.

"Go try to feed him, Xavior. If you need my help, call. I'll be in your reading room doing some quick research." She put on a pair of glasses, the tech inside them creating a hum that told me it had connected with the house WiFi. I watched as she took a seat in the comfy leather chair next to the reading lamp.

My concern for Greg grew when he didn't respond to me or the food near him. I picked up one of the clay containers, and heated it with my breath until the contents were steaming. I carefully opened Greg's mouth and lodged it in far enough that when I tipped his head up, it slid down his throat.

The first few tries, Greg gasped and coughed. Though, for a dragon, it was like he gasped and regurgitated. But enough went into him that he finally opened his eyes. The bright ruby color seemed pale compared to earlier in the week. "Greg, you're sick. I have a doctor here, but I need you to drink this." He blinked in response, and I replaced the empty container with a new one. When most of the liquid was in his stomach, I let him catch his breath and returned to where Catherine was doing her research.

"Did you find anything?"

She nodded. "One of my daughters recently digitized all our family's patient notes. It's been helpful to cross-reference hundreds of years of information." She sighed.

"What's wrong?"

"Xavior, he's in an aging cycle. And based on the notes I have, it doesn't look good."

I conjured another chair to sit in across from Catherine. "Wait, that can't be possible. He's not even a dragon."

"Well, his body thinks he's a dragon, so it's acting like one. Rapid aging cycles aren't unknown among dragons. Especially when they first enter one."

"Okay, that makes sense," I said, and hoped that maybe if we kept Greg going, it was only a matter of getting him through this rough patch, and then we could wash off the magic afterward.

"But from the symptoms I'm seeing, it's possible it could kill him. My great aunt Consuela wrote notes about another dragon that had similar symptoms. The dragon died, Xavior."

I sat forward. "What?!"

"I know you don't want to hear this, but unless you can make Greg move from the den to wash off the magic, he might not make it through his cycle."

"I barely got him to drink the broth. How am I supposed to get him to leave our den, let alone walk down to the lake?" After everything we'd been through already, despair threatened to set in. How was I going to have Greg help me save his own life?

"It's a long shot, but is there anyone he might feel jealous of or threatened by? Aging cycles are closely linked to mates and mating, as you well know. So maybe all he needs is the proper motivation."

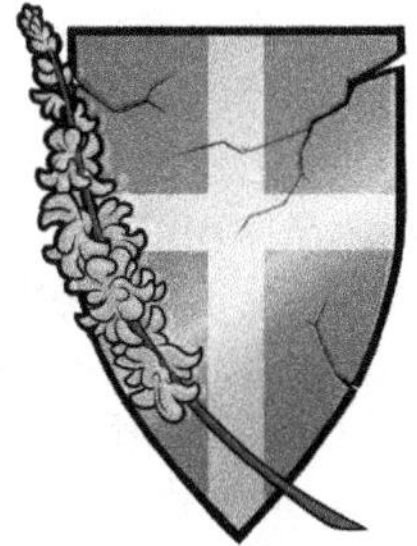

THE FAE GAMBIT

GREGOR

The broth Xavior forced down my throat still coated my tongue. It was hard to think about anything but breathing. I was aware someone else was in our den, but I didn't know who, and their smell didn't offend me. I felt trust from Xavior, so I trusted whoever was with him, speaking in Spanish. Though I caught the low tones of worry in their voices.

As far as I knew, I was tired. I only needed to rest. So I did until Xavior fed me again. It occurred to me that I was still a dragon. While I was surprised, I was also pleased. It meant that I thought of myself as a dragon, though I could certainly do without the pain.

Each time I woke up, the pain was more significant. It was fatigue that grew from my lower extremities and traveled in different directions. I tried to move a few times, but nothing responded like it should. It was perplexing, but I figured if it was what I needed to endure, I would, for Xavior's sake and my own. I could be the dragon he needed.

The next time I woke up, a smell intruded on my senses. It was too close and too foreign to be Xavior. I didn't like it, and Xavior was frightened. When I opened my eyes, a fae I recognized stared at me.

"I told you to be careful, did I not?" Jordan said.

I slid my eyes closed, tired of this intrusion. I tried to sense Xavior until I felt something slide into my front leg that caused an excruciating amount of pain and made me roar. It was sharp, and it hurt more than the rest of my body. I came to, panting.

"Good, you're awake, you shit." Jordan stood a few paces away. Xavior was behind him, but something was wrong. Xavior didn't look right. "Do you see him?" He paused. "I hope you do, because you're slowly killing each other. Xavior is set to die with you. But I'm not so content with that."

I made a noise and felt pain and grief. Had I done that to him? Was he not eating? I hadn't meant to overuse the potion, but other than being deaf, there hadn't been any other risks until now.

Xavior looked at me, clearly in pain. The knife Jordan had put in my shoulder meant something else was wrong. He shouldn't have been able to do that. He leaned close now and whispered. "If you pay attention to your mate, you'll know that you're not just killing each other." Jordan took hold of the knife and yanked it out. I roared in response, though the pain subsided a little. "But humans are selfish. It's no matter. After you waste away, I'll be here to care for him and the whelp you'll leave behind."

When Jordan backed off, I found the energy to stand. He moved toward Xavior, and I roared my anger at him. "Oh, so there's still some fight in you yet. Good." He walked toward Xavior. "Do you still love him, Gregor?" He grabbed Xavior around the waist like he was a rag doll. "Then fight me for him."

The fae ran faster than I'd ever seen any fae move, but Jordan was old. I paid no heed to my body's aches and fatigue and went after him. I followed their scents into the woods. It was nighttime, but that wasn't a problem with my dragon eyes.

Jordan taunted me all the way. I stumbled after him, fueled by all the rage and pain I felt. When we reached the lake's edge, I knew I had them. I barreled in after the two figures swimming away from the shore. My feet could touch the bottom, and I continued to move toward them until the bottom suddenly disappeared. I went under. I tried to use my wings to stop my descent into the water, but they folded and I sank.

I didn't know what happened after that. The next thing I felt were my lungs burning as I coughed up water on the shore of the lake. Xavior's face appeared above mine, and I smiled. The pain was gone, but my shoulder hurt. It hurt a lot, actually.

"Greg, are you with me?" I wanted to cry at the sound of his voice. Maybe I was dead after all. I reached for him and noticed fingers and then the feel of his face—the scruff there was much longer than he'd usually leave it.

"My shoulder hurts." My voice sounded strange after not hearing it for so long. Someone was tying something around my arm. I glanced over and saw Jordan. I tried to swing at him, but Xavior stopped me. "You! You stabbed me!"

Jordan was dripping wet, his brown hair in disarray. I'd never seen him like that. He looked annoyed. His skin was the color of a dark stormy sky as he sniffed slightly, then stood. "You're welcome."

"Xav, why did he stab me?" I glanced between them, trying to understand why Jordan stabbed me and why Xavior looked unwell.

"Never doubt the ability of pain or jealousy to motivate an individual," Jordan said as he washed his hands in the lake. Xavior helped me sit up, and my head felt like it was fit to split open.

"Dr. Alexander is back at the house. She can heal you. Can you move?" Xavior asked.

I nodded slightly as Xavior helped me stand. Jordan returned and took my other side. I didn't protest. I don't think I could have made it back to the house on my own, and I was concerned about Xavior. There was something under the worry I sensed from him.

Once we were back at the house, Jordan helped Dr. Alexander lay me down in the spare bedroom. She examined me and then did something to the wrap on my shoulder. A few minutes later, it was less painful to move my arm.

"I'll be staying in the guest room on the other side of the house. Once I'm satisfied that you and Xavior are on the mend, I'll be on my way. My recommendation to you is to limit your use of magic for now. Additionally, you should never use transformational magic on yourself again. I don't think you'll be so lucky a second time."

She stood to leave, and I reached for her arm. "Is Xavior alright?"

"He's exhausted, but he'll be alright. You both need rest, fluids, and plenty of protein."

"What about…" I remembered what Jordan said, "…is he?" She removed my hand gently and placed it on my stomach.

"Sleep, Gregor." She must have used a spell because I didn't wake until the next day.

EXPECTATIONS

XAVIOR

"Vitals are healthy. You look much better than you did a day ago, Xavior." Dr. Alexander put her tools back into her bag and removed her recording glasses. They were for notes, of course. Today she added another file to her extensive index associated with my family. Well, two, if you counted Greg's.

Plenty of food and bed rest had helped, but not being near Greg gave me anxiety. Dr. Alexander wanted to ensure that our mating frenzy was out of our systems. Jordan had stayed just in case, though where he was at the moment, I couldn't say.

"Is it safe to tell him? I don't want to get his hopes up."

"It should be, but everything comes with risks. Pregnancy is no different. We'll want to keep more of an eye on you since you're older and this is your first. I don't know how Jordan detected it, but he was right."

"Fae can read lifeforce as well as auras." Which was what Jordan explained after he congratulated me. It had been days, maybe a week at most. I wasn't really aware of it until Jordan pointed it out.

"As the pregnancy advances, you shouldn't have to worry about overwhelming pheromones, at least not from your aging cycle."

I stood, vacating the chair next to the fireplace. "I'd like to see him please."

Dr. Alexander tilted her head. "Of course, but make sure you have someone with you when you're near each other for the next few days. It would be best to abstain from any more intercourse until you're both healthy again."

The irony of having a chaperone at my age was not lost on me. I imagine Greg would find it equally as ridiculous of a precaution if we hadn't recently had another near-death experience. But this time, it was courtesy of our collective biologies rather than an external factor.

Dr. Alexander escorted me into the guest bedroom, where we found Jordan reading a book. It looked like one of the old leather tomes from my library in the living area. Greg was asleep. I ventured over to wake him up under the watchful eye of our family doctor and my best friend.

"Gregor?" I brushed his hair off his forehead, and the gentle touch gained the desired reaction. He smiled before he opened his eyes.

"I was dreaming." His voice was soft, and he sounded relaxed.

"About what?" I felt his exhilaration and desire. Maybe being chaperoned wasn't such a bad idea after all. I tried to tamp down my own desires and be responsible.

"The night we went flying." He gave me another smile, then looked around. The smile faded slightly as he sat up. He glanced at Jordan, then at Dr. Alexander. His eyes came back to me, his hand reached for mine. "Is everything alright?"

"Do you remember what happened at the lake?"

He nodded. "I also remember what he told me." His gaze cut to Jordan, then back to me. "Is it true?" I nodded.

I brought him in for a hug as he cried. I cried with him. We were overwhelmed. Somehow, with everything that happened, we'd ended up with something we'd only imagined before now.

"How?" Given all the cautions and warnings I'd given Greg about hoping for something that might not happen, it was an obvious question.

"When two species are physically attracted to each other . . ."

Greg nudged my arm, then let go of me to look me in the face. "Don't be an ass." We chuckled together. "How did it happen if you were never in heat?"

"Turns out, if you have as much sex as we did, you tend not to notice when it happens."

"Oh," Greg said. "Well, good to know for future reference."

I explained what the doc told me about my aging cycle. While Greg looked disappointed, he was also concerned enough for me in my new condition to not want to push things.

"How do you feel about lunch?" I asked.

"If it includes solid food, I'm in." He grinned and held my hand.

"Good. Let's go figure out what casserole we're warming up."

"Casserole?"

"While you were recuperating, my family has been sending food and presents. We've missed family dinner, so they assumed what one might assume with a newly mated pair."

"Ah. Well, I'm not picky at this point. I'll eat anything as long as it's not broth."

Jordan stayed quiet the entire time, even as we all sat at the table and ate. I was worried, since Jordan used Greg's insecurities to motivate him to save his life and mine. The last thing I wanted was for two people I cared about to be at odds with each other. So when Greg spoke, it surprised me.

"I am very grateful for your assistance, Jordan." Greg faced Jordan and Greg held out his hand, "You're Xavior's best friend, and I hope we can become friends as well."

Jordan glanced at Greg's hand, then reached out to take it. "I hope you understand how lucky you truly are. You can consider yourself my friend, and I yours." They shook hands on the words, and I sat with my astonishment. I hadn't asked Jordan to do that, so he had to have seen something in Greg to move from neutrality to friendship.

Or he was willing to wait. For fae, humans were a blink of an eye. I tried not to think about it. We had plenty of time ahead of us, though the activities of the last few days made me think about how many close calls we'd had this year alone.

"Maybe my parents are right about taking on a security business and bodyguard work."

Greg put down his fork, and Jordan glanced between the two of us. Dr. Alexander kept her head down.

"You said yourself, it's mostly for show. So if we take the right assignments, it should pose minimal risk. But if you're worried about it, we'll figure something else out," Greg stated.

"Far be it for me to tell either of you what to do, but Xavior, you've always done exceptionally well at research. Plus, there's enough of a mystery there to keep you managed. You don't necessarily have to run off to the four corners of the earth to seek adventure. As for you, Greg, have you ever considered being a stunt double? Considerably less dangerous than being a bodyguard, though it presents much of the same physicality." Jordan continued to eat as if he'd said nothing at all.

Greg looked at me, and I shrugged. "He's not wrong." I had nearly forgotten about the production house investment. It produced everything from holo movies to holo games. And we'd recently started old film restorations, which made 2D movies into 4D ones so they could be experienced as if you were standing there with the actors in their make-believe environment.

"We have time to plan for that, don't we? At least until the new year," said Greg. "We still need to talk about finances, and you mentioned helping me invest and diversify what I have in savings."

"My parents are going to be ecstatic," I chuckled.

"Speaking of your parents, I'm oathbound not to tell them about your private life. But when do you plan to tell them you're expecting?"

I looked at Greg. He smiled and offered his hand, and we laced our fingers together. "Christmas, of course."

A Lively Nativity

GREGOR

When I agreed to have Christmas in Spain and invited my parents, I expected the usual dragon hospitality. Too much food, hot chocolate, sangria, and lots of wine. However, life with Xavior was full of surprises, and our life in Spain was no exception. It's just one of the reasons I loved him so much.

"So, we have this family tradition, or well, one of them, that we put on a live nativity for the village every year on the night of the twenty-second," Xavior said. I was with him so far, but I was already three glasses into an excellent bottle of wine that one of his parents had brought out for the evening. I smiled and nodded, because sure, dragons put on a nativity for the village, made total sense.

"Your family is religious?" It wasn't unheard of, though it was a surprise if true. The family dynamics didn't give me the impression that they were all that religious.

Xavior shook his head. "We're not active participants in the Catholic Church. Or well, we haven't been in a long time. Dragons had plenty of politics without getting into the middle of human centric religion, no offense."

"None taken," I said as I laughed softly. I hadn't remained part of the church after being pushed out of my family, even though the Catholic Church was the origins of the original Order of Saint George. It started with three brothers, and only one of them was named George, but that's another story.

He continued, "However, the village down the hill my parents support is mostly Catholic. To honor the village, we honor practices that are easily accepted by everyone. Mainly, lighting candles in the manor windows through the holidays and performing a live nativity."

"That's cool, so does your family hire a group or something?" I'd heard of such things back in the states but never participated in one.

"Not exactly." Xavior grinned. "All the adults visiting for the holidays get together and drink the night before, and we pick roles from a barretina. Whatever role you pick, you dress as for the nativity tomorrow night."

"Okay, that doesn't sound like too much trouble. Everyone participates?"

Xavior nodded. "As a guest of honor and the youngest adult, you can pick first."

"Sure," I shrugged, completely unaware of what I was about to get myself into.

The red hat with a black band magically appeared in front of me. Xavior held it out, and I stuck my hand in the hat. I pulled out a slip of paper and read it.

"What's a caganer?" I'd never heard of such a thing, especially in a nativity scene. Xavior couldn't stop laughing, and Faith came toward me with a figurine in her hand.

"It's a Catalonian tradition," Faith said. She handed me a small statue of a man wearing a red hat, white shirt, black pants pulled down, squatting over a solid turd on the ground directly under his bare ass.

"Wait. This is part of the nativity?" There were at least twenty dragons in the room. Some started laughing, others began arguing, or at least being really loud in Spanish. Xavior piped up and tried to let me pick something else. My parents glanced at me and kept drinking. I didn't blame them.

Suddenly feeling very sober, I stood and whistled loudly enough to grab everyone's attention. Considering dragons had better than human hearing, that wasn't too hard.

"Hey, it's alright. I drew the caganer; I'll be the caganer."

Everyone was quiet for a moment, then they burst into cheers and laughter. They poured more wine, brought out more food, and more roles were drawn from the hat. Xavior ended up picking Mary, so I felt a little vindicated, as I wouldn't be the only one without pants.

"So, there's another part I should tell you about." Xavior leaned close as his family continued celebrating.

"Oh shit."

"Close, but not quite."

The following night, they dressed me as a traditional caganer, sitting on a stool, handing out little dragon caganers. Apparently, Xavior's family had them made every year for visitors. Each little dragon caganer, if broken open, contained a small amount of actual dragon shit.

As magical beings, parts of dragons were very prized throughout history. Scales, claws, and hearts were the most sought-after. After the Magical Species Pact, all of that was very hard to come by legally. However, one magical thing which remained relatively accessible and inexpensive was excrement.

Given the long tradition in Catalonia of the caganer and how it symbolized fertility and good fortune, Xavior's family celebrated it in their own way. They gave each village family an allotted amount of dragon shit to help them with their crops and gardens. As the village grew and word spread of the tradition, they came up with a more clever way to give a shit, so to speak.

Some families collected the figurines and used them in their own nativities. Others literally used them to ensure they prospered the following year during harvest times.

Freezing my ass off didn't seem so bad considering it helped the village and let them enjoy seeing the dragons play pretend. The family made funny faces and joked as the crowds would come up to take pictures with the scene or chat with someone. The whole point was to put on a spectacle and bring some levity to the holidays and "humanize" the story of Christ. It was certainly a less radical and serious approach to religion, and I appreciated that.

Xavior took the opportunity to shut off his glamour button for the time he was dressed as Mary.

Glamour buttons were little devices that could be attached to the wearer via body glue. They then turned on or off to hide a particular body area by shifting small amounts of mass. Individuals used them for anything from vanity to shape wear to hiding small pregnancy bumps. But it only handled so much. It was never good to use glamour long-term.

He got comments about how realistic his belly looked for the part. He ignored the teasing and would make suggestive jokes about the "caganer" knocking him up. Everyone got a kick out of that. The amusement and delight Xavior got from keeping our secret right under the noses of a houseful of dragons amused me too.

The twenty-third was taken up by a large family dinner to celebrate the success of the live nativity, and Gavin, the family historian, sought me out.

"Gregor," Gavin started. Xavior disappeared, supposedly to refill our wine glasses. Dragons handled alcohol much better than humans did. I was gently scolded about the difference when I had said something in private about drinking while pregnant. "Did you realize that you have roots here, too? Or well, your Order does. All of Spain obsesses over dragons, Barcelona especially. Catalonia pronounced Saint George their patron saint in 1456."

"Was your family living here by that time?" I asked.

"No, not yet. My great-grandparents, Xavior's parents, were children then, and Ransford was still in England. They wouldn't settle here until the early 16th century."

"Don't you think it's odd for a country to have a patron saint that killed a dragon while many of its cities revere them?"

"Not really," Gavin said with a smile. "Life is full of contradictions, and history points to a time that The Order and dragons weren't so at odds with each other. Dragons and nobility are often intertwined. It's plausible that your long-ago distant relative was protecting one dragon from another."

My mouth went dry. "You're saying the princess might have been a dragon?"

"Some of my research suggests it's possible. Many of the royal families have dragon bloodlines. Most of the noble families of Europe have dragon icons on their heraldry. It stands to reason that some of them might be related or could have been part of one or more dragon lineages."

"Wow." I couldn't think of anything else to say. My mother's sect didn't talk about the origins of The Order much. It made me wonder what they were willfully ignoring, especially if Gavin was right.

"It's all a matter of perspective and history."

"And family."

"Indeed," Gavin said. "Even the story itself was likely appropriated by Christianity. There are pre-Christian versions of similar stories. It's not surprising considering dragons have been around much longer than a majority of human civilizations."

"What did I miss?" Xavior asked as he reappeared with full glasses of wine.

I smiled. "Well, Gavin has a fascinating hypothesis that the princess my very distant relative saved, might have been a dragon herself. Or the story could be completely myth given its origins."

"Huh. That is interesting." Xavior had a moment of contemplation, then took a drink of his wine. "It's a mystery for another night, though. Tonight, we celebrate! Salud!"

"Salud!" Gavin and I repeated as we tapped our glasses together.

"The Christmas holiday seems to be a huge deal here." Both Gavin and Xavior laughed.

"Mi amor, you haven't seen the half of it. We celebrate the season until January sixth," Xavior said with some amusement.

"Seriously?" Xavior nodded, and I must have grinned like a kid because he laughed. "I think I could get used to this."

Xavior leaned close. "I hope so because I'd really like our whelp to have this, too."

I kissed him, and then it turned into something lustful and needy. When I focused on Xavior's emotions, I realized he was ahead of me in that department. "Where?"

He took my hand and placed it on his left side vest pocket. I felt the keystone for his den there and smiled. "Balcony window in our room."

We exchanged another quick kiss before Xavior disappeared, and I slowly made my way out of the party to follow him.

There weren't a lot of places to have some privacy with this many dragons in the manor. It's one reason why Xavior had his own villa, but waiting thirty minutes to return to his home seemed like waiting a decade. The doors didn't lock in the manor. They were too old for that. And who worried about it when you could retreat to your den. Dragons could enter dens of course, though many didn't as they were considered more private than bedrooms.

Our room was quiet and dark as I entered. I caught the shimmer of the portal in the balcony window that looked out onto the manor's garden. I smiled as I made my way to the window and went into Xavior's den.

The den's darkness matched our room, and I took a cautious step forward, wondering why Xavior kept it dark. I sensed him before I felt his hand take mine and lead me to the comfortable leather chair I knew was in his reading room.

His was so urgent with his desire, and yet gentle, as he kissed me while undoing my pants. Each kiss was branded on my lips as I reached up and unbuttoned his vest and his shirt, then slid both from his shoulders to the floor next to us.

Xavior's hands slipped into my trousers, then my boxers, avoiding the obvious and easing around to my buttocks where he lifted me so he could slide the material off my body. It was moments like this that reminded me how much power he had and what he could do with it, and what he let me do with it as his partner and mate.

My shirt was next as he unbuttoned it and slipped it from my shoulders. I reached for his slacks and he stepped away momentarily. "Afraid I would take advantage?" I asked, hinting that I very much wanted to.

"Not if I said no. However, it's hard for me to say no to you, Gregor."

I couldn't deny him either. I loved having him pant for me, to bring him to the edge and have him beg for another taste or tease or another thrust. Mostly, I tortured myself because I wanted him so much, and so often, I felt greedy with it. But I also wanted to make each moment, each time, with him last as if they were entire lifetimes unto themselves.

"How's the glamour holding up?" I asked as my eyes adjusted to the near darkness. I rested my arms on the chair and waited.

"Pretty good so far. No one suspects." Whatever direction Xavior was going with this, I was happy to follow. "What's your color?"

"Green," I said, excited about what he might do next. He didn't take control very often, but when he did it was always thrilling.

Xavior's knees landed on either side of my thighs, pressing my legs together. Before I could reach for his hard-on, he trapped my wrists on the arms of the chair.

A soft growl floated from his throat, a needy one. "Suck," was all he said in a gravel-filled voice. A needy shiver went through me that started in my abdomen and went to my extremities. Another soft growl chased the shiver and wound me up more, making my dick leak onto my stomach.

I opened my mouth wide to take him as he slowly pushed himself to the back of my throat and thrust a few times before he pulled away. I panted, then opened my mouth again. Xavior could see much better in this light than I could, and he unerringly found my mouth time and again.

Each time he plunged into me, I did as much as I could to his cock before he pulled it out again. Licks, sucks, small nibbles, the scrape of teeth. Taking him as far down my throat as possible and swallowing around him. Small thrusts against the roof of my mouth. Dragging my lips across his leaking dick. Whatever I could think of to do that would make him lose control.

I lost count of how many times he teased my mouth. He was edging his high for as long as he could take it as I did every trick I knew to make him spill down my throat. When he finally gave in, he threaded his fingers into my hair and fucked my mouth with a few quick thrusts, then finally let go. His load hit the back of my throat and I swallowed while he groaned with pleasure.

With a hand free, I reached for my dick and was denied as Xavior caught it before I could do anything to relieve the pressure.

"That's mine," he said before his mouth and tongue met mine to taste himself and torture me all the more. I gasped when he pulled away.

"Xav, please." I was not above begging, especially not for him. He would always leave me wanting no matter what role we played for each other.

"My knight pleads for mercy?" I loved it when he called me that.

"Yes," I said in a breathy voice as I shook from desire. As Xavior knelt above me again, our shared pheromone connection made its presence known. Emotions flowed around us and the glamour Xav was wearing rippled with scales, nearly disrupting the deception of his flat stomach. I almost asked about getting rid of the glamour when I became distracted by how he smelled. It wasn't just our sweat or sex, it was more.

Xavior was a forest, fresh porcelain clay, and a merry fire, burning with warmth and love. He was home and would forever and always be home. I took a deep breath of that scent and held it in my lungs, focusing on it. It was the strongest it had ever been. I had picked up hints of it before but this was like a puzzle coming together.

I kept my hands clenched into fists on the arms of the chair to keep from touching him. He reached for my dick, and a moment of sheer pleasure zipped up my spine from the contact until he sank himself slowly down on my cock.

The sensation practically choked me as I tried to breathe and not come the moment his ass pressed against my hips. He shifted slightly to put his feet under him as his hands moved to grip the back of the chair.

His half-hard cock slipped along my abs as he pulled himself up, then slid back down again. I couldn't tell if it was the lube he had used to prepare himself or how badly my dick was leaking that allowed him to ride me so easily.

I was drowning in his scent, my lust, admiring his determination, and the throbbing pain in my palms from the bite of my fingernails. Then, somewhere in my brain, I decided that my mouth was fair game, so I licked his chest as he moved on top of me. The gasp from him was my reward as I felt him harden against my chest.

"Mmm, Greg," Xavior moaned.

"Yes, my dragon?" I crooned, then gasped as he pressed all the way down again and squeezed around me. "Fuck."

His desperate chuckle let me know we were close to ending this play. I dared to reach for him as we panted in our momentary pause. His hands found my face and raked through my hair.

"Greg . . ." The plea from his lips was enough. I wrapped my arms across his back and shoulders. Then buried my face in his chest as I slammed myself up into him with quick thrusts, then slowed when I was right at the edge and thrust hard into him a few more times before I shot everything I had inside of him.

We froze like that in our pleasure-filled haze. Our pleasure was a living thing between us that seemed to stretch time itself until it snapped back as small physical signals registered.

My scalp hurt from where Xavior had pulled at my hair. I'd scratched his skin and cut my palms with my finger nails. My wrists were slightly bruised, and we were both a serious mess and not one that would be easily remedied.

We laughed as we took stock, giddy with our fucked out high but reluctant to do anything about the result.

"How long do you think we've been gone?" I asked.

"I have no idea, but we're newly mated, so we can blame it on that."

I laughed and wrapped my arms around him as he laid against me at an awkward angle. "You expected us to go back, though. You made sure our clothes weren't involved."

"True."

"Did you also plan how we'd clean up?"

One very well-designed and heated camp shower later, along with soft towels, a comfy nest of pillows, blankets, and rugs, meant we didn't go back to the party.

"Should one of us sneak out for food later?" he asked.

"Maybe. But at the moment, I'm content right where I am."

"Me too, mi amor, me too."

I kissed him gently as we dozed off in each other's arms.

CHRISTMAS IN SPAIN

GREGOR

As Christmas eve saw the whole Brantley family together again, eating and drinking the day away, while the evening spent with a log that poops presents. I thought people were joking about it when they brought it up, however, they weren't. They called the log Tió de Nadal.

When most of the house had retired for the evening eager for Christmas Day, Xavior and I ventured into the kitchen for leftovers.

"Glamour still working alright?" I asked in a whisper to his ear while he filled a plate from the various covered dishes left out for late-night snacking. Dragons liked to snack, and pregnant dragons were even worse.

"It's alright, but it won't last for much longer. Especially if you keep rubbing my belly like that." I kissed his ear as he grinned, removing my hand from his swollen belly. He had the glamour off while we were by ourselves.

"We could tell everyone now," I offered.

He shook his head while he handed me his full plate, then picked up another empty one and filled it. "No, we agreed on tomorrow. The glamour button will hold until then."

We'd been pretty lucky to keep it a secret this long. Xavior's birthday party with his family was a small affair, and no one caught on then. Xavior didn't look very pregnant, and the family chalked up our changing scent to being a newly mated pair. We traveled to different places after that. Xavior showed me around Europe with a more extended stop in Italy to meet with the Saint George Society at their headquarters. The meeting went well. By all appearances, they weren't like my mother's organization. But we stayed cautiously optimistic where they were concerned.

Even though we had valid reasons, his parents thought we were avoiding them, and that something was wrong. It didn't matter if we reassured them. Something in our scent said we were telling the truth but being sneaky. Dragons were tough to fool or surprise.

My parents were easier to manage since we only talked on holo, and we could frame that however we liked. This week was the first time they'd seen us since March. They were so overwhelmed by Xavior's family that they paid little attention to us.

We brought the plates of food over to the kitchen table. I couldn't help but reach out and touch his abdomen after we sat. Scales appeared across the surface and disappeared as I moved my hand. Sometimes they would show up a lighter color of green than I would typically see on him. It made me wonder if the whelp would look more like Xavior when they were born, or like I had when I used the potion.

"It reminds me of Gina and Sissy's last kid, but different." Xavior patted my hand, and I pulled it away. I tried not to annoy him with my fascination, but sometimes I couldn't help myself. "Is it odd that you don't feel them kicking?"

Xavior shrugged. "Mostly, I feel the weight change. And my size. Sometimes I can hear a heartbeat."

I smiled at hearing the details. Xavior told me things all the time, but each time he talked about his experience it made the pregnancy more real for me. I could sense things from him at times, and that was helpful too. We had two more months to go according to Catherine. In the meantime, I was working as a stunt fighter on one of Jordan's movies so I wouldn't annoy Xavior so much. Apparently another effect of the pheromones was to cause the non-pregnant partner to be attentive to the point of annoying. Having work to distract me helped, especially since the movie was being filmed close enough I could be home within an hour if Xavior needed me.

As Xavior finished one plate, then took the other and started working on that, I stole a piece of cheese. He grumbled, but when I broke off a bit and held it up for him, I was forgiven with a sultry look. He took it from my fingers and licked them clean.

"Well, if that didn't look cute. And here mum and papa thought you two were having relationship troubles." We turned to look at Faith as she came over to sit at the table. Xavior activated the glamour as she sat. "What was that?"

"What do you mean?" Xavior asked.

"Do you think I don't know when someone is using glamour to hide something after ten whelps, Xavior Brantley?"

"My ring has a glamour on it." I pointed at it to distract her, and she narrowed her eyes at me.

"Don't you try to cover for him, Gregor. That smells old. New glamour smells like someone farted flowers. What are you two up to?"

Xavior shoveled food into his mouth faster as I leaned forward. "Do you really want us to answer that question?"

She took another sniff, and I let her draw her own conclusions. "It's the kitchen, for fuck's sake! Couldn't you two wait until you got back to your room or his den?" She pointed with her fork. "Seriously, anyone could walk in here."

I know I was a rosy shade of red, mostly because I was thinking of it not even five minutes before Faith announced herself. Plus I'm sure we still smelled like we'd had sex recently, which was also true. We sat quietly through the rest of Faith's admonishment while Xavior finished eating.

After we cleared our mess, we left Faith to eat half a chocolate pie on her own. Once we were down the hall and headed for our room, I whispered to Xavior, "Did she seem tense to you?"

Xavior shrugged. "She's missing Trevor, more than likely. He took Lena with him to visit his family. They'll be back tomorrow, but it's always this shuffle when the whelp is younger. Everyone has family traditions to keep, and it puts a lot of strain on them."

"Why didn't she go with them?" I felt a pang for Faith's concern. Even if it seemed necessary, I don't know how I'd handle being separated from Xavior and our child.

"Family responsibilities here. Don't worry. It'll pass. They've done this every time they've had whelps, and once the whelp hits puberty, they are so sick of each other they are ready for a break."

We walked into Xavior's room and I closed the door as he dropped the glamour again and took a breath. His belly popped out, and the effect made me chuckle, then sigh as I put my head on his shoulder. "We're not going to be like that, are we?"

"No way. You'll be the younger, older-looking dad that likes strict schedules and decent bedtimes, and I'll be the fun one that spoils them rotten, and you'll catch us in a food fight and make us clean it up." I wrapped my arms around his shoulders, and we swayed to his little story. "We'll put our whelp to bed, and they'll only get one story because of the food fight." He turned in my arms, and I could feel his rounded stomach press into me. "Then we'll wait until they're sound asleep, and you'll give me my punishment for encouraging such inappropriate behavior."

I laughed. "Punishment, hmm?" Xavior had sounded wistful, and I loved how he thought of our growing family and us. "You didn't get enough earlier?" I received a kiss as my answer. We kept kissing as I walked us toward the bed. Xavior reached to turn on the glamour but I stopped him. "Leave it off. Hiding yourself to surprise our families is one thing, but you shouldn't feel like you have to hide from me."

Xavior smiled. "There's no way I could have fucked you in my reading chair without it." That was only a night ago. I'll forever have fond memories of the reading chair in his den.

I shrugged. "Then we'll figure out other ways." I kissed him and moved my way down his body until I was level with his stomach. I kissed it too and listened to Xavior softly laugh.

"Who knew you were such a sappy person? Should I expect this with all our whelp's milestones?"

"Yep. Get used to it."

The next day, Xavior and I dressed up a bit. With our button-ups and slacks, Xavior wore a belt styled to be a bow on a present, while I wore an overly large present tag that said: "To everyone, love Greg." Most of the morning and through breakfast, people were confused. Some thought it was some kind of couple's joke—which was close. But once everyone had gathered in the family room to exchange gifts, Xavior and I stood up first and handed our parents their cards.

It's a Dragon,

Merry Christmas!

A tiny baby dragon roared on the inside of the card. We'd borrowed an audio clip from one of Trevor's family media posts of Lena roaring to complete the effect.

"Greg, are you joking?" asked Jennifer. Philip looked concerned. I shook my head. When I looked at Xavior, he deactivated the glamour, and his stomach appeared in all its glory.

Xavior's mom jumped up to hug him, and Ransford immediately went for a bottle of champagne or three. The rest of the family helped with glasses and pouring.

"To a new family member. May they be healthy, strong, and look as handsome as their fathers." There were a lot of awws. "And! And . . ." Ransford continued, "and know that they are loved no matter what."

A round of "Salud!" and a lot of questions followed. My parents cornered me while the merriment went on around us.

"We're happy for you, Greg," Philip said, as he gave me a hug, and Jennifer followed.

"But we're concerned," said Jennifer. "Do the two of you have a plan?"

"What do you mean?" Because most of the plan right now was to make sure Xavior stayed healthy. We hadn't thought beyond that, really.

"Where do you plan to raise them? How often will we be able to visit? You know, plans," Jennifer said with a smile. "If you decide to stay here, we'll understand, but we'll want to visit."

I grinned. "No matter where we are, you'll know, and you're welcome to visit anytime." We rejoined the larger family circle and watched as my parents, along with Xavior's, toasted their surprise again. It was one of the best Christmas Days I'd had in a very long time.

We were both tired when we finally made it back to our room so Xavior could take a nap. We curled up in bed, his back to my front, my hand on his stomach. I'd never felt more content. In a short amount of time, there would be three of us, and it seemed like all the things I'd ever dreamed of were coming true.

IMPORTANT EVENTS IN HISTORY

MAGICAL SPECIES PACT OF 1452

As trade and expansion became more prevalent, territorial wars and colonization became more commonplace. While harvesting parts of magical beings had always been unseemly, the trade and expansion of different empires pushed it into high gear. It was at this point that the Council of Elders, the wisest and oldest magical beings in Europe, came together to create the Magical Species Pact to protect magical beings or anyone that used magic. The pact made magical beings inert or non-magical upon death. If any part of the being was magical, it would render any magic that part or person carried inert. It effectively enforced tolerance between species that shared the same continent.

What they did not understand at the time was how this would affect beings with regenerative powers, such as phoenixes. Magical species that go through a cycle of renewal, such as phoenixes, have a duality of power as their death generates magic that causes a rebirth, allowing the individual to keep their magical abilities, whatever those were. There's been some side effects attributed to the pact, as phoenixes have reported issues with memory loss since its enactment.

Nor was death magic taken into account. Of the number of elders that were represented by the council, very few had any domain over the dead or undead. This was the loophole that allowed Joseph Florentine to thrive.

NECROMANTIC WAR: 1873 TO 1878 (THE NECRO WAR)

The major theater of war was in Europe and the Prussia Empire, though it spilled over into parts of the Russian Empire as well. Joseph Florentine had been an exceptional necromancer who rose to power in the mid-1800s. His platform centered upon allowing magic users the rights and freedoms to use magic as they pleased. He and his followers wanted to abolish the Magical Species Pact created by the Council of Elders to protect magic users. Florentine considered it the height of hubris that one of the most powerful groups of magical beings in Europe had forced magic users on that continent into the pact.

It took many magical species, including necromancers, vampires, and non-magical species (mostly humans) to fight off Florentine's forces.

Author's Note

What you have right now was originally the beginning of Xavior and Greg's story. I wanted to skip over how they met, figuring out where they were in their lives, who they used to be, and why they were drawn to each other. I wrote their relationship before I wrote their meet cute. These two always seem to make me do things backward and this story is no exception.

In the original, they didn't get pregnant. I wanted to tell more story before that happened. But as I started to write book three (And before you ask, there are five books planned for The Saint George Chronicles.), I realize pretty quickly that sending them off into parenthood made a certain amount of sense.

Part of being in a fantasy setting is deriving from the world around you and also tweaking it. This book deals with the other side of criminal justice. Whether your an individual experiencing house arrest, incarceration, or temporarily detainment, I firmly believe we need to treat people like people. Unfortunately, all too often, we don't. This is of course a fantasy, which allows me to skirt some of the harsher realities of current justice systems. Also, Xavior has means, and family support where many others do not.

The US justice system is intentionally set up to dehumanize. I'd be absolutely lying if I said I knew how to fix it. But there are a lot of smart folks out there trying to do that, and I encourage you to do research on it if you are interested.

The ACLU, The NAACP, The Marshal Project, The Peace Alliance, and the National Institute for Criminal Justice Reform are just a few that are working to change the systems that are rooted in systemic racism and dehumanization.

I'd like to thank my beta readers, my awesome editor, and Tapas readers. I'm forever grateful for the feedback and comments I received while developing this story and its final form.

Additionally, I want to thank my crit-buddy group and the Inclusive Romance Project who talked me though a number of parts in this book and helping me shape it.

And finally, I want to thank the artists that put their time and talents into helping create visuals for the characters in this book. They continue to inspire me and my writing well past this particular story.

For anyone that picked up this book, read it, and left a review, my gratitude is heart-felt. I hope you enjoyed the book. If you didn't and left a review anyway, it's still appreciated.

All the best,
M.L. Eaden

About the Author

M.L. Eaden works by day in the tech industry, but at night, she reads books, writes stories, throws axes, and is an avid gamer with a current addiction to Azul. Originally from the sunflower state, she migrated to one with a lone star—and more sun. She tries desperately to keep up with two adorable cattle dogs that still act like they are five instead of the seniors their vet says they are.

There are more great things to find at mleaden.com – blogs, reviews, and her latest newsletter. Sign up today @ mleaden.com and receive a free downloadable short story!

ALSO BY M.L. EADEN

You can find more books from the
Mythical Desires Universe at:
mleaden.com/books

Or sign up for the newsletter:
mleaden.substack.com

www.ingramcontent.com/pod-product-compliance
Lightning Source LLC
Chambersburg PA
CBHW070412310726
48977CB00003B/657